D0437316

Scandal

VOLUME IV

SCANDAL

BY LAUREN KUNZE

IN COLLABORATION WITH

RINA ONUR

GREENWILLOW BOOKS

An Imprint of HarperCollins*Publishers*

Thank you so much to everyone who has seen this series through to *Scandal*, especially if you're a fan. I couldn't have done it without a phenomenal team, including my editors (special shout-outs to Tim, for never tiring of all the *drama*, and to Virginia, for teaching me most of what I know about creative writing while working on that very first draft); my agents (a round of applause for Rosemary!); my family (and their undying support); and my friends—fellow Harvard alums and otherwise—who provided specific soundbites and other endless sources of inspiration (you know who you are!). Whether you're here to reminisce about your college years or to anticipate them going forward, I hope you all had as much fun with the Ivy series as I did writing it.—L.K.

www.epicreads.com

The text of this book was set in Adobe Caslon.
Book design by Christy Hale

Library of Congress Cataloging-in-Publication Data

Kunze, Lauren.
Scandal / Lauren Kunze in collaboration with Rina Onur.
p. cm. — (The Ivy ; v. 4)
"Greenwillow Books"
Summary: Callie thought she had finally worked things out and chosen the right boy but Gregory suddenly disappears with no explanation, while she continues trying to prove herself innocent of authoring the anonymous Crimson blog and leaking sensitive information.
ISBN 978-0-06-196051-2 (hardback)
[1. Harvard University—Fiction. 2. Universities and colleges—Fiction. 3. Conduct of life—Fiction. 4. Interpersonal relations—Fiction. 5. Dating (Social customs)—Fiction. 6. Journalism—Fiction.] I. Onur, Rina. II. Title.
PZ7.K94966Sc 2012 [Fic]—dc23 2012022602
13 14 15 16 17 LP/RRDH 10 9 8 7 6 5 4 3 2 1
First Edition

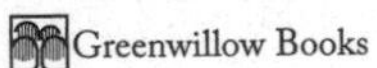
Greenwillow Books

For my readers

PROLOGUE

Monday, April 4: 2:43 A.M.

Gregory Bolton cursed and swiftly silenced the ringer on his cell phone. The incoming number displayed on the caller ID did not match the one he'd nearly finished dialing prior to the interruption.

"I'm coming." He answered the phone in hushed tones. "Just give me another minute."

"I'm afraid we don't have another minute, Mr. Bolton." The voice of Noel Rubenstein, the Bolton family attorney, crackled over the line. "We needed you back in Manhattan yesterday."

Gregory peered behind the shade of his bedroom window in Wigglesworth Dormitory overlooking Massachusetts Avenue. The street was completely deserted save for a black Lincoln town car parked directly below. "I had to make sure all of my 'affairs are in order' like you said," he muttered, turning back from the window, "and to figure out a way to tell—"

"To tell who what?" the lawyer interjected sharply. "Mr. Bolton, was there anything ambiguous about my instructions to say nothing to nobody? No e-mails, no texts, and no phone calls except to answer this number and this number alone."

"Right," Gregory mumbled, casting around his room. His eyes fell on the far wall, where his bookshelf stood next to his dresser.

"But what about . . . a note," he said, sliding his copy of Jane Austen's *Persuasion* off the shelf.

"A note?" Mr. Rubenstein yelped. "You're joking, right? Please tell me you're joking. Please tell me that you did not just suggest setting down your reasons for leaving *in writing*. Do you have any idea what could happen if anyone were to *find* such a note?"

"What if I left it," Gregory started, almost as if speaking to himself, "where only some*one* could find it . . . and only if she knew where to look?" Setting the novel on his desk, Gregory flipped to a particular section toward the end.

"Mr. Bolton," the lawyer began while Gregory uncapped a pen with his teeth. "If you do not cease whatever it is that you're thinking about doing immediately and get in this car—which, I might add, is draining the paltry remainder of your father's funds by the minute—then I will come up to fetch you myself."

"Uh-huh," said Gregory, fixated on the yellowed pages of the text.

"I mean it," Mr. Rubenstein barked. "Your father authorized me to use whatever means necessary, and I would have absolutely zero qualms about dragging you out of that dormitory by your hair—"

"All right, all right, I'm coming," Gregory conceded, though he'd made no move toward his bags. "Just remind me again: it's okay to leave my laptop as long as I turn it off, right?"

"WHAT?" Mr. Rubenstein sputtered, sounding apoplectic. "I said to *pack* the computer—that was the very first thing—have you even been listening to me at *all*, Mr. Bolton?"

"Not entirely, to be honest—no." Gregory almost smirked. His laptop, ready to go in its case, sat behind him, leaning against the rest of his things by the door.

"Young man, just because your father— Oh, shit—" A string of expletives exploded from the lawyer's end of the line.

Gregory froze, gripping his pen. "What?"

"The *Times* article just went live," Mr. Rubenstein spat. "The media vultures must've wanted to make this morning's edition—"

Gregory frowned, staring at the book on his desk.

"—a miracle the reporters aren't here already," Mr. Rubenstein continued ranting. "Now Mr. Bolton listen carefully for once in your life, because this is my final offer: if you are not down here within the next sixty seconds, this car is leaving without you, and you can find your own way back to New York and fight off the reporters—and who knows, maybe also the authorities—all by yourself. I hear the Chinatown bus is cheap."

Gregory closed his eyes. Then, standing, he threw his backpack over his shoulder. "See you in fifty-seven seconds," he said, hanging up his phone. Frantically he scanned the surface of his desk, his eyes alighting on a stack of Post-it notes. Plucking one, he stuck it onto the cover of *Persuasion* and then quickly scrawled a message.

A moment later he'd gathered his bags. Pausing, he looked at the book in his hands and then up at the door. It would take only several more precious seconds to cross the common room and exit into the hall, where he could easily slip it into the metal drop-box on the door directly opposite his suite.

Shaking his head, he turned and propped the book prominently on the top of his bookshelf, where it could be discovered by anyone—or make that some*one*—who might take the time to examine his collection. Then, with one last look over his shoulder at the slim volume, he left.

ONE

J'accuse...WHO?

To my darling Campus Scandalmongers:

My how the rumor mills have been churning! While I may not have all the answers re:

WHY a certain campus "It" boy is still mysteriously missing after vanishing in the middle of the night; and

WHO is the person responsible for the "Ivy Insider" articles attempting to trash the Hasty Pudding, one of the oldest, most elite clubs on campus; and

WHAT is going on with The *Crimson*–The Pudding?–The Economy!–The Country!

I *can* dispel one particular rumor right now: no, my new position as interim managing editor at the *Crimson* will NOT detract from my weekly duties as *FM*'s favorite advice columnist! I am pleased to report that with the proper delegating–and dismantling of the historically short-lived blog formerly known as FlyBy–I still have plenty of time to provide the guidance you so desperately need. And what could be more topical this week than:

How to Survive a Scandal Unscathed

1. Fire everyone in charge. Check! The Ad Board already took care of this one. For those who haven't seen it yet, the *Crimson* released a formal apology penned by the staff member whose oversight led to the disastrous publication of the Pudding's Punch Book, a private document in which club members recorded their, shall we say, *unflinching*, opinions of prospective members. Luckily there's a new sheriff in town: that's right, *c'est moi*!

2. Disappear in the dead of night. Campus "It" boy Gregory Bolton has successfully dodged answering any questions regarding his finance-maven father's *dodgy* behavior in the hedge fund industry by leaving campus on the eve before that scandal broke, and has yet to respond to anyone's–including this advice columnist's and serious girlfriend, Alessandra Constantine's–attempts to contact him.

Have *you* heard from him? If so, let us know he's okay by e-mailing tips@FMmag.com and remember: innocent of hedge fund fraud until the SEC takes you away!

3. Deny, Deny, Deny. Instead of lying, try denying–Bill Clinton style! How many clever interpretations can you future politicians/defense lawyers/Ponzi schemers invent? It was *borrowing* not *stealing; checking the answers* not *cheating*; résumé *perfecting* not *padding*. . . . "No, I did not have sex with that woman! At least not on Tuesday."

4. Frame someone else/Catch the true culprit. Used up the last of the toilet paper? Made a mess of the common room? Not to worry: just blame your roommate! Duh, that's what they're there for! But, on the flip side, if *your* conniving, toilet-paper-hogging roomie blames you, by all means, catch them in the act! (Note: TP hoarding is not advised.)

5. Pray that something bigger comes along. Fortunately for the Ivy Insider (whoever he or she might be), something even *more* interesting is happening in the *real world* (yes, that thing that occasionally occurs outside of Harvard's much-touted ivy-covered walls). Boltons, Bankruptcy, and Bailouts, oh my! Have hedge funds ever been hotter?

6. ~~Make drastic changes to your physical appearance.~~ Wait–whoops–scratch this one. We all remember how that haircut* turned out for Keri Russell's character on college-based drama *Felicity*. . . . Wait, what's that? You *don't* remember? Oh yeah, right, cause that show—and its ratings—faded into oblivion as soon as she chopped off her hair.

*The most drastic, damaging haircut in television history. Bad hair day? More like bad career day-turned-month-turned-years-turned . . . GAME. OVER. And "they" say "we" at the Pudding are superficial!

My parting thoughts are these. When you're beautiful and have it all (like Gregory and Alessandra), people will always try to kick you when you're down. Why? Because they're jealous. And when it comes to the most exclusive clubs on campus, haters always gone' hate. Why? Because they're jealous!

As expected, even though the club's secure server was hacked and the club members' privacy was breached, "popular" (oh, the irony) opinion on campus has cast the Insider as a champion of the non-belonging 80 percent (Occupy Final Clubs!). Sorry, Nerds, but your hero is not long for this world. While the Administrative Board has insisted on strict confidentiality regarding any suspects, there's no doubt that a Student-Faculty Judicial Board hearing awaits the culprit, who almost certainly won't be returning to campus next fall . . . or ever.

So scandal-magnets, keep your heads up and try to remember what Oscar Wilde said.

"There is only one thing in life that is worse than being talked about—
—And that is not being talked about."

Alexis Thorndike
Interim Managing Editor @ *The Harvard Crimson*
The Nation's Oldest Continuously Published Daily College Newspaper since 1873
Advice Columnist @ *FM Magazine*
Harvard University's Authority on Campus Life since 1873

Callie Andrews closed her eyes. Maybe I'm having a nightmare, she thought wildly, and in a minute I'm going to awake. My room will be clean. I'll know who to trust. And as for the past seventy-two hours: gone—*poof!*—erased.

Her lids flew open.

Damn.

Papers still covered every imaginable surface of her tiny bedroom in Wigglesworth dormitory. Annotated with highlights and sticky notes, they littered her twin bed and the desk beneath the window, spilling onto the small stretch of floor usually reserved for old soccer sweatshirts and dirty laundry. Various headlines confirmed the unfortunate reality of her present predicament.

Behind the Ivy-Covered Walls: Part IV

Insider Silenced or Still at Large?

RE: LOG-IN RECORDS
To: Callie Andrews
From: The Ad Board

How to Survive a Scandal Unscathed

Insider Oversight: A formal apology from the *Crimson* and its staff—By GRACE LEE

But the mess wasn't the worst of it. Matt Robinson, Callie's first-ever friend at Harvard University, had also just raised his voice at her for the first time, ever.

"I cannot *believe* that you would even *suggest* that I had anything to do with this!" he continued, slamming the highlighter he'd been using on her desk.

"I don't see what's so hard to believe," Callie replied, sounding out her words slowly like a foreigner speaking an unfamiliar tongue. "You were with me at the *Crimson* almost every day," she stated. "You knew my log-in and my password—in fact, you practically set up my account. And it's no secret that you hate the Final Clubs, and the Pudding, and everything that the elite campus societies stand for!"

Matt shook his head, appearing at a loss for words.

Callie held his gaze from where she'd perched on the edge of her bed, the comforter barely visible beneath the remnants of a crazed, three-day (and counting) paper chase to discover the true identity of "The Ivy Insider": the anonymous blogger who had posted a series of critical "exposés" about the Hasty Pudding social club from the offices at the *Harvard Crimson* using Callie's log-in name and password.

There it was in black and white, on the copies of the time-stamped log-in records that the Administrative Board had sent over that morning: "*candrews*" online during every single instance of an Insider posting. The times on the article printouts next to her knee, highlighted in pink, were a match.

Except that she hadn't written the articles. And she had no idea who had, or how to prove her innocence in time for her Student-Faculty Judicial Board hearing in May. Unless—

Her head jerked up and she locked eyes with Matt: one, two,

three, four, and then five seconds passed before her face finally crumbled, all angry words and accusations giving way to a wail.

"I'm sorry!" she cried, burying her forehead in her hands. "I don't know what I was thinking." The words sounded squished through her wrists. "I wasn't thinking. I can't think anymore because I'm just—so—*screwed*!"

"It's okay," said Matt, sinking next to her. "And it'll be okay." Gingerly he patted her shoulder. "We'll get this figured out."

"Will we?" She lifted her head. "We've been going through this stuff for *hours*," she said, gesturing at the papers, "and we still haven't gotten any closer to figuring out who the Insider is or why they decided to frame me!" Swallowing, she took a deep breath. "All I've done so far is to accuse people, including the one—" Her voice broke. "The only person who's been there for me from the very beginning . . ."

"Oh, stop," said Matt. "You're making me blush." For once, though, he wasn't blushing. In fact, he appeared utterly unruffled to be seated so close to Callie on her bed—a welcome change, as far as she was concerned, from the previous semester. These days, it seemed he had a new obsession: Grace Lee, Callie's COMP director and the managing editor at the *Harvard Crimson*. Well, make that *former* COMP director and *former* managing editor, since, effective two days ago, the Ad Board had officially banned Callie from COMP and removed Grace indefinitely from her post at the helm of the school's daily newspaper. The Ad Board had replaced Grace with Callie's Number One Ivy Insider Suspect, otherwise known as:

Thorndike[1] (*noun*)

1. The Campus Queen Bee
2. A Boyfriend Stealer*
3. One who is renowned in the arts of blackmail, trickery, and coercion
4. Exclamatory expression usually uttered when something terrible has happened

*Or, more specifically, the former-ex-now-current girlfriend Callie's now-ex boyfriend Clint.

Callie shuddered to think of the alternative: that somebody, somewhere out there, might hate her more than Lexi did. Lexi, who had taken extreme measures—including blackmailing Callie with a sex tape shot in secret by her Huge Mistake of a high school boyfriend, Evan—to keep Callie from joining *FM* magazine and dating Lexi's ex Clint Weber. (Both endeavors had succeeded even though Callie had eventually escaped Lexi's undue influence by preemptively exposing herself in an article written for the *Harvard Crimson*.)

"Who could possibly hate me *that* much?" Callie murmured aloud.

"What was that?" asked Matt.

"Nothing," she muttered.

"Well, hang on a second," said Matt. "I think you might be onto something. We need a fresh approach, right, so why not make a list of everyone who hates you!"

"Wow, sounds like fun," said Callie.

Alexis Thorndike.[1]

"We're going to need more paper," Matt said with a mischievous smile.

"Gee, thanks a lot!" Callie called as he opened the top drawer of her desk and fished out a yellow legal pad.

"Number one," he began, marking the page. "How about—"

"Alexis Thorndike," she interrupted.

"This again?" Matt asked. Sighing, he handed the pen to Callie. Under Alexis's name Callie wrote:

She did it:

a. She hates me

b. Access to the *Crimson* offices

c. Wants me out of the Pudding

d. Wants to run the *Crimson* (?)

Taking the legal pad, Matt frowned slightly as he read. Then, grabbing the pen, he added:

She didn't do it:

a. Would never jeopardize the Pudding/her social status

b. Already stole back Sweater Vest (sorry . . . Clint)

c. Already kept you off FM magazine

d. Already compromised by blackmailing you w/ high school tape

e. Usually in the upstairs, not downstairs, offices

f. How'd she get your password?

g. Haven't we already spent enough hours going over this already?

"Fine!" Callie snapped, looking up from the list. "We'll move on."

"Number two," said Matt, scribbling a name on the pad, "Vanessa Von Vorhees."

Callie grimaced. "I still don't think—"

"Reasons why she did it," Matt continued aloud as he wrote, ignoring Callie. "She might still resent you for violating her 'man-dibs' or whatever you kids call it these days, and ditching her on her birthday to join that stupid Pudding club without her, and stealing her diamond earrings and then blogging about how she's the second coming of Satan on Earth—"

"Now hang on just a minute!" Callie yanked the yellow legal pad out of his hands, where so far Matt had only managed to get down "*She might still resent you.*" "I never stole her diamond earrings; she just used that as an excuse to trash my bedroom back when we were fighting, which is *why* I wrote the draft of an article about an *unnamed* 'roommate from hell' intended purely for venting purposes *not* publication."

"I'm not saying I blame you!" said Matt, holding up his hands. "You know she's pretty high on the list of people that *I*—well, certainly have nothing nice to say about—"

"I know, I know." Callie cut him off. "You two have your differences, and she and I certainly had a rough patch—okay, very rough," she conceded at the look on Matt's face. "But after I put my own membership on the line to get her into the Pudding, I don't think she's feeling left out anymore. And besides," Callie added, thinking about the secret that only she knew, that Vanessa's parents were in the middle of a nasty divorce, "you never know what kind of other things a person might be going through... private things that are just too painful to talk about."

"Fair enough," said Matt. "I mean, yeah, just think about how no one had any idea with Greg—"

"REASONS WHY SHE DIDN'T DO IT," Callie said loudly, wanting desperately *not* to "just think about" anything having to do with *him*.

<u>She didn't do it:</u>

a. No access to the *Crimson*

b. Why would she try to destroy the Pudding when all she wanted was to belong?

"Well," Matt interjected, reading over Callie's shoulder, "what if, when she didn't get into the club during the fall punch season, she hatched a plot to take the entire organization down—only she had to make herself look credible by still *pretending* to want to join—"

Callie snorted and shook her head. "Sorry, Jack Bauer, but your conspiracy theory is missing one key piece of information."

c. Didn't join the Pudding until late spring—i.e., no access to insider information

"Huh?" said Matt.

"Whoever wrote all these articles," Callie explained, pointing to the pile of printouts titled "Behind the Ivy-Covered Walls," "was almost certainly *in* the Pudding already. How else could she—or he—have gotten access to all that inside information?"

"Hearsay?" Matt suggested. "Bugging devices? Wikipedia?"

"And," Callie continued, rolling her eyes, "in order to publish the Punch Book—

"Right, the list of people your club wants to *punch* in the face—"

"When did you get so snarky?" Callie asked, enacting said gesture lightly on his arm.

"When did you stop feeding me?" Matt retorted, eyeing the empty bags of chips and cans of soda in the trash can under her desk.

Callie laughed. "As you well know, the Punch Book was a secure electronic document compiled online at HPpunch.com where members wrote their anonymous and sometimes unnecessarily . . ."

"Snarky?" Matt volunteered.

"Yes, their sometimes *snarky*, or harmful, comments about prospective members. Meaning that, unless the Insider has some seriously genius level hacking skills—"

"We *are* at Harvard," Matt said.

"Right," said Callie. Even if *my* days here are probably numbered. She swallowed. "But still, the Insider probably had the Pudding's password to access the Punch Book, which is another indicator that the Insider is a member."

"Let's not forget," said Matt, "that whoever it is had *your* password, too."

"Eugh," Callie groaned. "Don't remind me."

"As did Vanessa," Matt pressed on, making a note of it on the legal pad.

"And a little someone I like to call . . . *you*," Callie shot back.

"Fine," said Matt, handing her the pen. "By all means, add me to the list."

Callie searched his face, but signs of the earlier spat had dissipated. "All right," she said, turning the page with a sigh. She wrote in silence for a minute or two then handed him the list.

He did it:

a. Access to the *Crimson* offices

b. Had my password

c. Hates the Pudding/Final Clubs/other forms of elitism or exclusivity on campus

He didn't do it:

a. Greatest friend a girl could have

b. Thinks I'm super-awesome

c. Would never do anything to get me in trouble/kicked out of school

d. Would never do anything to get his CRUSH (!!!) in trouble/demoted

e. Lexi in charge @ the *Crimson* probably = his worst nightmare

f. Is super-duper-super-awesome

Matt tutted when his eyes neared the end of the list. Then he smiled. "I have no idea what item *d* is in reference to," he said, emphatically crossing out the word *crush* and replacing it with *managing editor*. "However," he continued, "*f* is an excellent point, and as for *e* . . ." Frowning, he picked up that morning's edition of the *Crimson*. "Just look at this!" he cried, flipping to an op-ed authored by Alexis entitled "In Defense of the Hasty Pudding Social Club's Punch Process and Right to Privacy."

Clearing his throat, he began to skim, muttering certain segments aloud. "'Anne Goldberg, secretary, stated this morning . . . all prospective members tacitly consent to the punch process by appearing at our first event. . . . This proves, if anything, why secrecy is so fundamental to our process . . .' Oh yes, here it is. '*Crimson* staff writer Matt Robinson noted in an internal e-mail: "The Insider's decision to target what is arguably the most progressive of these institutions is puzzling. Clearly the all-male Final Clubs are a much larger part of the problem."'

"She quoted me—*me*!" he cried, tossing the article aside. "From a staff e-mail about the Insider. I didn't consent to that comment, but I can't do anything about it since she's suddenly my *boss*! Only two days in charge and she's already writing exactly the kind of socially biased articles that Grace loathes. . . ."

Callie cringed. Grace, a junior, had taught Callie more about writing and editing than most of her professors. Unfortunately Grace probably also belonged on the list of "People Who Hate Me," since a series of miscommunications over the course of the semester had led Grace to suspect that Callie was the Insider. As a result, Grace had believed she was doing Callie a favor by publishing the Insider articles on FlyBy without editing or alteration in their "mutual" quest to expose socially unjust organizations on campus.

Callie sighed, remembering the look on Grace's face when Callie had insisted to the Ad Board that she was innocent—

throwing Grace, as far as the older girl was concerned, under the bus. "I should probably add her to the list."

"Are you kidding?" asked Matt. "She didn't do it."

"Yeah, but she does hate me," Callie pointed out.

Matt pressed his lips together.

"And who knows?" Callie continued. "Maybe she could have used her admin access to figure out my password and then posted the articles herself." Even as she said it, Callie knew it wasn't true. Grace, who disapproved of publishing anonymously, never shied away from expressing her opinions—happy to print her feminist, anti–final club rants on the front page of the op-ed section. It also seemed highly unlikely that Grace would violate any of the journalistic ethics she so passionately preached to the COMPers at the start of each semester, including the importance of never hacking into a password-protected site.

Grace's replacement, on the other hand, had no problem playing dirty to gain access to private material. In fact, Callie was willing to bet her favorite (and only) pair of Converse that Lexi had wasted no time installing a locked drawer in Grace's old desk on the first floor of the *Crimson* offices: a place to stash other peoples' secrets for a rainy day when the new interim managing editor needed a favor she couldn't accomplish by asking nicely. . . .

"But I guess 'everyone's a suspect until proven otherwise,'" Matt finished, rousing Callie from her thoughts. He had, albeit begrudgingly, added Grace to the list. "Who's next?"

Rap-rappity-rap-rap . . . RAP-RAP! A knock sounded at the door.

Matt raised an eyebrow. "'Shave and a Haircut'? Really? Is that *really* necessary?"

"Come in, Vanessa," Callie called, ignoring him.

Slowly the door inched open, creaking on its hinges. A huge pair of oversized sunglasses peeking over the popped collar of a Burberry trench coat appeared through the crack.

Matt leaned forward. "Were you followed?"

"I don't think—" Vanessa started breathlessly. Then her eyes narrowed. "For your information," she announced, pushing open the door, "*I*, unlike *some* people present, am actually taking this seriously." She dragged several large shopping bags into the room. "And no"—she enunciated every syllable—"petty sarcasm aside, I was not followed. It's only me and my entourage," she continued, gesturing at the bags.

"*Reeelax*, girlfriend," Vanessa ordered Callie, who was peering over her shoulder to make sure the common room was empty. "Marc Jacobs won't say a word—we have Retail Therapist/Patient Confidentiality."

Callie smiled weakly. "Still," she started, gathering some of the papers off the floor, which, with three sets of feet and all the bags, was now completely congested. "You can never be too caref—"

"I won't say a word either!" a voice chimed from one of the other bedrooms.

Matt looked scandalized. "Dana knows?"

"Roger that, D-meister!" Vanessa yelled at their roommate Dana, who was holed up working, most likely, on her advanced chemistry homework.

"It didn't feel right to have her be the odd woman out in the suite," Callie whispered, standing and struggling to shut the door, which had gotten jammed by all the papers.

"Mimi knows?" Matt yelped, his voice cracking.

Callie shrugged. "They're my roommates. They're like . . . family."

"Why?" Vanessa snorted. "Because you can't choose them but you have to live with them anyway?"

"What's with all these bags?" Callie changed the subject, giving up on the door.

"Ah yes," Vanessa said, reaching down. "I got you a present!" she explained, pulling a bulletin board out of the largest bag. "You know, to help you catch the perp?" she elaborated in response to their puzzled expressions.

"Exactly how is a bulletin board supposed to help?" Matt demanded.

"Um, *hello*," Vanessa snapped. "Haven't you ever seen CSI? You stick all the evidence on the board," she continued, pulling a packet of thumbtacks out of another shopping bag, "and then you pace, and think, and then you catch the dirty bastard!"

"Well," Matt started, picking up the yellow legal pad, "we already sort of have a system going. . . ."

"Is that so?" Vanessa asked, snatching the list of "People Who Hate Me." Before either Callie or Matt could protest, she started scanning the pages. Then, to Callie's relief, she smirked. "You forgot to add that I couldn't write a newspaper article to save my life!"

"For once we agree," Matt muttered. "As you can see," he added, raising his voice, "we're already on top of this, and it's getting sort of crowded in here so—"

"So you figured out who did it, then?" Vanessa put her hands on her hips.

Callie and Matt were silent.

"That's what I thought," she concluded. "Now where to put this," she murmured, eyeing the walls. "Looks like the only place with enough room is right . . . oops."

Vanessa had frozen in front of the stretch of photos taped above Callie's bookshelf, staring at one in particular.

"Oops," Callie echoed, quickly pulling the photo of her ex-boyfriend Clint off the wall. "I've been meaning to, er, take some of these down. . . ." She stared at a photo from last November taken at the Harvard-Yale football game. She and Mimi had posed for the picture at the beginning of the tailgate, only at the last second before the shutter snapped, two boys had sneaked into the frame: OK . . . and Gregory. The camera had captured the sudden shock and delight that had registered on Callie's and Mimi's faces. Callie remembered how they had howled with laughter when the boys had seized them, pretending to tackle them and tickling their sides. The photo depicted what looked like two happy couples. Except OK's love for Mimi had always seemed hopelessly one-sided, and as for Callie and Gregory, well—

"Earth to Callie," Vanessa called. "Come in, Callie."

"Sorry," Callie muttered, plucking the photo off the wall and shoving it between two books on the shelves below. "Just give me a second to clear some space," she added, reaching to remove a photo of Jessica, her best friend from high school, standing next to Callie on a surfboard at their favorite beach. Quietly detaching the rest of the photos, Callie tried to tune out Matt and Vanessa, who were bickering.

"You want to cut up *this* list?" Matt cried, waving the legal pad. "With *scissors*?"

"Yes, genius, with scissors."

"Why?"

"To stick under the photos."

"What photos?"

"The ones we're about to print from Facebook!"

"Doesn't that seem creepy?"

"Doesn't the fact that someone pretended to be Callie for a few months to post all those articles seem creepier?"

"For the record," Matt muttered, "I still think *you* did it. . . ."

"And *I* still think *you* did it!" Vanessa chirped, hoisting up the bulletin board and grunting under its weight.

"Guys," Callie started, backing away from her bookshelf and stacking the photos on her desk.

"Allow me," Matt cried, grabbing the bulletin board from Vanessa.

"No!" Vanessa shrieked, maintaining hold of one end. "You're doing it wrong! You're"—she tugged on the board—"doing"—she yanked with all her might—"IT"—Matt let go of the board—"wron—*ahghhh*!" Vanessa cried, catapulting backward onto Callie's bed. The bulletin board tumbled on top of her. Callie rushed to Vanessa's aid, but Matt beat her there, grabbing the board, which

Vanessa, still clinging to the other end, used to tug him down onto the bed. Callie dived in an attempt to separate them—and that was the exact position they were in when a voice called from the common room.

"Doing *what* wrong?"

Callie, Vanessa, and Matt all froze, their heads swiveling in the direction of the speaker, whose impeccable British accent made him instantly identifiable. OK Zeyna, ebony skinned and taller even than Matt, stood visible through the crack in Callie's door.

"Nothing!" Callie cried, recovering first and leaping off the bed.

"What is going on in there?" OK called, starting toward her bedroom.

"NOTHING!" Matt and Vanessa chorused, sitting up and slowly relinquishing the bulletin board.

"Why won't anybody tell me anything anymore?" OK demanded. "First my top mate disappears in the middle of the night"—Callie winced—"and won't return any of my phone calls, and then you all keep having these secret meetings—"

"It's, uh, just—a school project," Callie yelled, reaching down to scoop up the papers jammed under the door. "For . . . uh . . . linear multivariable algebraic derivative calculus."

OK, who had been steadily advancing, stopped in his tracks. "Ah," he said. "Say no more. I won't be a bother. I just stopped by to see if—"

"Mimi's not here!" Vanessa yelled wickedly.

Whirling around, Callie silenced her with a glare. Then she shoved the papers into Vanessa's arms, miming that Vanessa and

Matt ought to start clearing all the Insider materials off the floor. Not that she didn't trust OK—he had always been a solid friend; she just couldn't afford to trust anyone else right now.

Poking her head back out into the common room, Callie forced a smile. "Would you like me to give Mimi a message?"

"Actually, for everyone's *information*," OK boomed, "I came here looking for *Dana*—"

"What?" Dana called from her bedroom.

"Dana! You're here!" OK cried as Dana appeared in her doorway.

"Correct," she said shortly, eyeing him suspiciously. "Well, then—what is it?"

"Dana . . . Dana . . ." he began, furrowing his brow. "I've come to ask you . . . if . . . say!" His face lit up. "You don't happen to know why Adam is cross with me?" Adam, the fourth inhabitant of the suite directly across the hall, was Dana's boyfriend.

Dana's eyebrows knit together. "Just replace the toothbrush and all will be forgiven."

"Excellent," said OK. "Right. Maybe a color less similar this time or—"

"That should be fine." Turning, Dana looked at Callie. "Shouldn't you have left by now?"

"Huh?" said Callie. "Left for what?"

"Don't you have Literary Theory from two to four in the Barker Center on Thursdays?"

Callie's eyes went wide. "Shit!" she cried, grabbing her phone. It was 3:45. She'd missed almost the entire lecture. Maybe if she ran she could catch Professor Raja right after class.

"Shoot," Dana corrected.

"You memorized all of our class schedules?" Vanessa yelled through the wall.

"Someone had to do it," Dana called back.

"Dammit!" Callie cursed. "Sorry," she added, darting around Matt and Vanessa in search of her book bag.

"Darn it," Dana urged patiently.

"You couldn't have said anything earlier?" Callie cried, locating her bag under her bed.

"You seemed pretty busy . . . with *math*," Dana retorted primly. Dana felt the same way about lying as Mimi did about going to bed before midnight: it was something that ought to be avoided at all costs.

"Crap," Callie muttered.

Vanessa paused midway through piling papers atop Callie's desk, her head cocked toward the wall. "Poop?" she ventured.

Matt guffawed.

Shaking her head, Callie lowered her voice to a whisper. "Would you two mind . . . ?"

"Of course not," Vanessa reassured her.

Callie gazed at the bulletin board, still resting on her bed. "Shouldn't I—?"

"No," said Matt. "*Go*," he added. "Seriously. We've got this."

Reluctantly Callie backed out of her bedroom, dragging the door shut behind her. Trying not to think about what messes might await her when she returned if Matt and Vanessa got into another argument, Callie hurried across the common area. "Bye!"

she called to Dana, and to OK, who had settled onto the couch to ostensibly *not* wait for Mimi.

"Bye!" they replied.

Out in the hall she found herself face to face with the gold letters *C 23* that marked the entry to the opposite suite. Home to OK, Matt, Adam, and . . . *him*.

She knew she should be sprinting to make the final few minutes of Literary Theory. After all, the last thing she needed while facing impending expulsion was a sudden dip in GPA. And yet something behind that door seemed to be beckoning her, a clue to the other mystery that kept her up at night; distracting her when she should have been single-mindedly obsessed with discovering the identity of the Insider . . .

Gregory's disappearance.

It had been three days, and as far she could gather, no one had heard a word from him. Newspapers and gossip columns, however, could seem to speculate about nothing else apart from the scandal surrounding his father's declaration of personal bankruptcy.

However, while each new article offered another set of explanations, none could give Callie the answers that she wanted. When would he return to school? Or, at the very least, decide to break the silence?

(After going straight to voice mail for two days, his phone line had been disconnected. His Facebook and Twitter accounts: deactivated. And e-mails bounced back from his Harvard address with an automated reply about his inability to communicate with anyone from school at the moment, particularly via e-mail or cell, signed by the family's attorney. Callie knew all of this because she had exhausted every possible avenue of contact. She didn't even care about their "relationship status"—Friends? It's Complicated? In a Relationship?—anymore. Okay, fine, she cared a little; but mostly she just wanted to know that he was all right.)

Slowly she poked her head inside C 23. "Hellooo . . . Anybody home?"

Silence.

Every single door off the common space stood open, and every adjoining area empty, save for the door to Gregory's bedroom, which was closed.

Callie's heart thrummed in her chest. Was it possible that he'd returned? That he was inside, unpacking, after a brief trip home to Manhattan? Or had he gone somewhere else entirely? He could be anywhere right now, it occurred to her—though without any working credit cards his options were probably, for the first time in his life, rather limited.

The doorknob felt cool in her hand. Hesitating, she looked over her shoulder. Then she pushed open his bedroom door.

She'd been inside, briefly, only three days ago, struggling to process what OK meant by "gone" while Alessandra Constantine, her face stained with tears, explained that Gregory had left school.

He was supposed to leave *you*, Callie thought, catching sight of a small framed photo of Alessandra on one corner of his desk. The frustratingly gorgeous sophomore who'd transferred to Harvard at the beginning of the semester had been involved with Gregory since New Year's.

Callie smiled suddenly, noticing two ticket stubs for a Puerto Rican ferry ride also resting on his desk. They were dated for the final day of spring break: when Gregory and Callie had gotten stranded on the tiny coastal island of Vieques, forced to wash dishes at a local restaurant until they'd scraped together just enough for two ferry tickets back to the mainland.

The water had seemed so blue that afternoon, and the air so fresh, that even though it had only happened a few days ago, it was starting to feel like part of a distant dream. Had Callie only imagined the moment when he'd finally confessed his feelings for her? And when their lips had come so close to touching that her entire body had ached with agony when he insisted they wait until after he ended things with Alessandra?

No, she decided, shaking her head. As her mother and father frequently liked to remind her, she had an extremely active imagination, but even she was not creative enough, she decided, to invent the way his eyes had looked that day, the same color as the ocean, or how his dark brown hair had ruffled in the wind, or—

Dammit.

Spinning around in her reverie, she had spotted a tube of red lipstick on his dresser. It had to belong to Alessandra. Who, as far as everyone else seemed to be concerned, was still Gregory's girlfriend.

Callie heaved a sigh, turning back slowly even though she had no idea what she was looking for. On Monday his room had borne all the signs of his hurried departure. But someone had shut the dresser drawers and otherwise tidied up since then—probably OK, judging from the way the bed had been made (as if by someone who'd only ever had a manservant make it for him).

Today the room still appeared inhabited. There were dirty T-shirts in his laundry basket, the perforated metal trash can was full to the brim, and even an unfinished economics assignment was spread across the desk. Sinking into the desk chair, Callie touched the spot where he had scrawled his name onto the upper right-hand corner of the problem set, probably long since overdue. On his nightstand he'd left a nearly empty pack of cigarettes and a crimson-colored sweatband imprinted with a large white H, which he wore during squash games. She breathed in deeply, certain now that she *was* imagining the faintest scents of smoke and sweat and that other indescribable smell that seemed to materialize whenever he was near.

She could barely stand the sight of the bookshelf, its contents overlapping so much with her own, so instead she found her eyes falling back toward the trash can. Some tissues that seemed to have been used to blot red lipstick partially obscured several old copies of the *Crimson* and what looked like might be, at the very bottom of all the debris, a printout of an old Ivy Insider installment.

Recoiling in the chair, Callie closed her eyes.

But there was no escaping it: what was the use in obsessing about Gregory and wondering when—or if—he would return, when she might not even be there after her hearing in May?

She knew she should feel grateful that the Ad Board had granted her almost a month to build her case while they assembled a special Student-Faculty Judicial Board to thoroughly review the "facts," but part of her just wanted to hurry up and get it over with—

"What," a low alto said sharply from the doorway, "do you think you're doing?"

"Alessandra!" Callie cried, springing from Gregory's chair. "I didn't hear you come in."

"What are you doing in here?" the older girl demanded. Alessandra Constantine: rumored, and justifiably so, to have turned down a modeling contract back in LA before she transferred from USC.

"Just . . . um . . ." Callie faltered. "What are *you* doing here?"

"Picking up a few of my things," Alessandra explained icily, walking into the room.

Because . . . you broke up? But wait—wouldn't that mean—that of all the people he could have contacted first—he chose Alessandra? Callie clamped her lips together, feeling her mind whir into high-danger-of-accidentally-blurting-things-out-loud overdrive.

Alessandra bent down near Gregory's bed, giving Callie a front row seat to her irritatingly traffic-stopping cleavage. "And you are in here why, exactly?" Alessandra repeated for the third time, reaching under the bed.

"Oh," Callie mumbled. "I—um—also needed—for the—picking up—of some things. . . ."

"*What* things?" Alessandra straightened, holding a pair of red panties and looking murderous.

"Wha—ah—no!" Callie cried. Her cheeks burned. According to Gregory, Alessandra had learned the truth about what had happened between him and Callie last November: how they had spent the night together after the Harvard-Yale football game.

A few months ago Callie had allowed Alessandra to believe, by omission, that the "hookup" had occurred at the very beginning of freshman year. No wonder the older girl didn't trust her.

"I just came to pick up . . . a book! That I lent him . . . a long time ago," Callie declared, her eyes darting to the lowest shelf where her borrowed *Justice Reader* from last semester might still be lurking among his other textbooks. "But, um, I don't really need it right now, anyway, so I should probably—" Callie stammered, watching Alessandra yank open one of Gregory's dresser drawers and pull out some highly complex-looking, fire engine red lingerie to match the panties. Callie gulped. "Go."

Alessandra smirked. "Yes," she said, "I think it is best that you leave now and that in the future you stay away from my *boyfriend's* bedroom."

"Boyfriend?" Callie blurted before she could stop herself. "Um . . . still?"

"Why—did he say something to you?"

"I—haven't heard from him since he left," Callie said carefully. "Have you?"

Alessandra frowned. "I don't see how that's any of your business."

Callie stared at the wall. Regardless of whether it was her *business*, it certainly wasn't her place to break up with Alessandra on Gregory's behalf based on his confession on the boat. Besides, what if, given everything going on with his dad, he had suddenly changed his mind?

"You're right," Callie conceded finally. "It isn't any of my business."

"Good," said Alessandra. "Then we agree." Smiling, she removed the lingerie from where she had tucked it in her bag. "You know on second thought," she said, reopening Gregory's dresser drawer, "I think I'll leave this here. And I would ask you," she went on, turning to Callie, "to leave my boyfriend alone."

"Uh . . ." Callie faltered. Did she have a choice, given that he currently appeared cut off from all modes of communication?

"I'd hate to find out that it's true what some of the other Pudding girls say," Alessandra pressed on, "about how you're a serial boyfriend stealer who slept her way into the club."

Callie flinched. Since when had the sultry but sweet sex bomb formerly known as Alessandra turned into such a, well—pardon the French—*Thorndike*?

"Sorry," Alessandra muttered, seeing the look on Callie's face.

"No," said Callie. "*I'm* sorry. I'm sorry that you heard a nasty rumor about me, and I'm sorry that you chose to repeat it. But that's not the only thing I'm sorry about." Swallowing, she took another step toward Alessandra. "I'm sorry that I wasn't completely honest with you when you asked me directly about my history with Gregory. You haven't treated me like anything other than a friend since you got here—well, minus the past few weeks—and I have not done the same for you. So I apologize. Especially because I can't change the fact . . . that we both have feelings for the same guy."

Callie held her breath. Alessandra seemed to shrink slightly before her eyes, appearing suddenly younger somehow, and not just because she no longer held the lingerie in her hands.

"I . . . thank you," the older girl said finally. "I appreciate your honesty. I also would have appreciated hearing it from you—or him—earlier instead of finding out when I went through his phone."

"His phone?" Callie repeated, remembering that day in the library when Gregory had brought her lunch and asked her advice, as a friend, about what to do regarding Alessandra's trust issues, citing unsent texts she'd discovered addressed to another girl.

Was *I* that other girl? Callie wondered.

Alessandra shook her dark, wild curls out of her face. "It's not important. But so long as we are getting everything out in the open now . . . I have to ask: when you two were stranded on the island, did you—um—did he—I mean, did you and him . . . hook up?"

"No," said Callie. Hard as it had been to resist, she wouldn't trade a single kiss for the moment when he'd said, "I feel the same way," his fingers brushing across her shoulder, warm like sunlight. It was like every muscle in her body had tensed and relaxed at the same time, flooding her with simultaneous feelings of exhilaration and relief, of security and anticipation. "He made it clear that he would never . . . cheat on you," she added.

Alessandra grimaced, roused from what seemed like her own faraway memory. "You know, before I—came to Harvard, I never had much luck with men. I was what you might call 'a late bloomer.'"

"Why do I find that so hard to believe?" said Callie, taking in Alessandra's chocolatey brown eyes, her full luscious lips, and worthy-of-the-Victoria's-Secret-fashion-show-runway body.

"Believe what you want," Alessandra muttered, "but it's true. Before I met Gregory— Well, let's just say, I was a completely different person back then. I never knew what it could feel like to just . . . fit in. Or to fall in love."

Callie shuffled her feet, glancing at her dirty Converse.

"I do love him," said Alessandra in a tone that compelled Callie to look her in the eyes. "I didn't expect to . . . but I do. And so do you," Alessandra added softly.

Grimly Callie nodded. Since there was really nothing left to say, she began to retreat out of the room.

"Hey," Alessandra called suddenly. "Is this it?"

"Huh?" said Callie, turning.

"Your book," said Alessandra, picking up the volume that stood atop Gregory's bookshelf. "The one that you lent him?"

Callie's heart skipped. She had no idea how she had missed it earlier, for now the book was instantly recognizable. Battered and worn, it was Gregory's copy of Jane Austen's *Persuasion*. They had read it together in the New Haven hospital while waiting for Mimi to recover. Right before the first—and only—time they'd given in to their feelings that they had, up until spring break, been otherwise too cowardly to admit having.

A Post-it note was affixed to the cover.

"'Callie,'" Alessandra read slowly. "'My apologies for the delay.' Huh?" She frowned. "*What* delay?"

Callie shrugged and reached for the book. Just as she knew full well that the book did not belong to her—as Alessandra seemed to think—so she was certain that Gregory had concealed a secret note within its pages.

Reluctantly Alessandra handed it over.

"Well," said Callie, nearly tripping as she stumbled into the common room, "guess I'll see you around!"

"Yeah," Alessandra started to call after her. "See you—"

But Callie didn't hear the rest, slamming the door to C 23 shut behind her.

Out in the hall Callie could restrain herself no longer. Opening the book, she flipped through its pages. Then, frowning, she turned it upside and shook.

Nothing.

Maybe she'd been mistaken to believe there'd be a note. After all, their track record with notes wasn't so good, if the massive mix-up after Harvard-Yale—when a note from Callie to Vanessa had ended up in Gregory's hands and been woefully misinterpreted—was any indication.

Groaning, Callie thumbed through the pages a final time. While there was plenty of marginalia wherein Gregory had recorded his thoughts on the text, no slip of paper confessing his undying love or explaining everything fluttered to the floor.

Shutting the book, she reexamined the Post-it. *My apologies for the delay*, she reread, over and over until the words lost all meaning. Sighing, she opened the door to C 24. She'd been waiting—if she was honest with herself—for the entire year; what was a little more time? "And now on to more pressing issues," she muttered aloud, walking across the common room.

Matt and Vanessa had successfully erected the bulletin board in

Callie's absence, complete with pictures and items cut from the list of "People Who Hate Me" tacked beneath them. If only Vanessa hadn't decimated the yellow legal pad in the process, Callie thought ruefully, they could have added Alessandra to the list.

"Did you make the end of class?" asked Matt.

Callie shook her head.

"Are you okay?" he asked. "What's with the book?"

Callie shook her head again. "It's nothing," she said, sticking it on her shelf.

"Of *course* she's not *okay*," Vanessa said huffily. "Not while the asshole who is trying to frame her, ruin her life, and have her kicked out of the Hasty Pudding, and Harvard, and probably off the planet, too, is still out there plotting her imminent demise!"

Callie raised an eyebrow at Vanessa as if to say, *And that was supposed to make me feel better?*

"There, there," said Vanessa. "I have something that might cheer you up," she continued, snatching a large photograph of Alexis Thorndike and positioning it in the center of the bulletin board. Smiling, she handed Callie a thumbtack.

Grimacing in return, Callie speared it through Lexi's forehead.

Matt shifted uncomfortably. "I still don't think it's wise to expend all of our energy—"

"Oh, please," Vanessa snapped. "She's the only possible person who satisfies all of *your* criteria," she said to Matt, pointing to the upper left-hand side of the board where several index cards bore his handwriting.

FACT: The Ivy Insider had Callie's username and password.
FACT: The Ivy Insider had access to "inside" Pudding information=>is likely a verteran member of the Pudding.
FACT: The Ivy Insider had access to the Crimson offices=>is likely a staff member or COMPer of the Crimson or FM.

Callie stared at the list of "facts." Vanessa was right. There was only one person on the board who was in the Pudding, was on *FM*, and was certainly devious enough to have somehow determined Callie's password.

Alexis Thorndike.

A faint shadow fell across the photograph of Alexis as the sun started to sink behind the brick buildings and towering trees outside in Harvard Yard. Chestnut curls framed porcelain skin and a smile that—darkening in the wake of the setting sun—sent chills down Callie's spine.

"I know you did it," Callie muttered, staring at her archrival's likeness. What I don't know—yet—is how to prove it.

"Don't worry," said Vanessa, placing a hand on Callie's shoulder. "It's only a matter of time until you find a way. . . ."

Pursing his lips, Matt tacked a final item onto the lower right-hand corner of the board. It was the notice alerting Callie to her mid-May hearing date with the Student-Faculty Judicial Board: a grim reminder that, unfortunately, time was also running out.

TWO

I Pledge Allegiance

"TODAY'S GOSSIP IS TOMORROW'S NEWS."

>>IVY LEAGUE >>HARVARD >>STUDENT BODY SCANDALS >>GREGORY BOLTON

Harvard Student Flees Campus Following Father's Hedge Fund Fiasco

#FirstWorldProblems #RichWhiteBoyProblems #HedgeFundScandals #HarvardCampusCelebs

He may still have his smarts, looks, and a bangin' hot girlfriend, but Harvard University freshman Gregory Bolton's trust fund, estimated at way more money than our collective readership will probably see in a lifetime, has barely enough left to fund his tuition.

Cue "The Ballad of Rich White Boy Suffering"

No, but seriously, you've got to feel at least a little bit bad for the guy. According to sources at the *Crimson*, he's been absent from campus for over a week now, rumored to have fled in the middle of the night before the scandal broke surrounding his famed—now *infamous*—hedge fund founding father Pierce Bolton's alleged use of personal funds to pay off investors after a series of toxic investments. Well, shucks, you'd probably run away if Daddy lost all of your classmates' parents' money, too!

Perhaps the most ominous development for the younger Bolton in the unfolding scandal is the widely circulating rumor that investors at Bolton and Stamford Enterprises may have been paid off largely with assets originating from a trust fund in Gregory's name. (Prior to his eighteenth birthday, his father, Pierce, acted as trustee for the account.)

So exactly how complicit is the young Mr. Bolton? Did he have no idea Daddy was pilfering an account set up for him by his late mother, or did he, a former summer intern at Bolton and Stamford, authorize the transactions willingly? No doubt the SEC is also quite curious. Though a criminal complaint still has yet to be filed against Pierce Bolton, certain financial insiders swear that it's "only a matter of time."

It may be too soon, however, to predict that Gregory might eventually trade his single in Wigglesworth, a Harvard dormitory, for bunk beds with Daddy in a white-collar clinker.

Earlier today the *New York Times* reported that a huge "miracle investment" from Constantine Capital Investments in Bolton and Stamford Enterprises is likely to keep the firm afloat even in spite of the large number of withdrawals requested by clientele over the past week.

Is it just a coincidence, then, that the confirmed girlfriend of the younger Mr. Bolton is Alessandra *Constantine*, a sophomore at Harvard University?

We think not!

Ms. Constantine declined to comment, though a recent profile in [*FM* magazine] of the "Cutest Couples on Campus" has her swearing to "stick by [Gregory] no matter what happens." (Incidentally, Bolton—rumored to be under "house arrest" imposed by family attorneys in Manhattan—could also not be reached for comment.)

Constantine and Bolton met this past winter during a New Year's Eve party at the Ritz. According to various classmates, they have been "attached at the hip" ever since, and though the pair has been together only a few short months, friends describe their relationship as: "serious—very serious." Pictures of the couple can also be found in the aforementioned [*FM* magazine] piece.

Ooo la la! Is it just me or does it seem like those two could live on looks alone?

In conclusion, Gregory: whether you emerge unscathed or if the old adage "like father, like son" proves altogether too true, this reporter can be reached @lizbarker in the event that your relationship fails to withstand the scandal(!).

"Now repeat after me," said Tyler Green from where he stood at the head of the largest banquet table in the Hasty Pudding social club. "I solemnly swear—"

"'I solemnly swear,'" Callie muttered along with the rest of the club members who were seated in the dining room anxiously awaiting their lunch.

"That I am not responsible for any of the events that led to the publication of our Punch Book," Tyler boomed, peering slowly around the room.

"'That I am not responsible for any of the events that led to the publication of our Punch Book,'" the members chorused.

"Nor am I the author of the series of Ivy Insider articles," Tyler continued.

A sharp elbow caught Callie in the ribs. "Louder," Vanessa, who was sitting next to Callie, instructed under her breath. Callie glared at her but nonetheless raised her voice in time for Tyler's next missive.

"Nor am I the source for the aforementioned series of articles."

Mimi's stomach grumbled from where she sat on the other side of Callie. "*S'il vous plaît*, just confess already, before I starve to my death," Mimi murmured as everyone repeated, "'Nor do I have any knowledge of the individual or individuals responsible for these traitorous acts.'"

"Mimi!" Vanessa managed in hushed tones, keeping her eyes trained straight ahead. "This. Is not. The time. For jokes!"

"If anyone does have information pertaining to the events of the past few days," called Tyler, ending the session of Simon Says (otherwise known as "The Initiative to Reaffirm Our Loyalty") and pacing around the room, "please come forward immediately. Even the smallest seemingly insignificant details," he continued, making eye contact with first Vanessa, then Mimi, and then Callie as he passed their table, "could prove relevant to exposing the asshole who did this. Now Ian," said Tyler, turning to the computer science major responsible for club security, "are you still absolutely *certain* that this was an inside job?"

Ian nodded from where he sat at one of the other tables. "As I've told you already, it's simply not possible my system was hacked. Whoever did it had the correct password."

"Are you sure?" Tyler pressed.

"Do you think the United States Department of Defense would have just paid me an obscene amount of money to license my software if it *didn't* work?"

"No," said Tyler. "No I don't. But I would have preferred to believe that than the alternative: that the Ivy Insider is currently in this room."

Callie swallowed. From across the way a girl who had temporarily unraveled herself from the arm of the boy sitting next to her smiled.

This smile was different from her usual I-know-your-deepest-darkest-secret grin or the oft-appearing corollary, I-look-genuinely-happy-only-because-I-am-picturing-your-violent-or-publicly-humiliating-demise smirk.

This was the smile of victory, lighting the face that haunted Callie from the center of her bedroom's bulletin board.

Alexis Thorndike had finally won. The evidence was sitting right next to her, wearing one of his signature cashmere sweater vests: Clint Weber, Trophy Boyfriend of the Year, who looked perfectly thrilled as the salad course arrived to offer Lexi the first bite off his fork.

Seriously? Spoon-feeding already crossed a million PDA lines but fork-feeding? Since when were vegetables supposed to be sexy?

Callie's stomach rolled over and not just because she was hungry. Clint seemed content to act as if Callie had never existed, as if he had never scrawled *Callie + Clint* in the snow after they'd constructed an award-winning snowman, or built Callie a private ice skating rink, or brought her favorite Starbucks coffee drink to the *Crimson* offices nearly every evening she had to work late for COMP.

"Ahem-hem-*hem*." Vanessa cleared her throat. "Stare much?" she added, poking Callie under the table.

"Oops," Callie muttered, averting her eyes. "Still, I don't know why I agreed to let you two drag me to this thing, anyway."

Appearing scandalized, Vanessa brandished her knife. "Haven't you ever heard the phrase 'Guilty until she shows up at the next charity event dressed to the nines'?"

"Uh . . . no?" said Callie.

"*Oui, oui,*" Mimi offered between bites. "In cases like these you have simply got to keep calm and carry on."

Callie wrinkled her nose. "Wasn't that the British government's slogan created in case the Nazis successfully invaded?"

"Exactement." Mimi nodded.

Before Callie could respond, the main course arrived. As she took a bite of her lasagna, OK's voice carried from where he was seated on the other side of the table.

"Now, what exactly are you trying to imply?" he demanded of the boy seated to his left.

The boy, a sophomore Callie barely knew, shrugged. "Hey, man, it's not like I'm the first to suggest it! And all I'm saying is that it looks suspicious: not showing up at the emergency meeting about the Punch Book and then leaving school in the middle of the night. . . ."

Callie ducked her head, struggling to tune out OK's reply. Unfortunately everyone else in the vicinity appeared riveted, nodding and murmuring their agreement that there was something "very suspicious indeed" about how Gregory had vanished only hours before the final Insider article went live. Even over OK's protests, rumors began to sweep down the table like wildfire in a sudden wind.

Callie watched, horrified, Vanessa's viselike grip on her arm urging her to *act innocent* and say *nothing*—

Ding, ding, ding, ding, ding.

On the opposite end of the room Alessandra stood, summoning their attention by tinkling a knife against her water glass. "Fellow members . . . friends," she began, clearing her throat. "I can assure you, with absolute certainty, that Gregory is *not* the Ivy Insider."

The lingering whispers and murmurs ceased; silence fell across the room.

"He left before the Punch Book was published, so he had no idea that any of this was going on here at the club until yesterday"—her eyes roamed, pausing briefly on Callie—"when we finally had the opportunity to speak over the phone."

Callie stared at her, but Alessandra's gaze had shifted and she addressed the entire room.

"In fact, as it turns out, he's never even read a single Insider article!" She cleared her throat. "And so, with his . . . *blessing* . . . I'd like to take this opportunity to put any rumors to rest. Not only is Gregory *not* the Insider, but his father's company will *not* be declaring bankruptcy, thanks in part to an investment from *my* father's firm that I am now authorized and happy to confirm. I—*we*—are also thrilled to announce our plans to stay together through this despite any external . . . turmoil."

Callie could feel Mimi's and Vanessa's eyes on her, but she kept hers trained straight ahead, an odd ringing in her ears making it difficult to process the words that continued to flow from Alessandra's lips.

"Unfortunately a lot of the family finances still need to be sorted out, and we're not sure when Gregory will return to school. He sends you all his regards and thanks you for your support and your patience. He wants you to know that he's thinking of all of you even though he is going to be unreachable for some time except by his family members and . . . well, me, obviously!" Alessandra laughed. "And so . . . if anyone has any messages that they'd like me to pass on, let me know, and I'm happy to answer any questions, too. All I ask is that you continue to be supportive during this time in any way you can. Thank you."

"And thank *you* for the update, Alessandra." The clear, high voice cut in from the head of the table at the center of the room, midway between Alessandra and Callie. "Gregory has been a dear friend of mine and my family's for as long as I can remember, and I know that we're all rooting for him." Lexi looked at Clint, who nodded grudgingly. The black eye that Gregory had given him over spring break had all but faded, but Clint's hard feelings for his squash teammate evidently had not.

"Looks like somebody's still bitter about what happened between you and Gregory at Harvard-Yale," Vanessa whispered under her breath.

Mimi leaned in. "A little ironical, coming *de toi*, is it not?"

"Please!" Vanessa snapped in a hushed tone. "That whole crush was *so* last semester. Besides, it was always Callie who he . . . Callie? Callie!"

Callie wasn't listening. Instead, she could not tear her gaze away from Alessandra. Had Gregory really called her? Were they actually staying together?

She's lying, Callie decided. She could still picture that copy of an Insider article in the bottom of Gregory's trash: obviously he had read at least one of the "Behind the Ivy-Covered Walls" installments. And if Alessandra was willing to be dishonest about one thing, who's to say she hadn't made everything else up, too?

"She's lying," Callie said out loud. "I know it."

Mimi made a face.

"What?" Callie demanded, looking between her and Vanessa.

"It just seems like kind of a big thing to lie about," Vanessa admitted with a grimace.

Callie stared from Alessandra, to Clint, to Lexi, and then back to Alessandra. "I—I'll be right back," she managed, lurching to her feet.

Vanessa reached for her hand. "Are you all right?"

"Bathroom," Callie sputtered, heading for the facilities.

A dizzy spell threatened to overtake her. Gripping the edge of the sink, she tried to steady herself, willing the tiny room to stop spinning. Breathing deeply, she turned on the faucet and splashed cool water on her face. Maybe Gregory really had called Alessandra. Maybe they were still together; maybe he'd changed his mind. Or maybe he hadn't changed at all—and was still the same womanizing, unreliable, irresistible, unattainable a-hole that Callie had turned down at the start of that semester when she'd chosen Clint instead.

Oops. What had seemed like "better boyfriend material" then was currently out in the dining room fork-feeding Callie's worst enemy and probably experimenting with various ways to elide their names into a celebrity nickname (Clexi? Alexint? Clinexis? Kleenex!). He had also cheated on Callie (with Lexi) and lied about his friendship (with Lexi), which he had maintained, at least in part, due to parental pressure from his mother, who had urged her son to cozy up to Lexi's uncle, a governor, for the purposes of his securing a summer internship.

Eugh—another wave of nausea assaulted her. Was Gregory staying with Alessandra for similar reasons? Because her father had invested in his father's hedge fund and now he had no choice?

But then why apologize for the "delay" on a Post-it note instead of just pre-dumping (since they had never really dated) à la season six of *Sex and the City* ("I'm sorry. I can't. Don't hate me.")? *If* his Post-it was even recent, Callie realized suddenly. He might've written it eons ago—like, for example, in November.

Reaching into her pocket, Callie pulled out her phone.

What's the point? she thought as she dialed, preparing to hear the same automated message ("I'm sorry, but the number you are calling has been disconnected. Please hang up and try your call again") for the 202,678th time.

Instead, it rang.

Callie gasped at the same moment a click sounded and the line went dead. Redialing frantically, she placed the phone to her ear, only to encounter that same, robotic monotone—

A faint knock sounded at the door.

Frowning, Callie set her phone on the sink.

Vanessa, probably, come to insist that "innocent people never poo during a party"—or something.

Sighing, Callie unlocked the door. "I thought I told you that tandem peeing is creepy— Oh . . . um. . . ."

"You missed dessert," a clear voice said sweetly, its owner stepping into the bathroom.

Alexis Thorndike.

Callie backed up until she accidentally bumped into the wall. "What are you—what do you want?" she sputtered.

Lexi smiled, taking a step forward. "I wanted to check on you, of course! You must be feeling terrible, given the recent turn of events."

Callie swallowed. Well, this confirms it: out of all of Lexi's various personas, Playing Nice was definitely the most alarming.

"Really, I commend you for your courage in showing your face here today," Lexi continued, oozing sincerity out of every miniscule porcelain pore. "Most people in your position might be a lot less . . . *brave* considering that the only thing preventing everyone out there from finding out about what you did is—well—me."

Callie clenched her fists, fighting the urge to smack the smirk right off the older girl's face. "Dean Benedict insisted that their *suspicions* stay strictly confidential," Callie said quietly through gritted teeth. "Break that confidence and you have just as much to lose as I do, starting with your *interim* position as editor at the *Crimson*."

Lexi laughed. "Relax, would you?" she said. "I'm perfectly content to wait and see how it all plays out during your hearing in May. In fact, since the matter is so near and dear to my heart, I've already volunteered to serve as one of the students on the Student-Faculty Judicial Board."

Callie stared at her. "You . . . can't possibly . . ." Could she?

"Don't worry." Lexi smiled. "I plan to stay completely impartial until I've heard all the facts."

"I'm innocent," Callie stated flatly. "I'm *not* the Insider."

"You know what?" said Lexi, coming so close that Callie could smell her Chanel No. 5. "I'm actually inclined to believe you."

Callie's heart stopped. "Why's that?" she asked. Because *you* did it?

"Because whoever did it," Lexi started, her eyes dancing, "would have to be incredibly smart and incredibly sneaky . . . neither of which describes you."

Callie closed her eyes. "Speaking of sneaky," she said after a beat, "shouldn't you be getting back to Clint? I think we both know what happens when he's left unsupervised among so many eager freshman girls."

The effect was instantaneous: Lexi's smile melted, her eyes frosting over with a far more familiar glare. Her hand, which had been hovering near the doorknob, froze. To leave now would only validate Callie's implication: once a cheater, always a cheater.

Callie held Lexi's gaze, refusing to break the silence.

DudududuDU, du du du DU du du DU—

The sound of Callie's ringtone blasted through the air. Lexi, who stood closer to the sink, extended her arm as if to reach for the phone, the word *Restricted* lighting its screen. Callie dove to intercept her: watching in horror as their hands collided and the phone toppled and then fell with a resounding *plop*—straight into the toilet.

"Sorry," said Lexi, looking anything but as Callie stared down at her phone, which was bobbing like the last rotten apple in a barrel. The waterlogged screen appeared to have frozen, doomed to forever register that final, mysterious, incoming call. Callie bit back tears, knowing it could be a full month until she could afford a replacement.

Turning on her way out of the bathroom, Lexi offered one final sympathetic, simpering smile. "This just really isn't your year."

THREE

Going Once, Going Twice . . . SOLD!

HPSC presents . . .

THE 35TH ANNUAL

DATE AUCTION

ON:
Saturday, April 9

FROM:
8 p.m.—Midnight

AT:
The Hong Kong

ALL ARE WELCOME

ALL PROCEEDS WILL BE DONATED TO CHARITY

Preview our amazing auctionees online: auction.harvard/hpsc

"But you have to go!" Vanessa screamed through the wall between bedrooms in Wigglesworth suite C 24.

"WHY?" Callie yelled back.

"Because I signed us up as volunteers a month ago!" Vanessa shouted. "And because . . ."

"*Parce que* it will be *très amusant*," Mimi cried from where she was sitting in the common room on the couch next to Dana, her head gleefully Ping-Ponging back and forth between the two bedrooms.

"Yes, it will be *fun*," Vanessa insisted, mistaking the French word for *funny*. "And maybe, just maybe, you'll meet someone new and he'll sweep you off your feet by making the highest bid and—"

"Someone new," Callie started, stalking out of her bedroom wearing soccer shorts and a sports bra, "is the absolute *last* thing I need right now."

"Well, then do it because . . ." Vanessa's mouth hung open from where she stood in the doorway to her bedroom. "Because . . ."

"Because it's for charity?" Dana folded her arms.

"Yes!" Vanessa cried. "Yes, thank you, Dana. Do it for the penguins, Callie. *The penguins.*"

Callie stared at her. "What penguins? What?"

"You know, the penguins, with their little feet stuck in those plastic things from around my Diet Cokes that you're always yelling about," Vanessa fired back. "And the oil spills, and the otters, and their little paws—" She paused to do what appeared to be an otter imitation, raising her hands to her mouth like paws and widening her eyes. "And because of the hole in the ozone layer, which, if you don't allow yourself to be auctioned for just one little date tonight, is going to get bigger, and bigger, and bigger—"

"Okay!" Callie cried. "I'll go—so long as you promise to STOP—TALKING!"

"Deal," said Vanessa, bounding into her bedroom and returning with a dress. "Now put this on."

"*Ugghh*," Callie groaned. "Why do I let you talk me into these things?" Disappearing into her room, she threw on the dress.

"Because you love me," Vanessa called from her bedroom, where she was strapping on her high heels. "And because deep down you know I'm always right."

"Ear, ear," Mimi cheered, clapping her hands as both girls reappeared in the common room clad in cocktail attire.

"Don't think you're exempt from attending tonight either," Vanessa snapped at Mimi. "Just because you're not an auctionee doesn't mean you can't come and show us your support."

Mimi grinned. "I would not miss it for all the spices in India."

"Hear, hear," Dana muttered, stretching and rising to her feet. "We both promised to bid on OK," she explained in response to Vanessa's questioning look. "He wants us to form a 'ring' and collude to drive the price up as high as possible. It's for *charity*," she added at Callie's raised eyebrows.

Mimi chuckled wickedly. "More like he is worried that no one will be bidding on him at all," she supplied.

"Oh, *great*," said Callie, "yet another reason why—"

"Don't start!" Vanessa cried, grabbing Callie's hand and dragging her to the door. "Let's go—all of you—now!" And so they followed her, off to what was sure to be—or so Callie assumed—the latest installment in her weekly dose of humiliation.

A wooden stage had been erected in the upstairs lounge at the Hong Kong restaurant, Harvard Square's only equivalent of an underground nightclub, where the greasy Chinese food on the first floor served as the perfect 2 A.M. antidote to an evening of dancing and scorpion bowls. Tyler Green, Vanessa's on-again, off-again boyfriend (current status = "*NEVER*-again," according to Vanessa, meaning they'd probably be making out by the end of the night), stood center stage fiddling with a microphone as the auctionees trickled in "dressed to impress." Most were fellow freshmen, Callie noted, who like her had "volunteered" (i.e., had been strongly "encouraged" as the newer members of the club to participate in an age-old tradition that "in absolutely no way constituted hazing" regardless of whether or not they already had a significant other because it was for "such a good cause").

"Testing, one-two-three." Tyler spoke into the microphone, tapping the surface. "Good, it works," he muttered. "Looks like we're all here," he added, addressing the room. "Thank you for coming a few minutes early so we could go over the protocol. Essentially, feel free to mingle with the crowd once they arrive, but remember that you are being auctioned for a date, and so please, keep it classy." He cleared his throat. "No one wants to buy a nice date package with a picnic for two and a swan boat ride in Boston Commons and then see their date grinding with randos on the dance floor five minutes later, capiche?"

Vanessa rolled her eyes. "Control freak," she muttered. Callie elbowed her in the ribs.

"When I call your name," Tyler continued, "you will join me, the MC, on stage. Then I'll describe the particular date up for auction, as well as listing some of the fun, flirty, and *colorful* details we asked all of you to submit."

"What?" Callie said sharply, turning to Vanessa.

"No worries, girlfriend," Vanessa sassed. "I took care of all that for you."

Before Callie could respond that nothing could be *more* worrisome, Mimi materialized and handed her a drink. "Courtesy of his royal highness," she explained, nodding to where OK sat at the bar talking intently with Dana. No doubt he was reminding her of her promise to bid on him. Callie grimaced, taking a big gulp of her fruity-tasting beverage. Mimi winked. Meanwhile Vanessa returned to glaring at Tyler.

"Well, that just about covers it!" Tyler finished. A line of students had started to form behind the red velvet rope blocking the entrance to the lounge. "Thank you all for participating, and please remember that however high or low, those bids aren't *really* for you; they're for charity!"

Right, thought Callie, exhaling as Tyler unhooked the rope and the room flooded with her fellow classmates, clad in cocktail attire and gossiping openly about the auctionees. Callie recognized

Tom, a reporter from *FM* magazine, standing next to Marcus who, equipped with his camera, had already started snapping candids. It's not for me; it's for charity. It's not for—crap! She ducked behind Vanessa—out of sight of Clint, who had just appeared with Alexis on his arm. Several seconds later Matt walked into the room, followed by Grace Lee. A date or *Crimson* business?

Crimson business, Callie decided, sneaking a quick wave at Matt before turning away to avoid catching Grace's eye.

"WELCOME, ladies and gentlemen," Tyler boomed suddenly, "to the thirty-fifth annual Charity Date Auction, brought to you by the members of the Hasty Pudding social club! Thank you for joining us this evening. We've put together some wonderful date packages for you all with some of your favorite underclassmen! For those new faces out there who don't know the drill: if you see something you like"—Tyler winked—"raise your hand, and when I point to you, yell out your bid. Bidding will start at the face-value cost of each individual date package, but there are no upper limits from there! So open those wallets, grab a drink, and get ready to have some fun!"

The crowd cheered. Callie swallowed. The whole school was there, or at least what felt like it, ready to witness her sell for approximately zero dollars and zero cents.

"So now, without further ado, allow me to introduce our very first auctionee, hailing all the way from sunny California . . ."

Frack. Callie gripped Vanessa's hand. Please don't tell me that he's calling us in alphabetical ord—

"Callieeeeee Annnnndrews!" Tyler yelled.

Callie barely heard the applause over the thundering sound of her pulse in her ears.

"Go on," Vanessa urged, giving her a gentle shove.

Callie's legs trembled in her heels as she mounted the stage. Turning, she faced the crowd, keeping her eyes trained on a neon Bud Light sign mounted on the far wall.

Glancing at her, Tyler covered the microphone. "Smile," he whispered, offering her one in return.

Callie nodded, exposing her teeth. Hopefully it didn't look like a grimace.

"Callie is a freshman planning to concentrate in English literature," Tyler began. "When she isn't studying, she's usually blogging about how much she loves her roommates or cru— cruising?—yes, cruising for books—er, books is in quotes—at the front desk in Lamont Library. She's traveled to all seven continents and, extremely coordinated, can last for seven minutes in some of the most complicated positions in yoga. Finally, while she holds a high school title of state champion in soccer, her true passions include competitive fly-fishing, competitive pie eating, and competitive figure skating."

I'll kill you, Callie thought, shooting a death-glare at Vanessa. Vanessa shrugged, struggling not to appear amused. Tyler continued, detailing the dinner-and-a-movie date package up for auction, but Callie stayed intent on Vanessa, willing her roommate to hear her interior monologue, which went along the lines of: Fly-fishing? Competitive Pie Eating? EXTREMELY COORDINATED?

Vanessa held up her hands and next to her, Mimi beamed, giving Callie two thumbs-up.

"So," Tyler finally finished, "the bidding for this package starts at sixty dollars. Do I hear sixty? Only sixty dollars for dinner and a movie and the priceless company of the lovely Ms. Andrews . . . Anyone?"

Callie closed her eyes. Worst fear = realized. Despite the hustle and bustle from the excited crowd, not a single person had raised his hand. Even Matt and OK stayed silent: the former probably prevented by the presence of his crush and the latter, his status as an auctionee.

"Come on now, guys," Tyler said. "Don't be shy. All it takes is one look at her to know that sixty dollars is a real steal—wha—er—ah, yes, and it seems we have our first bidder?"

Callie's eyes flew open, just in time to see a suspended arm being yanked down by the girl standing next to its owner.

Alexis Thorndike, looking far more murderous than Callie had only moments earlier, maintained her viselike grip on Clint's arm, muttering furiously. "Er . . ." Tyler faltered, watching his roommate turn to address his girlfriend.

Callie felt her cheeks flush scarlet. The only thing that could possibly be worse than no bid at all was a pity bid from your ex, who apparently still felt guilty for screwing you over.

Clint lowered his hand, shaking his head at Tyler.

Scratch that: a *retracted* pity bid was definitely worse.

Tyler made a face at Callie. He had never, as he'd once confided in her, liked Alexis, and even though to call his relationship with Vanessa "rocky" would be putting it lightly, he and Callie had always gotten along.

"Uh, right." Tyler cleared his throat. "Just to clarify, if you'd like to bid simply raise your hand and I will call on you. . . . So let's try this again. The bidding starts at sixty dollars, just sixty dollars. . . . Ah yes, you sir, there, on the left," he pointed.

"One hundred dollars," said the boy, lowering his hand. It was Bryan Jacobs, Callie's old classmate from West Hollywood High, now a junior in the same Final Club, the Fly, as Tyler and Clint.

"ONE HUNDRED DOLLARS!" cried Tyler, speaking quickly, one eye still trained on his roommate. "Going-once-going-twice-and-SOLD! And what a way to start the night!" he boomed over the crowd's applause.

Callie tried to smile at Bryan, but her face felt frozen. Fortunately her legs took over with only one mission in mind: exit stage right.

Vanessa's outstretched arms were waiting. Callie lacked the energy to brush them off. "You did great," Vanessa reassured her. Callie scoffed but allowed her roommate to lead her to where Dana and Mimi were waiting, seated now on stools around a small table near the bar at the back of the crowd. Mimi conjured up another drink while Dana nodded at Callie. "I had no idea you were such a seasoned world traveler," she said.

"I'm not," Callie muttered, rounding on Vanessa. "Seven continents!? Why—"

"Because fun facts are supposed to be funny! And greatly exaggerated!" Vanessa insisted. "Trust me. This is not my first rodeo."

"*Ceci n'est pas* her first bachelorette auction," said Mimi, appearing delighted to be translating for once.

Callie folded her arms. "Thank god it's only Bryan," she murmured, smiling weakly at him across the room. "Otherwise I might have had to learn how to fly-fish or, heaven forbid, become balanced enough to do yoga!"

"Speaking of dates," said Vanessa, "how crazy was that when Clint—"

"BOLTON?" Tyler's magnified voice rang across the room.

Callie spun around so fast that she tumbled off her stool. Steadying herself against the table, she searched the crowd—

"Gregory Bol— Oh," Tyler stopped himself, crossing a name off the list. "That's right. He's not . . . here." Callie heard him mutter into the microphone.

"And speaking of balancing," Vanessa picked up without missing a beat, ushering Callie back onto the stool, "you need to take a serious chill pill."

Mimi started rifling through her purse. "I believe I have a Valium or at the very least a Xanax playing seek and hide in here somewhere. . . ."

Dana shook her head. "I'm sure if he could be here, he would have bid on you," she said, placing a hand on Callie's wrist as Tyler called the next auctionee's name.

"Not like he could afford it!" Vanessa exclaimed.

"Vanessa!" Dana snapped.

"What?" Vanessa was indignant. "I'm just saying that if anything, Gregory's the one who *needs* charity now—"

"That's enough!" Callie commanded, tilting her head pointedly at the group of *FM* reporters congregating nearby. Fortunately Alessandra stood out of earshot, readying for her onstage debut, where she would no doubt fetch a gazillion and ten dollars for charity.

"Sorry," Vanessa muttered, chewing her lip. "I guess I was being a little loud."

"Smile!" Marcus Taylor cried, stepping forward from the *FM* crew and brandishing his camera. There was a blinding flash, followed by the deafening roar of applause as "the moment you've all been waiting for," i.e., "MISS ALESSANDRA CONSTANTINE!" took the stage. Callie blinked, fairly certain her face was going to look deformed in that photo.

"So what'd it feel like to be the first auctionee?" asked a girl Callie recognized as one of Lexi's evil *FM* spider monkeys, joining Marcus and pulling out a notepad.

"Uh," said Callie, struggling to tune out the fierce bidding war brewing among several men in the audience. "Somewhat objectifying?" she offered, thinking of Grace, who in the days before her probation probably would have loved to get a quote condemning the auction.

"Going once . . . going twice . . . and SOLD! For a record breaking—so far—amount, especially given that she's taken." Tyler beamed at Alessandra, who smiled back.

"No further comments," Callie announced loudly. A gazillion and ten dollars wasn't too far off. "That's right," she added to Mimi, who had just placed another drink in front of her. "Keep 'em coming. Bottoms up," she muttered, spying Lexi and Clint, who appeared to have made up, in the corner. Well done, Sweater Vest. You two deserve each other, Callie thought bitterly. So you can take your *charity* bid and shove it up your—

"Bryan!" Callie shrieked, leaping to her feet and hugging the boy who had just approached. "My hero," she intoned, stepping back but keeping her hands on his water-polo-and-swim-team-enhanced shoulders.

"Excellent," Marcus encouraged them, the bulb in his camera flashing. "Now one more, for the cheap seats in the back!"

Callie rolled her eyes and moved closer to Bryan, who threw a brotherly arm around her shoulders. "Thank you," she said quietly when the camera had stopped flashing, frowning at the lingering *FM* reporters.

"For what?" asked Bryan with a sportsmanlike grin.

"For being the one and only person to bid on me," Callie replied.

"It was my pleasure," said Bryan. "Anything for a good cause, right?"

"Exactly," Vanessa chimed in, flipping her strawberry blond locks. "Won't you join us?"

"Sure," he said, pulling up a stool.

Callie smiled. Some of Vanessa's mannerisms vaguely reminded Callie of her best friend, Jessica, whom Bryan had briefly dated back in high school. He's all yours, Callie attempted to will her roommate.

Unfortunately Vanessa seemed to have the exact same thought in mind as far as Callie and Bryan were concerned: singing

Callie's praises in between stopping to giggle at some of the other auctionees "fun flirty *facts*," ranging from "her fourth-grade science project inspired CERN's Large Hadron Collider" to "he starred as a backup dancer in a Lady Gaga video."

And yet, even in spite of Vanessa's clunky, obvious attempts at matchmaking, the evening flew by. Before Callie knew it, Tyler was announcing the winning bid on Penelope Vandemeer, a fellow freshman who had remained in the Pudding despite her threats to quit after reading the nasty things the older members had to say about her when the Insider published the Punch Book.

"You're next," Callie said, smiling at Vanessa. "Revenge will be so, so sweet."

"I, for one, couldn't be more excited," said Vanessa, standing and smoothing her dress. "Just picture the look on Tyler's face when he sees how many other men are interested in—"

"AND NOW . . ." Tyler paused, glancing in their direction. "OK ZEYNA!"

"*What?*" Vanessa gasped.

"OK Zeyna to the stage please," Tyler repeated, grinning wickedly. "And here he is, ladies and gentleman," he cried as OK appeared, "our final contestant of the night!"

"What!" Vanessa shrieked again. "Did he just—deliberately—*skip* me?"

"*C'est la vie*," said Mimi, winking at Callie. Even Dana cracked a smile. "Whoever digs a pit will fall into it," she intoned, "and a stone will come back on him who starts it rolling."

"English, please," Vanessa snapped.

"That. Is. Life!" said Mimi.

"Karma can be such a Thorndike," Callie added, patting her on the back.

Vanessa gaped. "But I—"

"Educated in London but with origins in Nigeria, our final contestant's claim to royal roots is no secret," Tyler boomed, eliciting cheers from the crowd.

"But now for a few things you probably didn't already know about his majesty," Tyler continued. OK grinned, hamming it up for the audience. "He loves any and all reality TV shows with America in the title, from *Top Model to Idol.* He likes long romantic walks on the stone pathway between Wigglesworth and Annenberg, virtual race car driving, and all music with the exception of the—and I quote—'horrendous posers in Sexy Hansel'"—this incited some spirited boos—"and finally, would like all the ladies in the house to know that while he's only twenty-five percent British and fifty percent royalty, he is a resounding one hundred and ten percent SINGLE!"

Mimi rolled her eyes. "I suppose this is our cue to start the bidding," she said to Dana. "Would you prefer to go first or should—"

"TWO HUNDRED AND FIFTY DOLLARS!" an upperclassman girl screamed from the center of the crowd.

Tyler smiled into the microphone. "Ladies, please remember to raise your hands if you'd like to bid. Now I heard two hundred and fifty; do I hear two sixty? Yes, you there," he cried, pointing to another girl. Several other hands had shot up in the meantime.

"I guess we won't be needed after all," said Dana.

Mimi narrowed her eyes. "This is just—"

"All right, now we have three hundred from the lady in the back!" Tyler cried. "Next up—yes, you there, on the left—"

"—*absurde*." Mimi finished.

"Is somebody—dare I say it—*jealous*?" Vanessa demanded.

"*Absolutement pas!*" Mimi denied it with a wave of her hand.

"And we have three hundred and fifty," Tyler announced. "Going once . . . going twice . . . and—what the—"

OK, eager, it appeared, for more bids, had removed his shirt and started circling it above his head. The crowd went wild.

"Well, this is certainly a first," Tyler remarked over the shrill sound of female screaming. He laughed as OK chucked his shirt across the lounge.

"Four hundred dollars!" belted a senior who'd wrestled the garment away from her peers like a bouquet-crazed bridesmaid.

"Ladies, please wait until I've called on you," Tyler urged while OK, who'd been sauntering up and down the stage, reached to undo his belt. "Let's try to keep this civilized—"

"FIVE HUNDRED DOLLARS!" It was Marcus Taylor, *FM* photographer and bartender at the Cambridge Queen's Head pub, whose interest in OK had always been abundantly clear to everyone with the exception of his highness.

Up on stage OK froze. Then, with a shrug, he beamed, sliding his belt out of its loops.

"Is it over yet?" Dana asked, her fingers plastered over her eyes.

"Going once . . ." Tyler warned. "Going twice . . ."

"FIVE HUNDRED EUROS!" Mimi screamed, standing.

"Five hundred . . . euros?" Tyler repeated. "Er, how many dollars is that?"

"Approximately six hundred and fifty-eight," called a boy near the stage.

"SOLD!" OK yelled, grabbing the microphone. "To the lovely Miss Marine Clément—"

"Now hang on just a minute," Tyler interjected, yanking back the mike. "You there," he called, pointing to the girl who, still clinging to OK's shirt, had just raised her hand.

"One thousand dollars!" she screamed, jumping up and down.

OK's face fell. Mimi, by contrast, appeared quite serene as she reassumed her seat.

"One thousand dollars: by far the highest bid of the night!" Tyler echoed loudly. Then, with his hand only partially obscuring the microphone, he added with a stern look at OK, "Bro, seriously. The pants stay on."

OK frowned.

"Going once . . . going twice . . . and . . . SOLD, for a whopping one thousand dollars to the lucky lady holding the shirt! What a way to end the bidding, folks! But wait—don't head for the door just yet! 'Cause my man DJ Damien Zhang's about to start spinning some serious tunes, so get ready to grab your favorite auctionee and hit the dance floor!"

Half an hour later, after some halfhearted dancing, Callie stood making conversation with Bryan. Vanessa had abandoned them to go yell at Tyler. Dana had excused herself and Mimi had just flat out disappeared, much to the dismay of OK, who'd been cornered by his winning bidder and appeared unable to retrieve his shirt. And Matt, Callie felt certain, would be found wherever Grace might be—probably back at the *Crimson* offices, overseeing other reporters' draft coverage of the auction.

"So . . . you keep in touch with Jessica much?" Bryan asked, confirming Callie's suspicions that her best friend was a heartbreaker.

"Only about twice a day," said Callie. "Even if it's just a stupid Facebook poke."

Bryan laughed. "That's good to hear. She planning a visit soon?"

Callie sighed. "She keeps promising to come and then flaking out when I try to make her commit to actual dates— Oh, excuse me," Callie apologized, spotting Vanessa who, having finally tired of Tyler, was motioning frantically at Callie from the bar.

"Sorry to interrupt," Vanessa gushed. Callie rolled her eyes. "But here," Vanessa continued, thrusting her iPhone into Callie's hands. "Call your dad."

"What?" asked Callie.

"He called a few minutes ago looking for you."

"My dad . . . called *you*? Looking for me?" Callie repeated.

"Yes, but since you seemed *very busy* dancing with a certain handsome gentleman from California, I explained that you were otherwise occupied." Vanessa beamed. "You're welcome, by the way."

"But . . . how did he get your number?"

"Probably because you gave it to him after that five-pound hunk of scrap metal you called a phone finally put us all out of our misery by kamikaze-ing into the toilet, remember, genius? 'If my parents don't have a number where they can reach me, they will freak and think I *died*—'"

"Oh, right," said Callie. "Thanks," she added, glancing at the phone. "I'll be right back."

"Ask him for an iPhone!" Vanessa called after her.

"Oh, to be you!" Callie shot back as she headed for the stairs, well aware that her paychecks from working the front desk at Lamont Library could only stretch so far.

Outside, Callie dialed her dad's cell. After a few rings it went to his voice mail. That's weird, she thought, staring at the iPhone's call log. It showed no record of an incoming call from any of her father's lines. Instead, the only incoming call was from a restricted number, registering above several other missed calls, also labeled *restricted.*

She shivered even though it was a relatively temperate night. What if . . . ?

"Oh my god," she muttered aloud, dashing back into the Kong.

"Vanessa!" she called breathlessly when she reached the upstairs lounge, weaving her way across the crowded dance floor. "Vanessa!"

Vanessa turned around from where she still stood near the bar. "Is everything okay—"

"What did my dad say—*exactly*—when he called?"

"Um, I don't know, just that he was looking for you, and then when I said you were busy, he hung up?"

"Yes, but did he actually *say* that he was my dad?" Callie demanded, grabbing Vanessa by the arms.

"Huh." Vanessa frowned. "To be honest, it was somewhat

difficult to hear over the sound of DJ Damien mixed with Tyler's colossal stupidity . . . but what other deep-voiced dude would be calling my phone looking for you at this time of night other than your da— Oh." Vanessa paused. "You don't think . . . ?"

"What about all these missed calls?" said Callie, holding up Vanessa's phone. "*Also* from a restricted number?"

"They could be from anyone," Vanessa said gently, examining the call log. "Sorry, but I try to screen as often as possible, even when it comes to the numbers I do recognize."

"What?" cried Callie. "Why?"

"Answering the phone the first time someone calls is, like, *so* overeager. Do you want whoever's calling to think you've got nothing better to do than sit around waiting for it to ring? Screening a call or not responding to a text is the fastest way to let a guy know how desirable you— Oh, what's the use trying to teach you these things when you're clearly not even listening?"

"It was Gregory," Callie whispered, her eyes bright. "I know it."

Vanessa scrunched up her nose. "Just like you *know* Alessandra is lying about the fact they're still together?"

"Yes, I do know and I think I can prove—" Callie stopped short, glancing suspiciously over her shoulder. "Any chance you're ready to leave?" she asked.

"Sure," said Vanessa. "This party's a bust anyway. I wouldn't go on a date with anyone here even if they'd had the fair opportunity to pay me."

Callie laughed. "I'll get our coats."

When they were outside, Vanessa rounded on her. "So what's the deal?"

"Before Gregory disappeared, he left me . . . a note," Callie confessed quietly as their heels clicked along the cobblestones.

"What?" said Vanessa, stopping outside Dexter Gate. "Where? When?"

"On a Post-it . . . right before he disappeared, I think."

"A Post-it?" Vanessa repeated skeptically, starting to walk again. "What'd it say?"

Callie took a deep breath. "'Callie: My apologies for the delay.'"

"That's it?" Vanessa frowned. "I mean . . . sorry."

"It was significant," Callie persevered. "He stuck it on a book that we both love and then left it for me to find."

"Left it where?"

"In his room."

"So you found this note in his room?"

"Actually Alessandra found it."

Vanessa stared at her. "Was it even signed?"

"Initialed. G. B."

"Let me get this straight," Vanessa started slowly, halting in front of Wigglesworth, entryway C. "Out of everything he could have done to explain his absence or tell you how he feels, he chose a Post-it, and you think 'sorry for the delay' actually means 'wait for me, baby,' except it's in, like, code or something because even though it's addressed to you he somehow . . . knew that Alessandra might find it before you did?"

"Exactly," said Callie, though for some reason it sounded incredibly far-fetched when Vanessa said it out loud. "Or maybe he meant to write more, but he . . . ran out of time?"

"Okay," said Vanessa. "I—er—hate to be the voice of reason here, but when I think back to your track record with notes and to his track record in general . . ." Vanessa made a face as if she didn't like what was about to come out of her mouth. "This isn't the first time he's vanished in the morning and left you with no explanation," she pointed out, recalling Gregory's behavior after Harvard-Yale.

"Yes," Callie admitted, "but that was because of Clint—"

"Clint—Alessandra—there's always someone else, or something else, keeping you two apart," Vanessa interrupted. "When are you going to stop making excuses for him and admit that maybe it's just not meant to be?"

Callie recoiled, stunned.

"Sorry!" Vanessa wailed instantly. "I'm sorry, that came out—ugh! What I'm trying to say is it's not you, it's me. It's not me, actually, it's my mom. Her therapist and her spiritual guide from the Manhattan Kabbalah Centre are both on vacay this week, so she won't stop calling me and spewing all this psychobabble bullshit about my dad and—"

"It's okay," said Callie, placing a hand on Vanessa's shoulder. "You don't have to explain yourself. Let's just . . . go inside." She scanned her key against the lock. "Anyway," she continued as they mounted the stairs, "you might be right. Maybe I should stop making excuses for him. Maybe we really aren't . . . meant to be."

"Are you okay?" Vanessa asked, pausing at the top of the stairs.

Callie swallowed. "I'm fine. But it's true: if he really wanted to reach me, wouldn't he have found a way? And definitively dumped Alessandra?"

"Eh." Vanessa shrugged. "Look on the bright side: if you're right and she's lying, then at the very least he hasn't contacted either of you."

"She *is* lying." Callie furrowed her brow. "And you know what? I can prove it!" Grabbing Vanessa's hand, she dragged her down the hall, stopping in front of suite C 23.

"Callie, what are we—"

"Shh," hissed Callie, holding a finger to her lips. Then, opening the door, she pulled Vanessa inside.

It was dark, but they could hear noises coming from OK's bedroom.

Noises of a certain nature known to inspire giggles, which Vanessa succumbed to but quickly stifled. "Looks like someone got more than just a date tonight," Vanessa whispered as they tiptoed across the room.

Callie shook her head, ushering Vanessa into Gregory's empty bedroom and shutting the door softly behind them.

"What are we doing in here?" Vanessa asked, flicking on the light.

"Proving that Alessandra was lying," Callie said, crossing to the desk. "Ah-ha!" she cried a moment later, holding up an old copy of the *Crimson*.

"So what?" said Vanessa.

"The other day at the Pudding, Alessandra said that when Gregory called her, he told her that he'd essentially never even *heard* of the Ivy Insider."

Vanessa appeared unimpressed.

"Look!" Callie insisted, pointing to the headline for an op-ed about the Insider.

"I don't see how that proves anything," said Vanessa. "Just because there's a copy of the *Crimson* in our bathroom right now doesn't mean that *I've* ever read a word of it!"

Callie narrowed her eyes.

"What!" Vanessa cried. "It's not like you're COMPing anymore . . . eesh—sorry. My bad, again."

Callie sighed, setting the newspaper back down on Gregory's desk. "Hey!" she called in hushed tones. "Come here and take a look at this."

"What now?"

"There," said Callie, pointing to the trash can. "All the way at the bottom. I think it's a printout of an Insider article!"

"Ew!" said Vanessa, whacking Callie's hand away. "Don't touch that—it's garbage."

"Precisely," said Callie, dropping her arm and straightening. "And what do you think he was doing with that article *before* he threw it away?"

"What?" asked Vanessa, her eyes going wide. "Are you saying . . . ?"

"Yes." Callie nodded. "He—

"—wrote it!" Vanessa exclaimed at the same time Callie cried, "read it!"

Callie stared at her. "Wait, wha—"

A high-pitched moan sounded from somewhere in the vicinity of OK's bedroom.

Callie froze and then motioned to Vanessa that it was time to leave. Quickly they turned off the light. Racing across the common room, they shut the front door just in time to block out what sounded like OK doing a Tarzan yell.

Catching each other's eye, they burst into giggles.

"Gross," said Vanessa when she could speak again.

"So gross," Callie agreed, opening the door to their common room. "I mean, I love the guy, but that doesn't mean I want to hear him . . . uh, you know . . ."

"Hear who what?" asked Dana, poking her head up from over the top of the overstuffed armchair, where she had curled up with a book.

"Hey, Dana!" Callie called, starting to giggle again.

"It's nothing," Vanessa assured her. "Nothing at all. Where's Mimi?"

"Lampoon initiation, probably," said Dana. "She mentioned that it started today."

"Oh," said Vanessa with a yawn. "Well, I don't know about you two, but I'm exhausted!"

"Same here," said Callie, heading for her bedroom. "Good night, you guys!"

Once inside she kicked off her shoes. She was halfway out of her dress when she paused, staring at the bulletin board on her wall. Frowning, she shook her head.

After pulling on pj's, she plucked Gregory's copy of *Persuasion* off her shelf. The photo from Harvard-Yale fluttered out alongside it. She glanced at Gregory's face, and then at the thumbtacks on her desk, and then back at the board, Vanessa's words reverberating like a bad echo. Could he be . . . ? No, she decided, sticking the photo back on her bookcase and plopping on her bed with the book. "Definitely not," she muttered aloud as she started to read.

At least I definitely *hope* not.

FOUR

Eat, Party, Love

(Harvard) Society Pages

*All the gossip that's fit to print**

The toast of the weekend social scene was, quite obviously, the HPSC's Annual Charity Date Auction. Almost *everyone*–with one notable exception–was there, but for those unfortunate few who missed it, a recap.

The auctionees were called in alphabetical order, and luckily the bids grew increasingly higher as the night wore on, starting with a measly one hundred dollars and ending with a rousing thousand.

Callie Andrews, the first auctionee, was seen canoodling with her purchaser, Bryan Jacobs, for the remainder of the evening. Looks like she's moved on to her next upperclassman in the prestigious Fly Club for Gentlemen. The two new lovebirds haven't even been on their date yet, and we hear she's already referring to him as her "one and only."

Other notable auctionees included Alessandra Constantine (duh), Aaron Thomas (lacrosse hottie alert!), and Penelope Vandemeer (jet owner), who all stood tall on behalf of their club, the Hasty Pudding, even though all were anonymously slammed in the Pudding's Punch Book by their (now) fellow veteran members. For these three, among others, agreeing to be auctioned on behalf of the club (in a pretty transparent attempt at image rehabilitation) was certainly charitable in more ways than one!

(Incidentally, of the seven people questioned over the course of the evening, not one guessed the charity correctly. Gee, how embarrassing.)

OK Zeyna was the highest-priced ticket item of the night, with Alessandra Constantine coming in a close second. No doubt her incredibly high-profile relationship held her back. Or maybe it was OK's shirtless antics that sealed the deal for one lucky senior in particular, spotted leaving the party around the same time as everyone's favorite "prince" . . .

The auction wasn't the only memorable event of the evening. Alexis Thorndike and Clint Weber, already on the rocks after the inevitable reconciliation, have returned to resume their roles as costars of the popular campus reality drama *Breakups and Makeups in Prominent Public Places*.

Of course, nobody's presence was of greater interest than a certain individual's conspicuous absence. You could have heard the straw from a scorpion bowl drop after his name was accidentally called. And, as if the silence didn't say it all, the evening's very first auctionee could be overheard articulating what was on everyone's mind, suggesting that Bolton might now be better suited as the beneficiary of the charity, and adding wryly that he "couldn't afford [her]."

And that's saying something because, as previously stated, she sold for only a hundred dollars.

*Compiled anonymously by the editors at *FM*

"I need a favor."

"Yeah, what else is new?" Callie said without bothering to look up from the Ec10 problem set spread out across her desk as Vanessa slipped into her room.

"Two favors, really," Vanessa continued. Callie heard her bed springs creak, meaning Vanessa had probably sat down. Refusing to turn around, Callie continued working, hoping that her roommate would take the hint.

"The first thing I need is for you to take a break from working and this Insider detective obsession thing, and come with me to an event. It's literary; you'll like it!"

"Mmm," Callie grunted, turning to the final page in her problem set.

"And the second thing I need," Vanessa continued, oblivious, "is for you to tell me what you think . . . of my new outfit."

"Vanessa," Callie said, throwing down her pencil, "I really don't have time for th—"

Her mouth hung open and she stared at Vanessa. Her roommate, whose signature style involved sporting designer labels as conspicuously as she could, had morphed from New Money Manhattan Diva into Grungy Brooklyn Hipster. She wore a red-and-black-checkered flannel shirt tucked into tight black jeans ripped along the thighs and knees. A pair of black suspenders matched the frames of her oversized hipster glasses and the fedora perched atop her head.

"What on earth are you wearing?" Callie demanded, rotating in her desk chair.

"You like?" Vanessa asked, tugging at the sleeves of her shirt.

"It's definitely different. . . . But you look . . . cute?" Crazy, but cute.

"I know, right!" Vanessa smiled.

"Urban Outfitters?" Callie asked, naming one of Harvard Square's staple clothing suppliers.

"Please," said Vanessa, widening her eyes dramatically, "don't make me talk about it."

Callie laughed. "So what's brought on this sudden—er—change?"

"Well," said Vanessa, "I've really been getting into EPL these past few weeks. . . ."

"Oh jeez," Callie started. "Please do not try to tell me that just because you read Mimi's *tabloids* about all the crazy English Premier League WAGs making their husbands get hair implants or having sex with other players on the team, you suddenly understand soccer!" Callie glanced at the photo of Gregory on her bookshelf, remembering their impromptu, thirty-second soccer scrimmage the night of Pudding elections, which, thanks to an interruption from Clint, had basically ended before it had even begun. Kind of like our entire relationship, she thought bitterly.

"Uh, *no*," Vanessa was saying, "though I am impressed that

you've learned to use the acronym for Wives and Girlfriends in a sentence. I was talking about the book *Eat, Pray, Love.* Essentially, if you replace the *Praying* part with *Partying*, then the scenario becomes highly applicable to our lives."

Here we go again, thought Callie, steeling herself for one of Vanessa's epic speeches.

"Much like us, Julia Roberts has been through a bad breakup."

"Isn't the author named Elizabeth Gilbert?"

Vanessa shrugged. "Movie, book, it's all the same these days. Anyway, Julia tries to heal the pain of her divorce with James Franco. Except it doesn't work. You would think, as any sane woman would, that James Franco," Vanessa continued, lifting the photo of Gregory off of the bookshelf and holding it up, "heals everything. But you would be wrong. James Franco just creates even more problems than you had when you started," she declared, tucking the photo in between two books. "Meaning that it's time to forget *James Franco* and start focusing on *you*, and your own personal spiritual journey to self-actualization and independence."

Callie laughed. "Is your mom's kabbalah instructor back from vacation or something?"

"Callie!" Vanessa admonished. "I'm being serious!" Her smile faded as she placed a hand on Callie's shoulder. "I worry about you, you know? It seems like all you do these days is go to class, do your homework, and then spend every other waking moment obsessing about that bulletin board," she said, tilting her head at the wall, "or obsessing about . . . you know, James Franco. Don't you think it's time to take a break from all the conspiracy theories and do something else for a change? Something extracurricular and—well, I don't know—fun?"

Callie sighed. "I had an extracurricular activity. It was writing, remember? But I got cut from *FM* magazine and suspended from *Crimson* COMP, so now . . ."

"So now *so what*?" said Vanessa. "You don't need to be part of a paper or a magazine to keep writing! You can write anywhere, about anything, and there are plenty of other publications out there besides the *Crimson* and *FM*. Which brings me to my next favor." Vanessa's lips curled into a sly smile. "I need you to come to an event with me at the *Harvard Advocate* that starts in approximately fifteen minutes."

The Harvard Advocate was one of the oldest literary magazines in the country, and boasted many famous alumni and contributors, including T.S. Eliot, Norman Mailer, e. e. cummings, Jack Kerouac, and Tom Wolfe.

Callie shook her head. "There's no way I'm COMPing another editorial board ever again. Even if I weren't emotionally and literally exhausted and even if the *Advocate* didn't have an even more exclusive editorial department than the *Crimson* or *FM*, I still couldn't do it because it's too late: this semester's round of COMP is nearly over! And as for next year . . ." Callie swallowed. I might not be here next year.

To Callie's surprise, Vanessa grinned. "Yes, but *anyone* can submit poems or fiction or essays or whatever whenever they want! Meaning, all you'd have to do is bang out one little short story and you're in! Published! Wildly successful! People are fighting for your autograph in the streets! Men want to sleep with you, women want to sleep with you, and babies stop crying when you touch their tiny foreheads."

"I don't think writing a short story is as easy as you're making it sound," Callie remarked. "And I don't have anything prepared. . . ."

"Oh," said Vanessa, "I didn't mean that you should submit something today. The deadline for their spring issue submissions isn't for another month!"

"Well, than wha—"

"Today you and I will be attending . . . wait for it . . . a poetry reading!"

"A poetry reading?"

"Yep," chirped Vanessa, "so get your purse and let's get going."

Callie cast around her room, searching wildly for an excuse. She glanced down at her problem set, but she still had plenty of time to finish before the Friday due date. "I—uh—is that why you're dressed so—"

"Can I borrow these?" Vanessa interrupted, holding up Callie's tattered Converse.

"Um, I guess," Callie replied, watching Vanessa pull them onto her feet. After all, if it weren't for Vanessa and Mimi, who knows how many parties she might have attended barefooted and looking more homeless than Ke$ha or the people on HipsterOrHomeless.com.

"Come on," said Vanessa, grabbing Callie's hands and yanking her to her feet. "It'll be fun! And adventurous! And if it sucks, we can leave after twenty minutes."

"Promise?" asked Callie, finding herself in the common room. Damn you, Vanessa.

"Cross my heart and hope to die," Vanessa declared, bending over a pile of papers on the coffee table. "Now I just need to find that Admit Two Eventbrite printout," she muttered, sifting through the mess.

"What's that?" Callie asked, spying a page that looked like it had been torn out of the latest issue of *FM*.

"This? Oh, nothing," Vanessa said quickly, snatching the article headed "(Harvard) Society Pages" off the table and crumpling it into a ball. "Ah, there you are!" she added, grabbing the printout for the poetry invite.

"It didn't look like nothing," Callie called, following Vanessa to the door.

"Trust me," said Vanessa, turning to face her, the hand that held the article hovering over the trash. "You do not want to read this."

"Why not?" asked Callie, planting her hands on her hips.

Vanessa sighed. "It's a highly questionable, factually inaccurate recap of the Charity Date Auction, and I think"—she cringed—"that reading it would probably only upset you."

"Wh—oh." Callie frowned. "Let me guess. The *FM* editors go on and on about . . . *James Franco* and his undying love for Perky Boobs."

"Among other things," said Vanessa.

"Well then, by all means!" Callie cried, seizing the article from Vanessa and tossing it into the trash herself.

"Bravo!" Vanessa clapped her hands. "Way to take control and end the obsessing!"

Callie rolled her eyes. "To the Advocate?"

Vanessa linked arms with Callie. "Let the adventure begin!"

"The adventure" turned out to be far more painful than Callie ever could have anticipated. Eighteen minutes of sitting on folding chairs inside the reading room on the second floor of the little white house on South Street listening to fellow students share their feelings—often in rhyme—felt more like eighteen hundred hours. Callie wiggled in her seat, searching through her purse for her phone. Suppressing a curse when she remembered that it was still broken, she reached out and pinched Vanessa, who sat next to her.

"*Shh,*" Vanessa hissed, smacking Callie on the knee even though she'd been looking just as bored as Callie felt.

"But I didn't say anything," Callie whispered back.

Fortunately, the girl standing at the front of the room reading hadn't heard them from where they sat all the way near the back and continued to drone on about "lonely unicorn tears."

Nudging Vanessa, Callie pointed to the clock on the wall: nearly twenty minutes had passed.

"Just one more reader," Vanessa pleaded softly as the student at the front said thank you and the audience of roughly thirty students began to snap.

Callie snapped her fingers as loudly and as close as possible to Vanessa's face.

"I said just one m— Oh look, there he is!" Vanessa murmured, suddenly rapt with attention.

Callie looked. A guy whom she had never seen before was shuffling to the front of the room. His outfit, on the other hand, was highly familiar, right down to the suspenders and probably-not-prescription glasses. Callie, too shocked to say anything to Vanessa, simply stared as he stated:

"This is an erotic poem that I wrote about a complete stranger." He cleared his throat and then pulled a crumpled napkin from his pocket.

"The world spins . . . so fast.
Why can't we feel it?
All I feel is you
And me
And Me in you and yet
We drift
Away.
Like planets, in the galaxy.
No gravity.
Just gravitas."

He let the final *s* linger as he stared around the room, seeming to lock eyes with everyone. "Thank you," he said finally.

Vanessa snapped so furiously that it seemed like her fingers might pop off at any second.

Callie watched the boy who, tall and skinny and brunette,

might actually be cute under all that plaid, take his seat. Then, turning, she glared at Vanessa.

"You—me—outside, now," she said, without bothering to lower her voice.

"But—" Vanessa protested. Several heads turned. Giving up, Vanessa followed Callie out into the hall.

Once the door to the reading room had swung shut, Callie folded her arms, an accusatory expression in her eyes. "Is there something you'd like to say to me?"

"Um," said Vanessa. "Thank you for coming? It was fun?"

"No, it wasn't!" said Callie. "But what's even *more* annoying is the way you tricked me here with all that BS about spiritual journeys to independence and self-actualization when all you really wanted was to stalk a cute hipster boy!"

Vanessa held up her hands. "Okay. I admit that this might have had something to do with the *love* portion of our spiritual journey—"

Callie snorted. "I thought the whole idea was to be *less* boy-crazy."

"Is is, but—well—I like him! But we don't have anything in common! So there isn't any other way except—what's a non-creepy term for *stalking*?"

"Why don't you just ask him out?"

"I can't!" Vanessa insisted.

"Why not?"

"Because then I'd have to dress like this all the time!"

Callie started to giggle. "How did you meet this guy, anyway?"

"We haven't exactly met, per se," Vanessa admitted grudgingly. "But he works at Café Gato Rojo," she explained, naming the artsy beatnik coffee house inside Harvard Yard.

"Of course he does," said Callie, still giggling.

Vanessa drew her lips into a pout. "Don't make fun of me while I'm wearing suspenders—it's too cruel."

Callie smiled. "Can I make fun of his poem, though?"

"Why?" asked Vanessa. "Didn't you like it? I thought it was very . . . sexy."

"Um, okay," said Callie. "Hey, maybe you should write a poem asking him out!"

"Keep your voice down!" Vanessa cried, glancing wildly at the door to the reading room. Then, digging her nails into Callie's arm, she dragged her to the end of the hall and down the stairs. They came to a halt in the building's empty foyer in front of a wall covered with posters and flyers for various campus events.

"Seriously," said Callie, "you should just ask. But maybe not until after you change back into your normal clothes."

Vanessa sighed. "What if he says no?"

"Then you'll probably be totally bummed for a while, but at least you'll *know* so you can stop obsessing and move on to the next . . . goatee-sporting, granola-breath graduate student that catches your eye? Either way, it's better to put yourself out there and keep trying instead of just giving up like a ginormous loser."

Callie stared at the flyers on the wall, for plays at A.R.T., more readings at bookstores around the square, and an open invitation reminding students that there was still another month left before the deadline for spring submissions for the *Advocate*. Maybe I should take my own advice, it dawned on her. Yes, she had been burned, first by *FM* and then by the *Crimson*—but that didn't mean that she should stop writing and give up entirely. On the contrary . . .

"How about this?" said Callie. "If you agree to ask him out, then I'll try to write a short story and submit it to the *Advocate*."

Vanessa's panicked expression slowly gave way to a smile. "How very devious of you! Challenge accepted! *If* you promise to buy me a pint of Ben & Jerry's when he says no and listen to me bawl my eyes out."

"Deal," said Callie, extending her hand so Vanessa could shake it. "*If* he says no, then we can eat as much ice cream as you want and I'll be right there to cry with you when the *Advocate* rejects my story."

"*If* they reject it," Vanessa corrected, throwing an arm around Callie's shoulders.

Callie sighed. Given all of her failed attempts at journalism, she highly doubted her foray into fiction would fare any better. But of one thing she was certain: that Vanessa's journey to Eat (with the hipster), Party (with the hipster), and Love (the hipster) was sure to provide an excellent source of material.

"Shall we?" said Vanessa, starting for the door.

"Sure, let's . . . Hey, hang on just a second." One of the flyers on the wall that Callie hadn't noticed before caught her eye.

IT'S NEVER TOO LATE TO SIGN UP

For

INTRAMURAL ATHLETICS!!!

The spring season for the following IM sports

starts April 15:

Basketball

Volleyball

Soccer

E-mail froshIMsports@fas for schedules and to sign up!

"You coming?" asked Vanessa.

"Just a sec!" Callie called, flexing her knee. Then, with a smile, she pulled out a pen and copied down the e-mail address at the bottom of the flyer.

"What were you doing back there?" Vanessa asked when Callie caught up with her.

"Just taking your advice," said Callie, walking out onto South Street.

"Oh yeah?"

"Yep," said Callie. "I think I may have found another extracurricular activity."

"Something new?" asked Vanessa.

"Actually," said Callie, grinning, "something old."

FIVE

I love you, Grace Lee

The Harvard Crimson

NEWS OPINION *FM* MAGAZINE SPORTS ARTS MEDIA ~~FLYBY~~*

*Readers please take note that the FLYBY Blog has relocated. To view the blog exclusively online visit the "More than Daily News" section of *FM* MAGAZINE

Administration to Cancel Introductory Latin

Students organize a campus-wide protest even as enrollment in the (former?) "Universal language of academia" reaches record lows

By GRACE LEE, CRIMSON STAFF WRITER
Published: Thursday, April 14

Latin enrollment has reached a record low on campus, according to a recent report from the Department of the Classics. The subject that was once a requirement and, up until 1961, was the language in which all undergraduate diplomas were written, continues to attract fewer and fewer students every year.

In response, the administration has elected to cancel all introductory Latin courses starting in the fall of the next academic year. Advanced offerings will still exist for those who have enjoyed the opportunity to engage in previous study of the language.

And now a look back on some of the most famous Latin

phrases that have shaped both the community at this university and our society at large.

VERITAS: *Truth*
If you learn only one thing in Latin, learn this. It's Harvard's motto and appears on the school's crest.

DIVIDE ET IMPERA: *Divide and rule/conque*r
Niccolo Machiavelli famously proposed this military strategy in *The Art of War*, still a popular read among Harvard students, though perhaps today the theory is more relevant to cutthroat social situations than to combat.

ALEA IACTA EST: *The die is cast*
Just like Julius Caesar, so you can use this phrase, perhaps when deciding to go out on Thursday night instead of finishing a problem set. (**Veni vidi vici**, another of Caesar's phrases, means *I came, I saw, I conquered*—useful if you *did* stay home with that problem set, went to class, and then aced the exam.)

COGITO ERGO SUM: *I think, therefore I am*
How do you *know* that you exist? This was the answer of René Descartes, the father of Western Philosophy.

CARPE DIEM: *Seize the day*
Life is short, and you shouldn't waste a single minute of it.

DEUS EX MACHINA: *God out of a machine*
In ancient Greek plays when a plot grew too twisted or complicated, the author would often drop (literally, using a crane machine) an actor playing a god onto the stage to solve everything in the final act.

Curious to learn more? Then join fellow students in a protest on the afternoon of Friday, April 15, outside the Science Center to *Salvum Latinae* (that's *Save Latin*).

"Grace, Grace, Grace!" Callie exploded suddenly over salad at the Science Center's Greenhouse Café. "Do you ever talk about anything else?"

Matt's face turned bright red from where he was seated across the table. Callie instantly regretted her outburst, staring down at her lettuce. "Uh, sorry," she mumbled, prodding a tomato with her fork. "I know I'm not one to talk about obsessing," she confessed. "But don't you think it's time to admit your feelings? If not to Grace then to yourself at least?"

Matt sputtered. "I'm not—I mean—I was just saying that she seems to be—relying—on me a lot more—at the *Crimson*, I mean, now that, you know . . . she needs me . . . I mean, needs my—"

Callie placed her hand over his. "You're right. It definitely sounds like she's developed a great amount of professional respect for you. The truth is," she said, spearing a crouton and popping it into her mouth, "that I'm only being bitchy because I'm jealous. Of the way Grace respects you and your work!" she added quickly. "She totally hates me now." Frowning, Callie took a sip of her triple-shot latte, hoping it would reinvigorate her after a particularly grueling hour of Science B-29, The Evolution of Human Nature.

"Hate is such a strong word," Matt said. "I'm sure she'll come around. You were her favorite COMPer, after all, and her mood seems to be improving these days now that she's publishing again.

Granted, she's still on probation and Alexis is assigning her the last pick of all the articles."

"Ugh," Callie groaned at the sound of the name. "If there's one reason I'm grateful for my suspension from the paper, it's that I'm able to avoid Lexi's Reign of Terror."

Matt chuckled. "No one's been beheaded—yet. But there's definitely been a huge shift in focus regarding the types of stories we're encouraged to pursue. You hear a lot of whispering among the older staff members: that pretty soon the paper is going to look more like the magazine. That Alexis ran a tight ship at *FM*, but now she's in over her head. That sort of thing."

"Dissention among the ranks," Callie murmured. "Excellent. Maybe her 'interim' as managing editor is going to come to an end sooner rather than later."

"Let's hope so," said Matt. "Though it doesn't seem likely while she has Dean Benedict's ear, and this Insider matter is unresolved—"

Callie groaned again. "Sorry," she apologized.

"No progress?" Matt asked, his brown eyes earnest with concern.

"None whatsoever," Callie replied.

"I've been keeping my ears open at the paper like you asked," he said, lowering his voice. "But I haven't noticed anyone acting strangely." He tilted his head. "Or at least no one person is behaving any weirder than anyone else right now, given the administrative changes and the whole . . . thing."

Callie scanned the room, but most of the nearby tables were empty. "Does everyone think I did it?" she whispered, leaning in.

Matt cringed. "Let's just say that your sudden absence hasn't gone unnoticed. But the official position is that you quit, and neither Lexi nor Grace seems to be contradicting it. Plus, the administration made it clear that we are not to pursue any stories speculating about the Insider until they've personally identified and disciplined the individual responsible."

"Well, I suppose that's something," Callie muttered. "How ironic that the person who's really responsible is still hiding in their midst, if she isn't actually *running* the paper as we speak—oh, um, hey, OK!"

Matt's roommate, who had just rounded the corner where the cash registers were, recoiled in surprise, nearly spilling the two coffee cups he carried in his hands. "Er, hi there, you two," he said, approaching slowly.

"Hey, man," called Matt, turning. "What are you up to?"

"Nothing!" OK cried, glancing over his shoulder. "I mean, nothing except getting coffee."

"Are you meeting someone?" Callie asked.

"Why would you—oh." He stopped, glancing down at the second cup. "Yes. Kind of. Well, no, not really. It's complicated, see. These are both . . . for me," he finished lamely, setting the coffee on a nearby table.

Matt raised his eyebrows at Callie. "We won't bother you if you need some privacy," she said, kicking Matt, who had probably also overheard OK's nighttime visitor.

"Privacy?" OK repeated, hovering above Matt's chair. "Well, I'm not sure that will be necessar— Mimi!"

Callie's roommate had just exited Science Center C, heading for the café.

"What are *you* doing here?" OK demanded once she'd approached.

Yawning, Mimi rubbed her eyes. "It seems that I have fallen asleep during the class."

"No!" Callie cried, feigning shock. "Really?"

"I am afraid it is so," Mimi affirmed, smirking. "Is that for me?" she added, pointing at the extra coffee on OK's table.

Eyes wide, OK shook his head. "No. It's for . . . me."

Matt stared at him. "Dude. Why are you acting so weird?"

"Why are *you*, dude, acting so weird?" OK shot back.

Mimi started to giggle.

"Fine—take it!" OK snapped, handing her the coffee. "I really ought to be getting home anyway."

"*Merci, monseigneur,*" Mimi thanked him. "*Veux-tu une escorte a* Wigglesworth?"

"I guess," OK said sourly.

He *is* acting odd, Callie thought, watching him closely. Normally he'd be screaming, "How high?" before Mimi had even said, "Jump." He must actually like the new girl—whoever she was.

"If some . . . girl shows up looking for you," said Matt, "should we tell her that you couldn't make it?"

"A girl!" yelped Mimi, appearing, yet again, on the verge of giggles. "*Ooh la la, qui est-elle, cette femme mystère?*"

"Yes," Callie echoed. "Who is this mystery woman?"

OK glared at Mimi. "You know very well"—he eyed Matt and

Callie—"that I am not meeting anyone! There's no mystery! None! Good-bye!" he cried. "Mimi?"

Laughing, Mimi followed him down the ramp that led out of the Science Center, turning back at the bottom and pressing a finger to her lips.

"Well," said Callie, watching them walk away through the enormous glass window overlooking the front entrance to the Science Center. "That was weird."

"No kidding," Matt agreed.

"Any idea who . . . ?"

"No," said Matt. "But OK has definitely been entertaining a regular guest recently, based on the—er—noises coming from his bedroom. You would think, what with Gregory gone, that all the crazy hookup—sorry."

"Maybe it's that senior who bid a thousand dollars on him at the date auction?" Callie said quickly.

"Good call," said Matt. "But I can't see what's so embarrassing about that or why else it would be worth hiding."

Callie shrugged. "Maybe it's the weather." Stretching, she continued to gaze out the window. Outside under the April sun, the stone fountain flowed merrily, splashing onto the surrounding grass as people strolled up and down the cement walkways. A small group of students clustered around the stone benches farther away toward the back entrance to Harvard Yard, some bent over what looked like a bunch of butcher paper and cardboard.

"What do you suppose they're doing?" Callie asked. Squinting, she watched a girl attach one of the sheets of cardboard to the edge of a large stick and then lift it above her head. A sign! Callie couldn't read it from so far away or make out any of the students' features, but still, it had to be: "A protest!" she cried. "Any idea what for?"

"Uh," said Matt, staring at the table. "Not exactly."

"What do you mean, 'not exactly'?" Callie demanded, rounding on him.

"Well, we did publish an article yesterday that briefly referenced a protest scheduled to take place outside the Science Center this afternoon . . . you know, to save introductory Latin?"

"Ooh," said Callie slowly. "So *that's* why you wanted to meet at the Greenhouse Café."

"I'm not sure what you mean," Matt muttered, going scarlet. "I happen to like the coffee here. And, you know, while we're on the subject, I like Latin, too!"

"You know who else likes Latin?" Callie asked. "Grace! Come on, Matt. Just admit it. You're obsessed. And besides, *nobody* likes the coffee here. It's terrible."

"That's not . . . entirely . . . Fine," he conceded suddenly. "You win! I like her! A lot! At least as much as any man can . . . like a woman . . . who barely knows he's alive."

"She knows you're alive!" said Callie. "Weren't you just saying how much she's been relying on you lately?"

"Yeah, but that's not the same thing as wanting to date me."

Callie chewed her lip, unsure how to proceed. She could take the Vanessa approach (i.e., "OMG _____ totally looooves you, you have to go for it!"), or try to discourage him the way Dana might (i.e., "Don't you have a project due tomorrow? Shouldn't you be concentrating on that?"), or refuse all involvement by feigning ignorance with the Mimi route (i.e., "Wait—*who* are we speaking of again?"). In truth, she had no idea whether to encourage or dissuade, having never known Grace to even so much as speak about any romantic interests.

"I guess," Callie started, "that things are slightly complicated by the fact that she is—or, uh, was—your boss, so making a move could lead to potential awkwardness around the office."

"I know." Matt moaned, burying his face in his palms.

"On the other hand," Callie continued, "if you don't tell her how you feel, you might never know if those feelings are mutual."

Pausing, they both turned to stare out the window. Callie could just make out Grace now, marching in a circle and carrying a sign with the rest of the protesters, some of whom wielded megaphones, which they were probably using to chant Latin phrases.

"To be honest," Callie started gently, "I don't know if you're her type—but that's only because I don't know if she even *has* a type! She always seems so strictly business that I'm having a hard time picturing what she'd be like on a date."

"Oh god," said Matt, who'd been inadvertently gnawing on his knuckles. "Do you think she's already seeing some other guy? Of course she is! How could I be so stupid! She's so much smarter than I am and her hair is so shiny and she always smells like freshly printed newspapers and—"

Callie reached for his hands, pulling them away from his mouth and slowly setting them on the table.

"Regardless of whether or not it works out with Grace," she said firmly, "you are a great guy and a total catch, and even if it doesn't happen today, or tomorrow, someday soon you *will* find that someone who is perfect for you."

"So you *don't* think she's already dating someone else?" Matt asked, transfixed by the protesters outside.

Callie sighed. "I think that if you really want to know, you should probably just ask her—maybe before trying to tell her how you feel?"

"So I *should* tell her?" Matt asked, tearing his eyes away from the window.

"Um . . ." Callie faltered. "I can't make that decision for you. But I think what it ultimately comes down to is this: are you willing to take that risk? Are you prepared for any outcome even if it doesn't end up being the one that you'd hoped for?"

Slowly Matt nodded.

Callie started to smile as his head continued to bob up and down with increasing vigor—until all of a sudden he started shaking it violently from side to side.

"Nope!" he cried. "Can't do it!"

"Matt," said Callie, watching him leap to his feet.

"Just forget this whole conversation ever happened. Hey, you finished?" he added, reaching for her nearly empty salad container and coffee cup.

"Um, sure, but—"

"We should probably get going, then," he called, tossing their garbage in the trash.

"Matt," Callie repeated standing. "I didn't mean to—"

"No, no, no, it's fine," he reassured her, slinging his backpack over his shoulder. "Really. I'm sure we both have a lot of work to do."

"Okay, yeah," said Callie, grabbing her book bag. "Let's go."

Matt still seemed highly agitated as they pushed their way through the double doors leading outside the Science Center.

"We could sneak around the back if you want," Callie suggested, tilting her head toward a path that would allow them to bypass the protesters. There appeared to be about forty of them in total, plus roughly fifteen other students who had stopped to stare.

"Don't worry," Matt muttered, striding in the direction of Grace and the rest of the group. "It's not like I'm going to grab her and announce my love right here and now—"

"Matt?" Callie turned, realizing he was no longer walking beside her.

A dreamy look had passed across his face as he watched the protesters march, waving their signs and chanting in Latin.

Callie glanced back at the crowd, where Grace stood out despite being brief in stature, holding one of the largest signs of all, which read, in huge purple lettering, CARPE DIEM.

Oh no, thought Callie, turning. "Matt, what are you . . . ?"

"Hey!" he cried suddenly, dashing past her toward the guy closest to them on the outskirts of the group. "Can I borrow that?"

"Matt!" Callie cried, running to catch up. She couldn't hear the guy's response, but she did see him shrug and hand Matt his megaphone.

Before she could cry out again, Matt had climbed onto a stone bench, his head towering several feet above the crowd. Callie cringed as he raised the megaphone to his lips.

"GRACE," he boomed. "GRACE LEE!"

The protesters paused, all eyes on Matt.

"I LOVE YOU, GRACE LEE!" he shouted into the megaphone, sounding almost drunk on his own adrenaline. "I've loved you since the moment you first yelled at me during COMP, and if you would just agree to go on one date with me, it would make me the happiest freshman that ever walked this campus!"

Callie could hardly bear to watch as Grace slowly lowered her sign.

The crowd drew silent. Grace grabbed a megaphone from a girl standing near her and yelled, "What the hell do you think you're doing, Robinson? Get down from there!"

Some of the protesters cheered and others laughed, while a few appeared sympathetically dismayed. No one, however, looked worse than Matt, whose face had gone a nasty shade of gray. Tossing the megaphone back to the boy he had borrowed it from, he jumped off the bench and started walking rapidly in the direction of Wigglesworth.

Quickly weaving her way through the crowd, Callie followed him.

"And what are the rest of you doing standing around and

staring?" she heard Grace bark, still speaking into the megaphone. "Are we here to gawk, or are we here to save Latin?"

"*Salvum Latinae!*" several people cheered, waving their signs. "*Protestatione curriculum mutationes!*"

Callie had almost caught up to Matt when she heard someone call her name. "Andrews! Robinson! Just a minute, please." As usual, that authoritative voice was impossible to disobey. "I'm flattered, Robinson," the former managing editor continued bluntly as they turned to face her, "but I'm also gay."

"Gay?" Matt repeated, his mouth hanging open.

"Yes," said Grace. "As in I like girls, not boys."

Callie stared at the trunk of the nearest tree. On the (long) list of her life's all-time Most Awkward Moments, this had definitely just skyrocketed up into the top five, eclipsing that time she dropped a box of underwear in front of Gregory on the first day of school and then flashed the entire freshman class when she slipped in the dining hall a few days later.

Matt continued to gape. Grace watched him, waiting for a reaction. The silence lingered until Callie couldn't take it anymore. "Thank you for, uh, choosing to confide in us," she blurted, struggling to remember the contents of the "Coming Out" section of an LGBT pamphlet passed out on Diversity Day back in high school. "We, um, appreciate how difficult this must have been for you," she continued, forcing herself to meet Grace's eyes, "but we want you to know that we fully support you and . . . your lifestyle choices."

To her great surprise, Grace started to laugh. "Don't tell me you thought this was my first time coming out!" she roared, throwing her head back. "And to you two, of all people!"

Callie glanced at Matt, who still appeared dumbfounded.

Grace wiped her eyes. "Ah," she sighed when she had regained her composure. "Sorry. I've been out for over a year—two years to my closest friends—and so I just assumed that by now everybody knew."

"Well, clearly not everybody," said Callie, almost cracking a smile. She poked Matt in the ribs.

He jumped, looking like a lovelorn puppy torn between embarrassment and relief. "Are you . . . sure?"

"Quite sure," Grace replied, patting him on the arm. "Otherwise, I'm quite sure I would have accepted your invitation. Though maybe next time you ask a woman for a date, you should consider doing so in a less dramatic fashion. I am, after all, still your . . . boss."

The last word hung in the air, technically no longer true.

Callie stared at the pavement.

"I will take that under advisement," Matt murmured, his features finally relaxing. "And, er, Grace," he said, glancing between her and Callie. "There's something you should know. Callie didn't write those Insider articles."

"Then who did?" Grace asked, narrowing her eyes.

"I don't know yet," said Callie. "But I strongly suspect that Alexis Thorndike is involved."

Matt grimaced. "That's just one theory. But we don't really have any evidence—"

"*Yet*," Callie interjected.

"And I for one," Matt pressed on, "am having difficulty believing that any one person could be so . . . well, evil. I mean, blackmailing and boyfriend stealing are one thing, but trying to ruin careers and get people expelled?"

"I wouldn't underestimate her if I were you," said Grace. "I believe she is capable of all that and more. But the question isn't whether or not she *would* do it. The question is *did* she do it and, if so, how to prove it."

Callie stared at her. If there was one person in the world who hated Lexi more than Callie did, it was Grace, though the reason why remained a mystery. Callie knew they had roomed together their freshman year and that Lexi had transferred to a different dorm around the same time that the *Crimson* had cut her from their first semester of COMP. Grace, obviously, had made it through and gone on to become managing editor, but even though Lexi rose quickly in the ranks at *FM* magazine, the relationship between the two girls had remained, to quote Marcus Taylor, "one hair pull away from a cat fight to the death."

"So you'll help me, then?" Callie asked. She waited, holding her breath.

"I didn't say that."

"But you believe me," Callie said softly.

Grace sighed. "I believe . . . that there is more going on here than meets the eye. And I also believe that as long as Lexi continues to run the *Crimson*, the integrity of the paper is at risk."

"If we could find a way to prove that she's behind the Insider articles," said Callie, "then maybe you could get your old job back."

Grace frowned. "You know, my position at the paper isn't the only job I lost because of this. Dean Benedict called the *New York Times* last week and they've since rescinded their offer for a summer internship."

"Oh my god," Callie said breathlessly. "I'm so sorry. I feel so . . ." *Responsible* wasn't the right word, since she wasn't. Still, she felt terrible.

"Don't apologize," said Grace. "At least not if you're innocent."

"Grace," said Callie, meeting her eyes, "I swear to you that I didn't do it—I am *not* the Ivy Insider. But I will do everything I can to help clear our names."

"By finding something on Lexi?"

Callie nodded.

"Okay, I'm in," said Grace. "We'll do everything we can at the *Crimson* to discover the identity of the Insider and see that Lexi doesn't last long as managing editor—right, Robinson?"

Matt shuffled his feet, appearing uncomfortable; perhaps because he didn't think they should be focusing all of their investigative efforts on Lexi, though maybe because he had just learned that his crush liked girls. "Sure," he said resignedly.

"Good," said Grace as students started to flood the yard. The clock above Memorial Church struck three. "I should get back to the protest," she continued, nodding toward the Science Center. "Robinson, I'll see you tomorrow. And I'll call you," she said to Callie, "if I find anything worth reporting."

"Great," said Callie. "I'll do the same. Shall we?" she added, turning to Matt.

Glumly he nodded, and they began to walk back to Wigglesworth.

"At least now you know," Callie said after a beat, placing a hand on his forearm.

"I guess," said Matt. "But unfortunately knowing didn't just magically make my feelings disappear."

"Fair enough," said Callie, scanning her key against the lock for entryway C.

"But you're right," he conceded as they walked up the stairs. "It is good to know that it's not personal—not really. I mean, it's not *me* she doesn't like; it's just my . . . man parts."

"Man parts?" Callie repeated with a giggle, turning the doorknob to C 24.

"Fine," said Matt loudly as she pushed open the door. "My penis!"

"What?" snapped Dana, looking up sharply from where she sat reading on the couch.

"*Je crois qu'il a dit 'mon pénis,*" Mimi deadpanned from the overstuffed armchair.

"Callie!" Vanessa cried, bursting out of her bedroom. "There's somebody here to see you!" She grinned.

"Huh?" said Callie.

"*Oui, oui,*" called Mimi, also smiling. "Someone is waiting in your bedroom."

Callie's heart practically stopped. She stared at the door. Could it be? Was he back?

"Who?" Matt asked, from where he stood in the doorway.

"*C'est une surprise,*" Mimi insisted, wagging her finger.

"Go ahead and look," Dana urged.

Slowly Callie crossed the common room, her heart now threatening to leap out of her rib cage. Hardly daring to breathe, she reached for the door. It creaked open.

The person sprawled across her bed sat up, wearing a mischievous grin. "Hey there, good looking. Did ya miss me?"

SIX

East Meets West

>> Gossip >> HOT TOPICS >> Spotted! *A space for readers to report any strange or suspicious sightings* >> Gregory Bolton

MANHATTAN, NY—

I live in a high-rise where 2nd Avenue meets E 85th Street, and a young man matching Bolton's exact description (but hiding out under a hat and sunglasses) has been going into the Gracie Station post office at the same time every Friday. Wonder who he could be writing to—and if the SEC knows about his secret PO box.

—Concerned Upper East Sider

Spotted! Yes, I love this section! I go to NYU and last week I saw (swear to god) Gregory Bolton in a super shady store downtown buying a "burner" (disposable) cell phone. (Don't ask why I was there!) I guess he's got as good a reason as any to place untraceable calls from blocked phone numbers—then again, so do most drug dealers.

—NYU Student "Snoop"er

I've seen Gregory entering and exiting the Bolton's old Park Avenue penthouse (supposedly on sale later this month) several times recently. (I nanny for a family that lives in the neighborhood.) What I have *not* seen is the string of accompanying entourages on his arm. Yeah, yeah, I know that he supposedly has a "serious girlfriend," but I haven't seen *any* women going in or out of the premises. (Incidentally, I'm starting to believe the rumors that stepmother, Trisha, has fled to the Caymans with all the purses and shoes she could carry.) What's the matter Gregory? Too blue to keep up your womanizing ways? Or did that hot little Harvard number dump you when she realized exactly how broke you really are now?

—The Park Avenue Help

Bolton sat next to me on a bench in Central Park just three days ago and proceeded to read an article on his iPad . . . about himself. It was like catching someone checking himself out in the mirror, only better. Was almost tempted to go home and Google the so-called "Harvard Society Pages" just to read the full article on what looked like a charity auction . . . for him. Who knew Ivy Leaguers had such a sense of humor?

—Dog walker & Harvard H8er

This update coming to you live from the Harvard campus, where I've overheard several students claiming to have "spotted" Gregory Bolton at various Cambridge locales over the past few days. Why all the supposed sightings? Probably because pre–punch season has started: when the elite all-male final clubs extend social invitations to a few select freshmen considered "high priority" punches. Gregory Bolton used to be at the top of every club's list and most likely received invites to some of spring's most exclusive pre-punch events, including the Phoenix Caribbean Party and the Spee's infamous "Eurotrash"—but naturally those were sent out *before* #BoltonBankruptcyGate. Do the invitations still stand? And were those students just hallucinating, or will this rager-filled weekend actually inspire the younger Bolton to stage his return to campus. . . .

—Ivy Insider Admirer

EUROTRASH

(noun)

1.

A human subphylum characterized by its apparent affluence, worldliness, social affectation, and addiction to fashion

2.

The best dance party of the year

Brought to you by The Spee Club
Friday @ 76 Mt. Auburn St.
10 p.m. until you can't dance anymore
Featuring DJs Zhang & Shifty
Costumes Mandatory
R.S.V.P. to add +1s to the list

"JESSICA!" Callie screamed, her tiny flicker of disappointment fading fast.

Not Gregory.

But just as good, if not better.

"BESTIE!" Jessica screamed back, hugging her and jumping up and down.

After several more seconds of squealing, Callie finally recovered herself. "How did you . . . ?"

"*I* helped her coordinate, thank you very much," Vanessa called from the common room.

"That's right," said Jessica, smiling broadly. "I Facebooked Vanessa and then she gave me your class schedule and agreed to let me into the building so I could surprise you!"

"Amazing," said Callie, grinning from ear to ear. "You guys are the best," she continued, pulling Jessica into the common room and then into a three-way hug with Vanessa. "Just the best!"

"*Et moi et* Dana?" Mimi demanded, indignant.

"You guys are *also* the best," Callie amended, grabbing Mimi and Dana by their hands and then heaving them up into the hug.

"Okay, okay, enough, enough!" Dana cried a few seconds later from where she was squished into the center of the embrace. "I have a lot more reading to do!"

Breaking away in a huff, Dana returned to the couch and spread her huge textbook across her knees. Mimi flung herself onto the armchair, her knees kicked up over one side, and continued reading the current issue of the humor magazine distributed by the Harvard Lampoon, a social organization to which they suspected she now belonged, though she technically wasn't supposed to talk about it.

Catching Callie's eye, Jessica smiled. Jessica didn't have to say anything in order for Callie to read her mind: *They're all exactly as you described.*

"Ahem-hem." Matt cleared his throat, still hovering awkwardly near the door.

"You must be Matt," said Jessica, walking over to shake his hand. Glancing over her shoulder at the girls she mouthed, "*Cute!*" before turning back to him. "I hear great things."

"Uh . . ." Matt stammered, somewhat dumbstruck. Back home in California people had often mistaken Callie and Jessica for sisters, Jessica being the longer-haired, blue-eyed and still—thanks to the miraculous weather at Stanford—tanner of the two. "Nice to wonderful things about meeting you, too," he blurted. "Uh—I should—get . . ." he mumbled, backing out into the hall.

Callie smiled. "Will we be seeing you at the party later tonight?"

"Oh yes, will we?" Jessica echoed, her blue eyes wide.

"Er—sure," said Matt to Callie's surprise. The Spee, one of Harvard's eight all-male Final Clubs, was hosting "Eurotrash," its craziest party of the year, later that evening. Matt, much like Grace and, for that matter, the Ivy Insider, normally had serious moral qualms about Harvard's elite(ist) secret societies. But apparently tonight he was willing to make an exception. "I'll tell OK that I . . . changed my mind. Nice to, uh, meet—already said that. I'll be seeing you—all of you—later!" He pulled the door shut behind him.

"Ugh," Vanessa groaned, rolling her eyes at Jessica. "Welcome to Nerdsville. Population: Matt."

Jessica laughed. "No way," she said, shaking her head. "If you want to see a *real* nerd you need to stop by my Tech Start-up Seminar back at Stanford. We've got geeks that make Mark Zuckerberg look like Justin Timberlake!"

"You really think he's cute?" asked Callie.

"Sure," said Jessica. "But, as you well know, I'm holding out for someone else."

"Oooh," said Vanessa. "Who?"

"OK!"

"OK?" Mimi repeated, peering at Jessica over the top of the *Harvard Lampoon*. "As in our neighbor, not an affirmative American exclamation?"

"Correct," said Jessica. "Unless—I mean—I'm not trying to step on any toes here, so if he's already spoken for . . ."

"*Non, non, non*," said Mimi. "It is nothing except that we are suspecting he is already involved with someone else. *Mais l'affaire est un secret.*"

"A secret lover?" asked Jessica.

"*Oui.*" Mimi nodded. "We do not know who she is, but we are suspicious it is quite grave."

"You mean . . . serious?" suggested Callie.

"*Oui, oui,*" said Mimi, returning to her magazine.

"Not to worry," said Vanessa, brandishing the invitation to "Eurotrash." "Much more hotness awaits us at the party tonight!"

"Awesome," said Jessica. "I can't wait. Whaddya wanna do in the meantime, Calamazoo?" she said, turning to Callie.

"Walk around Harvard Square and grab some tea or fro-yo?"

"Coolness," said Jessica. "Is there a good kombucha spot around here?"

"Kom-what-a?" asked Mimi.

"It's a type of fermented tea," Jessica explained.

"Fermented?" said Dana. "As in alcoholic?"

"No," said Jessica. "More like yeast and bacteria and all kinds of other fabulous acids and antioxidants that detoxify your body and energize your mind."

"Oh no," said Callie, "it's happened!" Rushing to Jessica, she grabbed her by the shoulders and started to shake. "You've been brainwashed by the Northern California yogalates pod people! And drinking the kombucha Kool-Aid!"

Jessica burst out laughing. "So says the girl who swore she'd never be caught dead in a sweater set!"

"This isn't a sweater set!" Callie cried. "This is just a normal sweater and yes," she said, pointing at it, "these things tend to come in handy when it's negative five degrees outside."

"Touché." Jessica laughed again. "How about we just go for regular tea, then?"

"Perfect," said Callie. "I know a place."

"Pre-party festivities start at eight," Vanessa called after them as, arm-in-arm, they headed for the door. "So don't be late!"

Several hours later, after raiding Mimi's closet for all the feathered, shiny lamé, metallic-colored, and any other vaguely "Euro" items they could find, "The Mini Me-mes" (or so Mimi had delightedly renamed Callie, Jessica, and Vanessa after seeing them in her clothes) had arrived. After checking their names off the list, an upperclassman wearing sunglasses and skin-tight white pants handed them glow-stick necklaces and then admitted them into the darkened lobby of the beautiful redbrick mansion on Mount Auburn Street that housed the Spee Club.

"What a scene!" Jessica declared. "At Stanford, a 'party' usually just means a couple of jocks standing around a keg. No paper invites, no list, and definitely none of this," she finished, peering into one of the dimly lit rooms off the hall. Glow-sticks pulsed in time to techno music like beacons through a fog, revealing flashes of cleavage and chest hair as scantily clad girls decked in gaudy jewelry mingled with boys rocking tight jeans and even tighter, low-cut shirts.

"This?" Vanessa repeated. "This is nothing! Security's way more lax than usual tonight because it's pre–punch season for the Final Clubs, so they're actually letting a few select freshman dudes in for a change."

"Like Matt and OK?" asked Jessica. "Where are they, anyway?"

"Upstairs, maybe, on the dance floor?" said Vanessa. "Anyway, you should have *seen* the setup at the Fly's Great Gatsby party back in March. I mean, the champagne fountain! The jazz band! The *boys* in their white tuxedos—"

"Shh!" Callie grabbed Vanessa's arm, nodding pointedly at the couple who had just entered through the lobby.

Alexis and Clint. Who had, ironically, rekindled their relationship at that same party back in March—the party where Callie had supposedly been Clint's date.

"Oh my god," Jessica started in a whisper, "is that who I think it is?"

"Quick—in here!" Callie instructed, ushering them all into a room on the left.

"Was that him?" Jessica demanded breathlessly. "The runner-up for World's Douchiest Ex, second only to Evan?"

"Shh!" Callie cried again, peeking out into the hall. Lexi and Clint continued to walk, eventually disappearing behind the club's "mascot," a huge fourteen-foot-tall stuffed bear at the end of the hall near the stairs. Sighing with relief, Callie rejoined her friends.

"Yes, that was him, with Satan herself."

"Wow," said Jessica, "she's gorgeous."

Callie gave her a pained look.

"Sorry," she said. "I guess I just expected warts or something . . . you know, to match the inner *witch*?"

"If only, if only," said Vanessa, tugging at the base of her metallic hot pink romper.

"*Pourquoi ne pas nous* numb this potential for an awkward

encounter with a little drinky," Mimi suggested, "and then we head upstairs and slap the dance floor?"

"*Hit* the dance floor," Callie corrected.

"Same difference, *mais non*?" said Mimi, strolling up to a bar in the corner of the room and ordering four shots.

"To dancing," Mimi toasted, raising her glass after she had distributed the others.

"To new friends," said Vanessa, smiling at Jessica.

"To best friends," said Callie.

Jessica chewed her lip. "To kissing random boys because you're only in town for the weekend!"

"*Whoo-hoo*!" Vanessa cheered while Mimi downed her drink.

"Upstairs?" asked Callie, throwing an arm around Jessica.

"Yes!" she agreed, sliding an arm around Callie's waist.

A few minutes later, the girls arrived at the top of the stairs. Callie paused midway to the enormous library-turned-dance-floor-for-the-evening, staring into a room with reddish walls and plush leather couches, where students already burned out from dancing lingered to catch their breath or carry on a quasi-audible conversation. Clint stood at the bar in the corner, mixing two cocktails.

"*Allons danser!*" Mimi cried.

"Yes, let's go dance!" Callie quickly agreed, following Mimi onto the floor.

At the far end of the room a DJ dropped beats from a table elevated on a mini-stage. Lights flickered across their faces as Mimi pulled them front and center, where they proceeded to clear an area by dancing as exuberantly as possible. Several "randos," or so Vanessa dubbed them, attempted to approach, but the girls shut them down, preferring to dance, according to Vanessa, "dudelessly."

"This is so fun!" Jessica called to Callie over the *badabups* of the intro to Papa Americano.

"It *is* fun!" Callie agreed, grabbing her best friend's hands and spinning her.

"Why do you look so surprised?" Jessica asked over the music, laughing and bouncing up and down to the beat.

Callie shrugged. "I guess things haven't been so fun lately!"

Jessica stopped suddenly and moved closer, gripping Callie by the shoulders. "Everything will be okay," she said, speaking firmly into Callie's ear. "You'll see." Backing away, she spun around, waving her hands over her head. "But for now," she continued, "the best thing you can do is dance!"

Callie laughed, letting Vanessa twirl her around. "You're so right! I love you guys!"

"*Je vous aime aussi!*" Mimi yelled. "*Oh, regarde,*" she continued, pointing to the other end of the room. "*C'est Matt et OK. Bonjour mes petits voisins!*" she screamed, racing over to join her "little neighbors."

"She loses her English when she drinks," Vanessa explained to Jessica.

"Let's go say hi!" said Callie, weaving her way after Mimi through the crowd.

OK, who wore a shiny silver jacket over a white button-down

shirt with only three bottom buttons done, appeared to be in much better spirits this evening, picking Mimi up and whirling her around in a giant bear hug when she reached them. Matt, on the other hand, looked extremely uncomfortable in a lime green, short-sleeved, button-down shirt that he seemed to have borrowed, based on the size of it, from Adam's closet.

He perked up slightly when he spotted Jessica approaching, who greeted him with a hug.

Careful, Callie wanted to warn her. He's very fragile right now. She had been so wrapped up with filling Jessica in on her own drama earlier that afternoon and grilling Jess about life back at Stanford that Callie had neglected to mention anything having to do with Matt's botched love confession.

"Ladies, hello," OK boomed in his British best when he'd set Mimi down. He kissed first Callie and then Vanessa on the cheek before turning to Jessica. "And this must be the lovely Ms. Stanley come all the way from Stanford University," he said, taking her hand. "*Enchanté, mademoiselle*," he added, kissing it. "You are as beautiful as your Facebook profile picture if not more so, a phenomenon I find rare in this messed-up, Photoshopped world."

"It's nice to finally meet you, too," said Jessica, batting her eyelashes.

Oh no, thought Callie. Here we go. She and Vanessa exchanged a look.

"Though after hearing so many hilarious stories," Jessica continued, "I feel like I already know you!"

OK froze, accelerating from suave to scared in approximately three seconds. "What stories?"

"Well," said Jessica, "there was the time you got naked and accidentally jumped into Dana's bed because you thought it was your own, and then that other time you got naked for Primal Scream and Mimi stole all your clothes, and then that other time over spring break when you got na—"

"Blondie!" OK interrupted in a menacing tone, shaking his fist at Callie. "Why must you constantly salt my game?"

"Sorry." Callie laughed. "But it's too late. Jess already knows you're with somebody else."

"Huh?" said OK, narrowing his eyes. "According to who?"

"Uh—Mimi? She said you've been sneaking around with some mystery lady?"

Mimi, who had started talking to Vanessa and Matt, stopped and waved. OK glared at her. "From Mimi, eh? Well, *Mimi*," he said, raising his voice, "should know better than most that I am *not* sneaking around with anyone because I refuse to sneak around on principle."

Matt raised his eyebrows. "Then what's with the nightly noises, man?"

OK balked. Then he smiled. "Previous suitemates at Eton have described me as a 'violent and aggressive masturbator.'"

"ALL RIGHT, TIME TO GO," Callie announced, grabbing Jessica and Vanessa and dragging them back toward the more crowded area of the dance floor. "We'll be over by the DJ if you guys decide to start acting more . . . civilized."

"Wait!" Jessica cried. "We have to rescue Matt!" Darting back, she took him by the hand, tugging him away from where OK stood glaring at Mimi.

Vanessa, seeing the worried look on Callie's face, placed a hand on her shoulder. "Just relax and let them have some harmless fun," Vanessa murmured into her ear.

Callie nodded, smiling at Matt and Jessica when they arrived. Then, forming a circle, they all started to dance.

Twenty minutes later Callie found herself scanning the crowd, searching for Mimi and OK. Neither was anywhere to be found. She did spot Clint and Alexis over near the window at the edge of the dance floor, talking intently. Her eyes continued to skim over the sweaty heads of her fellow students. She sighed, tired of doing a double take every time she spotted a guy with dark brown hair, or light blue eyes, or a vague shadow of that unbelievable, maddening, tantalizing *I know what you look like in your underwear* sort of a smile.

"I'm parched!" she cried hoarsely, turning back to her friends and motioning at her throat. "Anyone want to go find some water?"

"Yes!" Vanessa yelled. "Let's try that way!" she added, pointing in the direction of the reddish-colored room that Callie had noticed on their way upstairs.

"We can come, too," said Jessica, breaking away from Matt.

"No, no," Callie urged. "You stay. We'll be right back."

The room felt mercifully cool after the sweaty dance floor: the dim lighting a welcome relief following the flickering strobe lights.

"This way," said Vanessa, heading for the self-service bar. "Liquor, liquor everywhere," she muttered, sifting through the bottles on the table, "but not a drop I want to drink!"

"Check in that refrigerator behind the bar," said Callie.

"Is that allowed?" asked Vanessa.

"No one's gonna care," said Callie, noting that none of the students mixing drinks looked like members. She craned her neck so she could see above their heads, but the people sitting down appeared to be mostly couples on the verge of making out.

"*Pfft*," Vanessa snorted, opening the refrigerator door. "Who supplies a bar with plastic LED light-up ice cubes but no water?" she complained, rooting around in the fridge. "It's a serious design flaw if you ask me, not to mention sort of hazardous if you thi— Ah-*ha*! Found it!"

"What the fuck . . . ?" said Callie, who had been on the lookout instead of listening.

"What?" said Vanessa, turning around and handing Callie a water. "No 'thank you'?"

"Sorry," said Callie. "But seriously, what the fuck is happening over there?"

"Where?" asked Vanessa.

"There," Callie answered, nodding in the direction of a couch in the corner.

Alessandra, holding a martini glass in which the liquid was sloshing perilously, leaned into Tyler who had apparently abandoned all pretenses and unbuttoned his shirt entirely. Their faces were only inches apart, her hand rested on his knee, and they seemed about five seconds away from sneaking off to a Members Only section of the club so Tyler's pants and Alessandra's dress—if you could call it that—could go the way of his shirt.

"What the fuck, fuck, fuckitty, *fuck*," said Vanessa, slamming her water onto the table. "What the hell does your non-boyfriend's non-ex-girlfriend think she's doing with my ex-boyfriend?"

"Huh?" said Callie.

"Exactly," said Vanessa, seizing her hand. "Let's go find out."

"Wait—no—ah—stop—"

"*What*, may I ask, is going on here?" Vanessa demanded after marching across the room in spite of Callie's protests.

"Excuse me?" said Alessandra, her unfocused eyes sliding over first Vanessa and then Callie.

Callie cowered behind Vanessa, praying that perhaps no one would remember this in the morning.

Unfortunately Vanessa was doing everything in her power to make the encounter as memorable as possible.

"You," she said, pointing at Tyler, "should know better than to blatantly hit on someone whom you *know* to have a boyfriend, and *you*," she continued, rounding on Alessandra, "well, how could you?"

"How could I what?" Alessandra asked.

"Do this to Gregory!" Vanessa cried. "As his girlfriend you should be supporting him, not cheating on him in public!"

Alessandra rolled her eyes. "Please," she said as Tyler attempted to inch away from her, shrinking back over the arm of the couch. "We weren't even doing anything."

"Oh," said Vanessa before Callie could interject, "that's a good one. I wonder what else you've been lying about, hmm? Maybe Callie here was right after all—"

Callie cringed.

"Maybe you haven't even heard from Gregory or—"

"Maybe," Alessandra interrupted Vanessa, "you should mind your own business and stop yelling at people for hitting on other people's girlfriends when your friend here—yes, I see you, Callie—does it all the time!"

Tyler shook himself. "Whose girlfriend did she hit on?" he asked, perking up considerably.

"Nobody's *girlfriend*," Alessandra snapped. "*My* boyfriend. If anybody ought to be worried about being cheated on, it's me, not him!"

Several nearby partygoers had stopped talking, straining to overhear in between the pulsing sounds of the music pounding in the next room.

"As long as *you're* in the picture," Alessandra continued, rounding on Callie, "nobody at this school's boyfriend is safe!"

"Oh yeah?" said Vanessa, drawing herself up. "Maybe that's because Callie doesn't put the *trash* in *euro*!"

Tyler laughed. "Sorry," he apologized as three sets of angry eyes zeroed in on him. "That was . . . sort of funny."

"Vanessa," said Callie quietly, "I really think we should go."

"Don't go," said Alessandra. "Stay—while you still can."

"What?" said Callie sharply.

"I meant why would you leave," Alessandra elaborated, sloshing some of her drink onto the couch, "when there are so many other people's boyfriends at this party for you to steal?"

Vanessa gave an *oh-no-you-didn't* gasp. Slowly Callie shook her head. "For the record, I never tried to *steal* your boyfriend, and I refuse to apologize for the fact that we had a history before you ever even set foot on this campus."

"Oh yes," said Alessandra, her eyes hazy. "There you go again about your 'history.' I wonder what lie you'll tell me this time. You know, I thought I was sorry, but I'm not!"

"Sorry about what?" asked Callie.

"Trusting you!" Alessandra babbled semi-coherently. "You deserve him. I mean *it*. You deserve . . . whatever happens. . . ."

Tyler, who had been fidgeting, turned to Vanessa. "Is it just me, or are you suddenly feeling really hot?"

"Seriously?" Vanessa snapped. "Seriously! *That's* your opening line? Well, you'd better quit while you're ahead, sweetie, because that train has left the station—in fact, it left weeks ago, and it's an express train, so it won't be making any stops in Lonely-on-a-Tuesday Town or I'm-feeling-sort-of-fat-tonight City or—"

"No." Tyler shook his head emphatically. "It's hot in here. Temperature wise. Does anyone else smell . . . ?"

"Smoke," Callie supplied, noticing some wafting in from the foyer at the top of the stairs.

"Don't be silly," said Vanessa. "That's just fog from the fog machine on the dance floor."

"Really?" said Tyler. "Because it smells an awful lot like smo—"

"FIRE!" somebody screamed suddenly from downstairs. "THE BEAR—IS ON—FIRE!"

The music in the next room stopped. Students started pouring into the foyer, clamoring down the stairs.

"Somebody dial nine-one-one!"

"They're already on their way!"

"Quick—there's a fire extinguisher in the back office—"

"*It's too late for that—we need to get everybody out—NOW,*" the Spee's president screamed, darting up the stairs and barking orders at the other members on the second floor, instructing them to make sure everybody evacuated immediately.

Tyler was already up on his feet, one arm thrown around Vanessa.

"COME ON!" Callie screamed at Alessandra, who remained frozen on the couch. "Move!"

Alessandra didn't budge.

"CALLIE!" Vanessa cried as Tyler pulled her out of the room.

Shaking her head, Callie grabbed Alessandra by the forearms and dragged her to her feet. "Snap out of it!" Callie yelled, pushing the older girl toward the stairs.

Alessandra finally seemed to rouse, stumbling on her four-inch heels. "Oh my—what the—"

"Let's go," Callie said. Grabbing Alessandra by the hand, she followed Tyler, Vanessa, and what seemed like the last remaining students down the stairs through a haze of smoke.

Coughing by the time she reached the first floor, Callie glanced down the hall, over the arm of a member at the foot of the stairs directing people outside.

Flames flicked over the huge stuffed bear, blackening the white wall behind. Armed with a fire extinguisher, several guys gathered around it and worked to contain the blaze, which despite their best efforts continued emitting an enormous amount of smoke. A sudden shower of sparks shot up dangerously close to the staircase's winding wooden banister, and Alessandra shrieked loudly—

"You need to get her outside with the rest of them!" a guy screamed at Callie over the wail of approaching sirens.

Nodding, Callie tugged at Alessandra, who remained transfixed by the blaze. "Come on," Callie managed between coughs, finally leading the older girl outside.

From the looks of it, they were nearly the last to leave the party; students clad in outrageous costumes littered Mount Auburn Street, making room for the fire engines as they pulled up outside the Spee.

"Jessica!" Callie screamed, spotting her best friend in front of Schoenhof's Foreign Books next door. Matt, Vanessa, Tyler, Mimi, and OK stood with her. "Are you okay?" Callie cried, running toward them with outstretched arms and nearly toppling Jessica with the force of her hug.

"Yes, yes, I'm fine," Jessica replied, gripping Callie tight. "Matt and I were actually already on our way outside to take a break from all the dancing—"

"Oh, thank you!" Callie hugged Matt.

"I didn't really do anything," he mumbled while Callie embraced her friends in turn, save for Tyler whom she gave a tentative pat on the arm. Alessandra hovered awkwardly in the background, tottering unsteadily on her feet.

"*C'est la chose la plus exciter en quelques semaines*!" Mimi declared, clapping her hands rapturously and staring at the smoking building.

"Hey!" cried OK.

"What?" asked Vanessa. "What did she say?"

"Nothing," muttered OK.

"QUIET PLEASE!" A firefighter had just emerged from the Spee's red front door. "If I could have your attention," he continued. The crowd drew silent. Callie joined hands with Jessica and Vanessa, who stood on either side of her. "We have succeeded in putting out the fire. Fortunately the damage appears to be minimal, and no one sustained injuries beyond very minor smoke inhalation. Upon closer examination, the fire appears to have started due to an unattended cigar left near the taxidermic décor."

Several other firefighters exited the building and gathered behind him, crossing their arms or removing their hats.

"Is it wrong that I feel slightly aroused right now?" Vanessa whispered, leaning in. Tyler grunted derisively.

"Not at all!" Jessica whispered back at the exact same second Callie said "Yes, it is."

The firefighter who had been speaking continued. "We cannot stress enough how important it is to remain vigilant in the event that you choose to partake in indoor smoking, particularly in a party setting. Even small accidents like what probably happened tonight can lead to devastating consequences. Obviously tonight was an exception—but next time, you might not be so lucky. So please, in the future, be careful to watch where you throw those cigarettes."

"Okay, party's over!" barked another firefighter as the previous speaker descended the steps. "Time to stop hanging around and head home! Now, folks! HUPD will be here any minute for a follow-up investigation, and I'm sure they'd hate to find any intoxicated, underage individuals loitering in the streets!"

"You heard the man!" the club president yelled as the firefighters began loading up their trucks. "Clear out!"

"To Daedalus!" someone cried, naming a popular bar across the street while the fire trucks revved their engines. "Because this party's not over till we say it's over!"

A handful of students cheered. Callie turned to her friends. Alessandra still lingered nearby. Callie caught her eye. But before either of them could say anything, Tyler muttered, "Oh, crap on a stick . . . here we go again."

Following his gaze, Callie saw Lexi and Clint standing several dozen yards away, visible now that the fire engines were leaving. Even with all the commotion, their words were still audible.

"*Maybe*," Lexi shouted, "if you had listened to me and given up cigars like you promised, none of this would have happened in the first place!"

"Maybe if *you* hadn't been bitching about it so much," Clint bellowed back as everyone in the near vicinity turned to stare, "I would've been paying closer attention when I set it down!"

Callie's eyes grew wide. She had never, in all the months they had dated, seen this side of Clint. Even when she'd practically torn apart his bedroom searching for signs of an affair with Lexi and he'd caught her red-handed, he had remained disturbingly, robotically calm. And even when she'd admitted to having spent the night with Gregory when she and Clint were on a break (technically a "fuzzy gray area"), he had barely raised his voice. She glanced at Tyler, recalling with new appreciation the times he had described Clint's relationship with Lexi as volatile, characterized by a can't-live-without-driving-each-other-crazy kind of love.

"So let me get this straight," Lexi was screaming. "*You* broke your promise, and *you* could have very well set your lit cigar down near that highly flammable eyesore, and somehow *I'm* responsible for trying to burn down the entire Spee?"

Clint opened his mouth to shout a reply but suddenly stopped short, noticing the crowd that had begun to form around them, including several Spee members who watched them closely. "Er—nobody tried to burn anything down," he called loudly. "Though I can't say for certain, since we were on the second floor the whole night!"

"Is that so?" Lexi demanded, ignoring the crowd. "Maybe we should stick around until HUPD shows up and see what they have to say about that!"

"You *would* try to have me arrested, wouldn't you?" Clint yelled. "That is just *so* typical. So. Fucking. Typical!"

"Excuse me, ladies," Tyler said quietly to Callie, Alessandra, and Vanessa. "Duty calls." Dashing over to Clint and Lexi, he grabbed his roommate and attempted to drag him in the direction of Adams House. Lexi followed them, calling insults all the while.

"I take it back," Mimi said breathlessly. "*That* was definitely *la plus excitant* thing to happen all evening!"

"I should go," Alessandra murmured, looking shell-shocked.

Callie turned to her. "Uh . . . do you think you can make it home okay?"

"Yeah—fine," Alessandra muttered, backing away. "Thanks—and sorry. About . . . everything."

"That's all ri—" Before Callie could finish, Alessandra had disappeared into the crowd.

"*Whe-wee*!" Jessica whistled, throwing an arm around Callie's shoulders. "Just another normal night on the old Harvard campus, eh?"

Callie blinked, staring at the spot Alessandra had vacated. For some reason she couldn't shake the nagging feeling that she was forgetting something.

"Tell me about it," Vanessa answered Jessica. "I can't decide if I need a nap or a drink."

"*Buvez, buvez*!" Mimi cheered in favor of option number two. "*Je vote pour que nous allons à Daedalus. Monsieur*?" she asked, turning to OK.

"Fine," he said stiffly. "If everyone else is going."

"I'll go," said Jessica. "I couldn't possibly sleep right now after all of that. Matt?"

"Sure," he said. "Callie?" he added.

"*Caaleeee*," Jessica repeated, waving a hand in front of her face. "You coming?"

"Where?" asked Callie.

"Daedulus, duh!" said Vanessa.

"Oh . . . um . . ." Callie stared at her friends. Her eyes roved over each of their features, one by one. OK and Mimi, Matt and Vanessa, and Jessica, whose presence in the group—amazing as it was to have her—served as a stark reminder of another member's absence.

Gregory.

Callie closed her eyes. If he hadn't gotten tangled up in his father's hedge fund scandal or everything at Bolton and Stamford Enterprises was business as usual, would he be here now? Would he have broken up with Alessandra as promised—and would he finally be hers?

Callie swallowed. *Yes.* He would have been there, devastating and disheveled with five o'clock shadow and the top buttons of his shirt undone. Navy blue, she decided, to match his eyes, which would have stayed on her the entire night, filling her with that same sense of security and anticipation she'd experienced on the ferry. And when the fire broke out, he would have taken her hand and led her outside, instead of her having to help Alessandra, and only when he knew she was safe, would he act as if he'd never been worried at all. He would lean in so close they were almost touching and ask her, with that signature smirk, if she knew anyone klutzy enough to have started the fire. She would feign offense, insisting on her innocence and asking if *he* knew any smokers, and then his lips would brush up against her ear as he whispered, "*Caliente*, do you know the Spanish word for *fire*?" And then—

"—she used to space out like this all the time during last period back in high school," Jessica was explaining to the others.

"Ow!" Callie cried, rubbing the spot on her arm where her best friend had pinched her.

"Had to do it," Jessica said with a grin. "Now are you coming or not?"

"Actually," said Callie, "I'm sort of exhausted. . . . Would you murder me if I said I kind of just wanted to go home and crawl into bed?"

"Not at all," said Jess. "I'll go with you," she added with a sidelong look at the others.

"Er, *excusez-moi, s'il vous plait.*" Mimi planted her hands on her hips. "*Sa va pas te tuer*, but *I* will murder you."

Jessica laughed.

"*Je suis très sérieuse*!" Mimi insisted. "How often in life will your best friend be visiting while your neighbors are wearing *ces ensembles absoluement ridicules*?" she finished, pointing at Matt and OK's outfits. "We must stay up all night tonight at the very least. Probably tomorrow night, too. *Ce feu, c'est juste le commencement!*"

Matt shifted nervously. "What do you mean, 'that fire is just the beginning'?"

"*Exactement ça!*" Mimi cried delightedly. "It is going to get a lot hotter before *la fin due weekend*."

OK grinned. "Oh, it's already getting hotter, baby," he said, undoing another button on his shirt. Vanessa howled like a wolf while Matt laughed.

Jessica looked at Callie, her eyes gleaming with anticipation.

"Okay, *fine*," Callie conceded, eliciting cheers from Mimi, OK, and Vanessa. "Let's get crazy and stuff. But not too crazy, okay? I have a paper due on Monday."

"Famous last words, my friend," said Mimi, taking her by the hand and leading them all down Mount Auburn Street. "*Fameux mots de la fin.*"

SEVEN

The Hangover

Dear Party Animals in Training:

Sunday morning in college: a less than holy time that far too many of us spend praying to the porcelain gods. So what do you do when Saturday night becomes Sunday morning, your rage face becomes your worst face, and the contents of your stomach are about to become the contents of your toilet or (*yick*) your roommate's shoes? And where are your keys? Your phone?? Your dignity???

I won't insult your intelligence by telling you that you could have easily prevented that hangover by hydrating, knowing your limits, and never exceeding more than one drink–accompanied by one glass of water–every hour. Nor will I inundate you with crazy hangover cure concoctions like Grandma Thorndike's classic for the "Overindulgent Evening of Bridge" (essentially a Bloody Mary). No, this simple guide will not address the physical, Sunday morning pain that you all brought upon yourselves but rather this simple fact:

Sometimes even the smartest people do the absolute stupidest things.

And sometimes they don't even remember doing them. So in order to solve those Sunday morning mysteries here is my foolproof, five-step program (and here's to hoping you never encounter a certain other twelve-step program later in life):

Piecing Together the Previous Evening's Events

1. **Check your phone.** This is absolutely the number one, most important step. (Assuming you already checked under your covers, under your bed–assuming that you're in *your* bed–and, in some cases, your closet for any forgotten overnight guests.) Check your outgoing calls. If you drunk dialed any particular number in excess of three times: send a mass text apologizing for a smartphone software malfunction. Check your outgoing texts. If any of your exchanges resemble these:

COME OVER! Where? HERE! ! Where's "here"? Where are you? HIDING! ...Are you in your dorm room? HIDE N SEEK, LITTLE BO PEEP! Have you been drinking? HURRY UP! DADDY'S NAKED AND DON'T LIKE TO BE KEPT WAITING! Good night, Sarah. Call me in the morning.	LAKJSFLAKDSFKJAASF!! ? !#$!ASDKFJKL%$#&258Q98?? Huh? Who is this? !#&$TaslkjflaksjdOUSERKJa;kjf!?!?!? Is ur phone malfunctioning? ;0 ;) ;) I don't get it. ...You still there? BABY IM SRY! Ha. It's ok. But srsly, who is this? I LOVE YOU.	YO Uh... Hi? 'SUP? Not much. It's 2am?! 'S COOL. Did you want something? NAH. DID YOU? You txted me! RLX. NBD. ? G2G. GTL. YKHII. TTYMbL.

Then you should send the following follow-up text:

SORRY FOR PARTYING . . . SORRY I'M NOT SORRY.

Or if you *are* sorry (though you shouldn't be–don't ask for permission, ask for forgiveness, and never apologize if you can avoid it), log on to Facebook and update your status to: PHONE STOLEN LAST NIGHT! MSG ME IF YOU'VE SEEN IT! Then wait a few hours and repost: FOUND IT! THANK GOD! ROOMIES MUST'VE STOLEN AS A JOKE. APOLOGIES FOR ANY WEIRD CALLS OR TEXTS!

If any of your calls were actually answered . . . well, there's nothing you can do but pray. Do keep in mind: playing the *I don't remember card* makes you sound like even more of a mess.

2. **Check your wallet.** Are all of your credit cards still there? No? Whoops–go find them. Yes? Good. Now go online and check your bank statements. They will likely tell you where you were last night, what you bought, and in many cases, what you should *not* have bought. Drinks for everyone at the bar? How generous. Seven pairs of new shoes from Zappos? I'm sure you needed those! (Though far safer than drunk driving–duh!–Drunk Shopping can still be a dangerous game. Remember: "Beer goggles + browsing often = serious retail regret.") Three extra large four-cheese pizzas with extra cheese? Wait, really? So gross. Let's hope you shared.

3. **Check the trash.** Uh-oh. Sorry, kiddo: three empty pizza boxes just don't lie. At least that baby bump you woke up with is a food baby, not one of those screaming, crying poop machines.

4. **Check your relationship status.** Another risky subcategory of boozing + browsing behavior includes Drunk Facebooking. While sometimes alcohol facilitates bonding, it can also lead to fighting, often with your roommates or significant other. You might be surprised how frequently an exchange of angry words leads to a Facebook update–either from "In a Relationship" to "Single" or "It's Complicated" or to a good old-fashioned Defriending. Or worse, an actual status update along the lines of "So-and-so is a grotsky little biatch." Oops. Undo the damage as best you can, apologize, and if all else fails, pull a Jamie Foxx and "Blame it on the a-a-a-a-alcohol."

5. Check the mirror. Do *not* leave your room without assessing the damage done to your face/hair/person. Trust me: you don't want to show up for Monday morning class with a ginormous penis scrawled across your forehead (thanks a lot, roomies). Also, take a shower. You're not Ernest Hemingway, and that smell does not become you.

Here to help as always,
Alexis Thorndike
Interim Managing Editor @ The *Harvard Crimson*
The Nation's Oldest Continuously Published Daily College Newspaper since 1873
Advice Columnist @ *FM* Magazine
Harvard University's Authority on Campus Life since 1873

A tiny triangle of light suddenly stabbed at Callie's face. Moaning involuntarily, she rolled over on a hard surface, causing the book that she had spread pages-down across her face in place of an eye mask to topple onto the hardwood floor. Groaning again, she forced open one eyelid.

Persuasion by Jane Austen, she managed to read upside down. Scrunching up her eyes in pain at the now unmasked, early-afternoon sunlight streaming in from a nearby window, she wondered, What the hell had a book been doing upside down on her forehead? How did it get here? How did *she* get here? Where *was* here? Blinking warily, she reread the title of the book—a volume that belonged to . . . Gasping, she bolted upright.

No Gregory. There were, however, several other individuals lying fast asleep and, in some cases, snoring, spread out, like she had been, at various odd angles on the floor of the boys' common room.

Slowly she heaved herself up onto one of C 23's two black leather couches so as to better survey the scene before her.

In the corner under the potted plant Matt and Jessica were spooning. Correction: Jessica spooned Matt, assuming the role of big spoon to her foot-taller little spoon counterpart.

Oddly enough, this was not the most bizarre thing in the room.

Several feet away Adam lay curled up near the TV, wearing a blue-and-white polka-dot dress, stockings, and pumps. Red lipstick was smeared across his face. A pink wig and a purse had been abandoned nearby.

OK sprawled facedown, spread-eagle under the coffee table, his head, arms, and calves poking out from underneath the mahogany wood. His limbs were bare, and one quick peek under the table confirmed his total nakedness. Callie reached toward the coffee table, cringing as she slid a copy of the *Crimson* out from under a mostly fallen tower of Jenga Truth or Dare blocks. Then, ever so gently, she arranged the newspaper pages to cover his rear. OK didn't budge.

Sighing quietly, Callie slumped back onto the couch, her eyes traveling to the other side of the room.

Vanessa, wearing only a one-piece bathing suit, appeared to have passed out in the exact same position as OK except that she lay faceup rather than facedown. Her forearms, forehead, and thighs were covered with what looked like chemical equations written in different colors.

Frowning, Callie peered behind the couch. Dana sat slumped against it, a thin thread of drool pooling on the collar of her shirt. In her hands she clutched permanent markers in red, green, and blue.

Spinning slowly, Callie scanned the rest of the room.

Mimi was missing.

Many odd items littered the floor, including (1) pair of glasses; (1) pair of pants (plus suspenders but minus an owner); (3) bottles of wine (empty); (7) cartons of Chinese food from the Kong (also empty); (1) bottle featuring a large green fairy on the label (mostly full); (1) tiny silver hat, (1) tiny silver shoe, and (1) tiny silver motorcar (Monopoly pieces?); and finally (1) gold trophy that read WORST EVER. But no other people appeared to be present. Callie grabbed a bottle of water next to OK's foot and chugged for as long as she could stand it. Then, sinking low onto the couch, she placed the bottom of the bottle against her forehead, hoping the cool plastic might relieve her aching head.

Moments later Jessica began to stir. "What the—"

"*Shh!*" Callie called, placing a finger to her lips while her best friend batted at the leafy fronds of the potted plant that had engulfed her.

Using what felt like every last ounce of strength she could muster, Callie motioned at Jessica to join her on the couch.

"What on earth," Jessica started with a whisper, "happened to us last night?"

Callie shrugged, pointing at the coffee table.

Jessica peered under it and then clapped her hands over her mouth, trying to stifle the giggles induced by the sight of OK sporting only the latest campus headlines.

Callie shook her head and then handed Jess the water bottle, which she accepted gratefully. After gulping some down, Jessica tilted her head at Matt. *"Did you see us . . . ?"* she mouthed.

"Did I see you WHAT?" Callie mouthed back.

"You know," Jess whispered. Then, closing her eyes, she mimed passionately making out with the nearest pillow.

Trying desperately not to laugh, Callie whacked her best

friend with another throw pillow. "Cut it out!" she whispered between whacks.

"No, *you* cut it out!" Jessica retorted, yanking Callie's pillow from her hands and then proceeding to beat her with both of them.

Callie cried out, struggling to fend off the blows.

"Omigawd, MY *THIGHS!*" came a sudden scream from near the door.

"Thighs," Adam mumbled in his sleep, rolling over in the dress. "I prefer the breast, please. Chicken, of course."

Callie and Jessica froze, staring first at Adam and then at Vanessa, who, having woken, gazed down at her thighs in horror. "Who did this?" she demanded of Jessica, whose head was visible over the edge of the couch. Callie gasped with laughter from where she lay trapped under the pillows below.

"Beats me," Jessica replied in a whisper, letting Callie up.

"Callie?" Vanessa said, fixing her with a death-glare.

Still overcome with silent giggles, Callie shrugged and then pointed behind the couch.

Instead of attempting to stand, Vanessa hauled herself up on all fours and crawled over. Spotting Dana, her expression turned livid. "Why that little—"

Vanessa stopped abruptly as Dana twitched. Rolling over again, Adam mumbled, "But it's *not* little, in fact, according to Wikipedia. . . ." Eyes still shut tight, he yawned. "Perfectly average . . ."

Catching each other's eye, Jessica and Callie burst, once more, into mostly silent laughter. Vanessa turned to them sharply. "Shut up!" she hissed. "Not another sound! Now hold still," she instructed, sliding the red permanent marker out of Dana's hand, "while I teach this little . . . *studier* a lesson. . . ." With a worrisome gleam in her eye she uncapped the pen. "Congratulations," she said breathlessly, brushing a brown lock of Dana's hair off her forehead. "You're about to become the newest member of the Pen fifteen club."

Before Callie could say something to stop her, Dana's eyes flew open. "What in heaven's name are you— Cease that this instant!" she snapped, batting the tip of the pen away from her forehead, where Vanessa had managed to draw the long line of a *P*.

Frowning, Vanessa wielded the pen over Dana like a dagger. "An eye for an eye, just like Jesus said!" she stated in hushed tones.

Dana stared at her. "What are you talking about? Jesus never said that."

"What am I talking about?" Vanessa echoed. "*This*," she said, gesturing at her thighs. Her eyes grew wide as she appeared to notice the marks on her arm for the first time. "And *these*!"

Callie glanced over her shoulder to see if Vanessa's cries had roused the boys, but neither OK nor Matt had moved, and Adam, though occasionally mumbling unintelligibly, still seemed fast asleep.

Dana shook her head, looking just as furious at Vanessa. "You don't remember, do you? This is precisely why you should be practicing abstinence!"

"Not that it's any of your business," Vanessa retorted, "but I'm. Still. A VIRGIN!"

"Virgin?" a hoarse male voice called from over in the corner near the potted plant. "Where? What? Why are you yelling?" Matt continued, sitting up and rubbing his head. "And has anyone seen my keys?"

"Ugh!" exclaimed Vanessa. "I'm yelling because Dana drew all over me while I was sleeping!"

"I seem to recall that you were awake while that was happening," Matt said slowly, squinting around the room. "And that you asked her to do it. Now what did I do with those keys . . . ?" he mumbled, emptying his pockets with no success.

Dana smiled smugly. "Abstinence with regard to *alcohol*," she said primly, nudging a nearby empty bottle with her foot. "Although I am quite surprised—pleasantly, I should say—to learn of your hymenal sanctity."

"I agree," said Matt to a dumbstruck Vanessa. "I mean—about the alcohol! We all probably went a little overboard this weekend." Catching sight of Jessica, his cheeks grew pink. "I mean, not that it wasn't nice—a nice time with . . . everyone. I'm just saying we maybe went overboard. Not that I wouldn't do it again. Because I would. I mean, not everything, just—"

Callie shook her head at him.

"So . . . I actually *asked* you to do this to me?" Vanessa said, turning to Dana.

Dana nodded. "Yes. It was right after you and Mimi put on the bathing suits—"

"Meemeeee . . ."

Jessica giggled, pointing at OK, whose fingers had just fluttered.

"Say," Callie interrupted, "where is Mimi, anyway?"

"Meemeeee." Strange gargling noises emanated from OK's throat, his lips smushed down against the floor. However, apart from his fingers nothing else had moved.

"I don't know. But like I was saying," Dana continued, speaking to Vanessa, "you started going on and on about how you wish you knew more songs about science. And then you asked me to sing you some, and I said I didn't know any. So then you asked me just to teach you more about science, but we didn't have any paper— and that's when you told me to draw on you."

"Is this true?" Vanessa asked the others, though, from her guilty expression, the memory appeared to have already resurfaced.

Dana, still slumped against the back of the couch, glared at her. "Ask Adam if you don't believe me! Unless he did the smart thing and slept in my room for the night like I suggested."

"Uh . . ." Callie exchanged a look with Jessica. The couch currently blocked Dana's and Vanessa's view of the rest of the room, and given that neither had moved, aiming pens at one another like warheads, neither had spotted Adam. Yet.

"About that," Jessica jumped in.

"What?" Dana demanded, suddenly alert. Her spider sense with regard to mischief must be tingling.

Callie made a face. "Maybe you should—"

"What the . . . *heck!*" Dana had finally spotted her boyfriend. Though, at the moment, perhaps the term *lady friend* was more appropriate. Briefly she closed her eyes and appeared to be whispering some sort of prayer. "Adam!" she finally shrieked. "Adam, wake up this instant!"

"Oh—good morning," he said, springing into sitting position as if he'd been awake the entire time. "Dana, my darling, last night I had the strangest dream."

Dana gaped at him while the others looked on, momentarily stunned.

"I dreamed I was wrapped in robes of the finest silk," he continued, speaking, as he had a way of doing from time to time, like a middle-aged man trapped in the body of a prepubescent-sized boy. "They were roomy and airy and delightfully comfortable, like floating in a cloud, and then a wizard asked me if I would like to buy some chicken, but when I licked my lips, they tasted like cherries. Bright red cherries. And I was tall—several inches taller than I . . ."

He finally seemed to notice the women's shoes on his feet. "Huh," he said, tilting his head. "That's odd. I thought I took those off before I turned in for the evening."

"Odd?" Dana repeated. "Odd? Adam Nichols, have you been drinking?"

Shrinking away toward the pink wig and purse lying near the television, Adam held up his hands. "No. Not since . . . last night?" His voice cracked on the final phrase.

"What—were you—clearly *not* thinking—" Dana sputtered.

"Sorry," he apologized. "But you fell asleep right after you insisted you were staying to make sure nobody committed any unforgivable curses—I mean *sins*!—and then they started playing that game," he explained, pointing at the Jenga blocks on the table. "And it looked sort of fun. See, red blocks are dares, green blocks are truths, and for the neutral-colored blocks you get to write in your own dares. Every time you choose a block, you have to try not to knock down the tower—and drink. Those were the, uh, rules?"

Dana folded her arms across her chest.

"Rules are . . . rules," said Adam lamely.

"Oh yeah," Matt called, looking from the Jenga blocks to Adam's outfit. "That dare was my idea! 'If you picked this block, you have to cross dress!'" He laughed but quickly shut up as Dana rounded on him. Then, marching over to Adam, she held out her hands. "Come on, get up. We can discuss this later, after you've changed."

Standing in the pumps, Adam was, for the first time, taller than Dana.

"Hey, these things are a lot easier to walk in than I thought they'd be," he mused as he followed her toward his bedroom. "I wonder if—"

"Don't even think about it!" she cut him off, ushering him over to his dresser and opening the top drawer.

"We played Jenga last night?" Jessica whispered to Callie.

"I asked *Dana* to *teach me SCIENCE*?" Vanessa added, her head still poking up from behind the couch.

"Oh jeez," said Callie. "I wonder what else . . . ?"

Near the potted plant Matt stretched and then stood. Ambling over, he plopped onto his common room's second leather couch, eyeing the three girls warily. "One thing in particular stands out," he blurted, seeming to avoid looking at Jessica. "But the rest is all a bit blurry. . . ."

"Pants!" they heard Dana cry from Adam's bedroom. He sat on the bottom bunk, appearing reluctant to change. "Which drawer?"

"Hey!" said Vanessa, spotting the pair of pants plus suspenders on the floor. "I found them!"

"Those aren't mine," said Adam, coming out of his room with his dress unzipped and stockings pooled around his ankles. He still wore the high heels.

"Get back here!" they heard Dana snap from inside. "To think what this could do to your political career if anyone were to see or document—"

"All right, all right," Adam conceded, retreating back into his room. "Second to last drawer."

"If these aren't Adam's," said Vanessa, lifting the pants, "then who do they belong to?"

"Don't look at me," said Matt, gesturing at his jeans. "Maybe they're the property of his highness? Oh, your highness!" he called suddenly, giving OK's calf a gentle kick.

OK didn't budge.

"Oh, wow," said Matt, bending down. "I can see his highness's royal heinie." Grimacing, he rearranged the newspapers, which had slipped.

"He's not, like, dead or anything, is he?" Vanessa asked, crawling over the back of the couch and sitting next to Jessica.

"*Meemeeee*," OK grunted into the floor.

Chuckling, Matt tickled OK's feet. "Time to wake up, your majesty. . . ."

"*Hooo-yah!*" OK cried suddenly, shooting up and knocking the back of his head against the coffee table. "*Wah-owwwwww*!" he wailed.

"Don't look!" Callie cried, crossing her arms and throwing one hand over Jessica's eyes and the other over Vanessa's before closing her own. OK had rolled out from under the coffee table, leaving the newspapers behind.

"Oh, come on," said Jessica, giggling, "No fair—"

"Please," they heard OK say, "to think I would be caught dead in skinny jeans. Though the suspenders do add a nice bit of flair."

Callie heard the low, squeaking sound that bare skin makes against leather, followed by Matt's cry of: "Dude! Other people have to sit there."

Callie opened her eyes. Vanessa and Jessica looked on delightedly as OK spread another sheet of newspaper over his crotch like a loin cloth. "This just in," he said, emphasizing his accent. "Breaking news: I rather enjoy the way the leather feels against my ballsack."

"*Ahh*!" the girls screamed, breaking into more giggles. Matt buried his face in his hands.

Callie apologized to Jessica. "I swear to god this doesn't happen every weekend."

"Actually," said Matt, "it kind of does."

"What can I say?" said OK. "I like to take my tea in the nude."

Jessica howled with laughter.

"Speaking of nude," said Vanessa, "if you're not going to put those on, maybe I will," she said, picking up the pants. "I'm feeling a little bit . . . exposed," she added, surveying her thighs.

"Time for church!" a voice chirped from over their shoulders.

Turning, they saw Dana with Adam in tow. She had restored his normal clothing, but he still looked as frazzled as she appeared furious.

"You can't go!" Callie cried as they headed for the front door. "We need someone to stay and force OK to put clothes on!"

"Yeah and—"

"Have fun, you two!" Vanessa interrupted Jessica, clapping a hand on her knee.

"Wait!" Jessica cried, shaking off Vanessa. "You still have pen—and lipstick—on your faces!"

"Oh, boo," said Vanessa, pouting. "You're no fun."

Dana stopped in her tracks, wheeling around to face Adam. "How did I not notice . . . ? *Why* didn't *you* tell me I have . . . *Ugh*!" Looking livid, she pushed open the bathroom door. Soon the sound of running water met their ears.

Callie hoped, for Adam's sake, that Dana was being gentle—though from the sound of it, she was taking her frustration out on his face, one violent washcloth rub at a time.

Leaning in, Vanessa whispered, "And you say my relationship with Tyler was unhealthy. . . ."

"Ohmygod!" Callie blurted, her spine straightening suddenly.

"What?" asked Jessica.

"Your phone," Callie said, staring at Vanessa. "Where is it?"

"I don't know," said Vanessa. "Why?"

"I've got a bad feeling. . . ." Callie muttered, heaving herself off the couch and casting around the room in search of Vanessa's iPhone.

"It can't have gotten far," Vanessa said with a yawn. "Brad and I are in kind of a codependent relationship."

"You named your phone Brad?" asked Jessica.

"So what?" said Vanessa.

"Want me to call it?" Matt volunteered, pulling his own phone out of his pocket.

"Yes," said Callie at the same time that Vanessa said, "Whatever."

The techno beats of Sexy Hansel's latest single started thumping from somewhere near OK. He narrowed his eyes. A few more bars of the German pop star's vocals confirmed that the phone was definitely underneath the cushion, the only thing separating it from OK's behind.

"Oh, get over it," Vanessa said to an immobile OK.

"No," said OK, planting his feet. "Not until you admit that they are terrible, horrible, no good, very bad, talentless arseholes."

"I am very sorry that your high school girlfriend slash infamous socialite Sissy Smirnoff left you for the sexy manliness that is Sexy Hansel and that you still haven't recovered," Vanessa said cruelly.

"That's it!" cried OK, standing. The newspaper fluttered to the floor. "I'm about to go R. Kelly all over this thing," he continued, lifting the couch cushion and standing above the phone.

"It's not a *thing*," Vanessa shrieked. "It's *Brad*—and stop—what are you—*noooo*!"

"Matt—do something!" Callie yelled from the other side of the room.

Shaking his head, Matt seized the phone. "Seriously, dude," he said, "not on the couch."

"Seriously, dude," OK mimicked him with an abysmal attempt at an American accent. "I wasn't actually going to urinate," he muttered indignantly. Scooping up the newspapers, he headed for his bedroom. "If you would be so kind as to put on the teakettle while I'm dressing," he finished, speaking to Matt over his shoulder. Then, stepping into his room, he slammed the door.

Matt drew a long sigh. Then he stood, and after handing Vanessa her phone, he turned on the electric kettle the boys kept next to their refrigerator. "Would anyone else care for some tea?"

"Oh," said Jessica. "Yes, please. Green tea is just the thing for a hangover." She beamed at Callie. "He's really just the best, isn't he?"

Blushing, Matt busied himself with the kettle.

"Oh. My. Flipping. God." Vanessa's jaw hung open as she stared at her phone.

"I heard that!" Dana called from the bathroom. "And I don't approve! Stop squirming," she added, presumably speaking to Adam.

"This is bad," Vanessa said, her eyes glued to the screen. With every swipe of her thumb, her expression grew increasingly grim. "Bad . . . bad . . . bad."

"What?" asked Callie, the color draining from her face.

"Well," said Vanessa, "the good news is that Gregory's phone number is probably still disconnected. So it's unlikely that he received any of these texts. Which is great, lest he think that I . . ." Squinting at her phone, she read, "'Can't lib without u Ms. Your facez.'"

"What?" shrieked Callie. "Give me that!" she cried, reaching for the phone.

"Wait, this one's good, too," said Vanessa, dodging her. "'Rufor reals still dating Prky Boobies? Y?!?'"

"Ohmygod." Callie covered her eyes with her hands. "Kill me now. Seriously. Do it. Please. Put me out of my misery."

"Relax," said Vanessa as Jessica put a comforting hand on Callie's shoulder. "I'm sure his line is dead. Though there's really only one way to find out. . . ." Before Callie could stop her, Vanessa had dialed. "Yep," she said a few seconds later. "Still disconnected."

Callie heaved a sigh. "Good."

"Not so fast." Vanessa shook her head. "We're not out of the woods yet."

"Stop dragging it out and just tell us!" Jessica commanded.

"Fine," said Vanessa, "see for yourself." She held out her phone, which featured the following exchange with Tyler:

YO YO T-DAWG.

. . . HI VANESSA. I THOUGHT THE "TRAIN HAD LEFT THE STATION"?

THAT'S RIGHT. WE DON'T WANT 2 TALK 2 U.
BUT WE HAVE A MESSAGE. 4 UR ROOMMIEZ.

OH?

CLINT WEBER IS A POOPY PANTS!

POOOPIE POOOPIE POOPIE POO!

POOP POOP!

HA. I'LL LET HIM KNOW.

WOW, THANK YOU. MAYBE I WAS WRONG.
U DON'T SUCK WORSE THAN A BLIND DONKEY THRU A STRAW.

HAHA. NOW I HAVE A MESSAGE FOR YOUR ROOMMATES.
TELL THEM TO CONFISCATE YOUR PHONE.

"Oh no," said Callie as Jessica struggled not to laugh. "Did . . . *I* write these?"

"I have a vague memory of it being a group effort," said Jessica.

"Did we at least listen? Did we let someone take away the phone?" Callie asked, raising her voice and addressing Matt.

"I tried," said Matt. "But you ladies seemed to be on a mission."

"A mission to do *what*?" asked Vanessa.

"Well," said Matt, arranging some tea bags in mugs, "it's hard to say exactly, but there was a lot of talk about finding some guy's phone number and asking him to come over."

Vanessa bolted upright. "That would probably explain this," she said, looking nervous, and scrolling to another set of messages in her phone.

HEY YOU! COME OVER.

WHO IS THIS?

YOUR SECRET ADMIRER.

???

WIGGLESWORTH, C 23 IF YOU WANNA FIND OUT. –VVV

"These messages are time-stamped at two o'clock in the morning!" exclaimed Callie.

"I know." Vanessa moaned. "Do you recognize the number?"

The others shook their heads.

Suddenly a knock sounded at the door.

"*Ah*!" screamed Vanessa, grabbing a blanket off the couch and throwing it over her head.

"Shut up!" Callie hissed. "And maybe whoever it is will go away."

The knock sounded again, louder this time.

"I think we'd better answer it," Jessica whispered.

"*Nooo*," came the muffled sound of Vanessa's voice from underneath the blanket.

"You do it," said Callie to Jessica.

"Me? Why? No! I'm just the visitor!"

The girls locked eyes for a moment and then both turned to Matt.

"Fine," he said, turning off the teakettle. "Coming!" he added as the knock sounded for a third time.

Callie did a double take as the door swung open. Standing just outside was the tall, skinny, brown-haired poet that Vanessa had forced her to stalk at the *Advocate* a few weeks ago. Warily he took a step into the room.

"I'm just here to get my pants back," he said slowly, staying close to the door. "Then I'll be on my way."

Callie and Jessica watched as Vanessa slowly lowered the blanket from her face, which had become the same reddish color as her hair (except for the green and blue chemical equations written on her forehead). Everyone stared at her legs, on which she wore the mysterious set of skinny jeans, the suspenders dangling loosely at her sides.

"Uh . . ." said the guy, looking at Vanessa like she had inspired the song "Super Freak," minus the "she's all right" part.

Vanessa seemed to be paralyzed.

"Oi, Max is back!" The door to OK's bedroom flew against the wall. Finally clothed (in an oriental-patterned silk kimono), OK strolled out into the common room.

"It's Maxwell," said the guy.

"I prefer Max," OK replied nonchalantly, as if correcting someone's pronunciation of his own name, rather than of this almost stranger's.

Max(well) rolled his eyes, appearing more eager to leave now than Callie had been to flee that poetry reading, which was saying a lot.

"Maxwell," said Vanessa slowly.

"Yes," he said irritably. "As in, the person whose pants you're wearing?"

"These . . . are yours," Vanessa said quietly. Pulling them off as fast as possible and then wrapping the blanket around her lower half, Vanessa handed him the pants.

"Thanks," Maxwell said curtly, backing toward the door. "And a final word of advice, if I may," he added, pausing on his way out. "Next time you feel like finding someone's phone number on Facebook mobile and calling them up in the middle of the night—don't."

He pulled the door shut behind him.

Vanessa let out a wail, throwing herself onto the couch and pulling several pillows on top of her.

"There, there," said Jessica, patting the pillow that Vanessa hugged to her stomach. "We all fall victim to drinking and Facebooking at one point or another."

"I can't believe I . . . did. . . ." Vanessa struggled through her sentences.

OK let out a barking laugh. "Oh, you'd better believe it, baby! You," he continued, pointing at Vanessa, "couldn't stop talking about how much you wanted to 'call up the poet and make sweet, sweet poetry'—the kind that leads, according to you, to 'miniature hipster babies.' And so then you," he continued, turning to Callie, "said, 'Why not look up his number on Facebook?'" He looked at Jessica. "Then you chimed in with 'Call him, call him, call him,' but you refused"—he nodded at Vanessa—"and sent him some texts instead. Then, wonders that be, he came over."

"*Ugh*," Vanessa groaned from under the pillows. "Why is this happening to me?"

"Oh, but there's more," said OK, a spark in his eyes. "Blondie over here said that you should write him a poem, but Jess—or shall we call her, Blondie the Sequel—"

"Hey!" Jessica interjected, aiming a pillow at his head.

"Blondie Part Deux?" he asked.

"I prefer *Jess*," she said, smiling.

"Anyhow, Jess had a better idea. She said the fastest way to a man's heart is to turn up the heat, pretend to spill water or red wine on him, and then take off his pants!"

Callie raised an eyebrow. "*Gentlemen Prefer Blondes*?" she asked her best friend.

"There's no arguing with a strategy devised by Marilyn Monroe," said Jessica.

Vanessa poked her head out from underneath the pillows. "Oh god. Tell me I didn't . . ."

"You did," said Dana, emerging from the bathroom. "And I admit that of all the things that happened last night, that incident was . . . mildly amusing."

"You were there, too," Vanessa recalled with a sigh.

"We were," Adam affirmed, joining Dana in the common room.

Callie sat up. "Dana, exactly what time did we come home last night?"

Dana pretended to look put out, but her shoulders seemed to perk up slightly, no doubt at the opportunity to turn the story into a medieval morality tale. "Well, it was definitely after midnight, and while I can't comment specifically on the events that occurred before, Adam and I were here watching a movie when suddenly you all barged in. Vanessa kept singing something about how 'she blinded me with science,' and other people were singing, too. It was very loud and rather out of tune."

"Hey!" cried Vanessa.

"Mimi was carrying that green bottle and you all drank from it and then Jessica screamed 'dance party' and turned off all the lights. Adam and I decided it would be in everyone's best interest if we stayed and chaperoned, since you all seemed somewhat intoxicated and your judgment highly impaired."

Matt, looking sheepish, set down several cups of tea on the coffee table. Jessica shot him a grateful smile. He sat next to her on the couch, loosely draping his arm above her shoulders.

"After you were tired of dancing, you all decided to have a slumber party. Then you agreed you should play a game. The general consensus seemed to be that Monopoly was boring, so you asked our upstairs neighbors if you could borrow their Jenga. Then you proceeded to write the most ridiculous set of dares," she continued, lifting some of the neutral-colored wooden blocks off the coffee table. "'If you drew this block, you have to cross dress.' 'Send a "relationship request" to one of your Teaching Fellows on Facebook'—"

"Uh-oh," Callie mumbled, making a mental note to cancel that *asap*.

"'Put on bathing suits and go swimming in a pile of money,'" Adam jumped in. "'Torture OK until he confesses who his mystery girlfriend is—'"

OK gasped.

"Don't worry," said Dana. "They weren't successful."

Adam cleared his throat. "Dana eventually fell asleep after fulfilling Vanessa's request to draw on her, but I figured I had better stay behind to—er—keep an eye on things. We played Jenga for another hour or two, during which that Maxwell guy showed up and then left, *without* his pants, when he realized that you two"—he nodded at Jessica and Vanessa—"weren't going to give them back."

"I'm transferring to Stanford," Vanessa declared. "Jessica, take me with you!"

"But we were *where* before midnight?" Callie asked.

"Beats me," said Adam. "Did you check all of your phones?"

"The moral of the story is," Dana cut in loudly, "that none of you should ever drink again, ever."

Callie's eyes traveled from OK, who had sprawled out across one couch; to Jessica huddling next to Matt, sipping tea with a pained expression on her face; to Vanessa cowering under the blanket and pillows. Oddly enough they all seemed to wholeheartedly agree. Her head pounding, Callie nodded. "Never again," she murmured, which they all echoed with a series of grunts and moans. Absentmindedly Callie picked up Vanessa's phone and started scrolling through it, making sure nothing had been overlooked.

"Good," said Dana. "Now if you'll excuse us, we're off to church!"

"Why are you going to church on a Saturday?" asked Vanessa.

"It's not Saturday, it's Sunday," Dana said with a scathing look of disbelief. Then, shaking her head, she and Adam left the room.

"Sorry," Vanessa mumbled.

"Oh, hey, wait a second," said Callie, staring at the phone. "We forgot to check the pictures. Aha! Mystery solved. Before midnight we were at Tommy Doyle's," she said, holding up a photo. "And it looks like we were doing . . . karaoke? Hang on, there's a video." She set the iPhone on the table where they could all see it and then pressed Play.

Vanessa stood on stage at the bar, holding a microphone and singing the eighties one-hit-wonder "She Blinded Me with Science."

"Well, that certainly explains some things," said Vanessa, who, having perhaps reached her mortification quota for the weekend, appeared indifferent to the video.

The scene changed as Mimi took the stage when Vanessa was finished, belting out her favorite, Edith Piaf's "La Vie En Rose." In the background the audience booed. As her roommates had tried to hint gently to Mimi on numerous occasions when she sang in the bath, she was truly, unequivocally terrible. At the end of the video a man presented Mimi with a small gold trophy.

"And *that* explains *this*," said Callie, picking up the golden trophy that had WORST EVER printed across the base.

"Okay," said Matt. "But that still doesn't explain: where *is* Mimi?"

"Meemeeee!" OK yelled, eliciting giggles from the others. "What?" he demanded.

"Nothing!" Jessica and Callie chorused.

"Don't just sit there," OK admonished, though he himself had not moved. "Help me."

"Mimi!" the others droned. "MIMI, WHERE ARE YOU?"

"*Dans ici*!" came a faint call from somewhere inside the bathroom.

"Did you hear that?" asked Matt.

"*Oui, oui,*" said OK, dragging himself off the couch.

After helping each other up, they followed him into the bathroom.

It was empty.

Slowly OK peeled back the shower curtain over the bathtub.

It was filled with a mixture of one, five, and ten dollar bills, and multicolored Monopoly money. Mimi's head, shoulders, and knees poked out from beneath the cash.

"*Bonjour, mes amis,*" she said brightly, languishing with her head tilted back as if she were in a particularly luxuriant mud bath at a spa. "*Je me sens comme un million de dollars!*"

"Yeah," said Matt with a laugh. "No wonder you feel like a million bucks. I would, too."

"Care to rejoin me, fellow dare buddy?" Mimi asked, winking at Vanessa. "You look as if you could use a good scrubbing!"

Giggling, Vanessa hopped into the tub. "'Put on bathing suits and go swimming in a pile of money,'" she recalled. "Genius. Say," she continued, "do you know whose glasses are in the common room?"

"Yours," said Mimi. "You asked Callie to retrieve them to help you prepare before *le hipster est venu*, and then she returned with that book and proceeded to cry out in her sleep. 'Wentworth!'" Mimi mimicked Callie, naming the main love interest in *Persuasion*. "'Gregory!'"

"Okay," said Callie, ignoring Jessica's amused expression. "That's enough of story time!"

"Wait," asked Matt. "Any idea what happened to my keys?"

"*Non*," said Mimi.

"You didn't"—Matt lowered his voice—"*roofie* us last night, did you?"

"Ha!" Mimi laughed. "It was only a weensy splash of absinthe. Perfectly legal these days; in Europe we take ours in our tea. *Pfft!* Featherweights," she muttered. "Now be a dear, deary," she called to OK, "And fetch us *un* cocktail. I am simply parched!"

"A cocktail?" OK repeated, seeming too surprised to be offended at being told to fetch. "Right now?"

"*Mais oui,*" said Mimi. "*C'est la seule façon de réparer un* hangover."

Hours later, after gorging on greasy food and a brisk walk along the Charles River, Callie's hangover had finally subsided. She still felt terrible, however, and not entirely because it was time for Jessica to leave. Insane as the weekend had been and wonderful as it was to see her best friend, her overall predicament remained unchanged. She was two days closer to her hearing and yet no closer to proving that Lexi was the Ivy Insider. And, even worse, the ratio of time spent obsessing about Gregory to actual time spent *with* Gregory basically equaled a huge number divided by zero which was—in real life and in math—a problem with no solution.

"Can I give you two pieces of sisterly advice?" asked Jessica, breaking out of a teary hug near the escalators that descended into the Harvard Square T station.

"Of course," said Callie. "I need all the advice I can get."

"Okay," said Jess, propping herself up on the handle of her carry-on. "Here it goes. . . . Number one: you've gotta stop obsessing about Gregory."

"Who me? Obsess?" Callie feigned weakly.

Jessica laughed. "Look, I'm not saying you should give up completely because I still think that you two are meant to be . . . well, at least not like *this*. Howsoever, no amount of obsessing or calling out for him in your sleep—"

Callie groaned.

"—is going to bring him back any sooner. He will return when he is ready. And when he does, maybe he'll have good reasons for going totally AWOL—or maybe he won't. Either way, it's not going to change the fact that you have more important things to worry about right now."

"I know," Callie agreed with a sigh. "I've been trying to tell myself the same thing since that Monday after spring break."

"It's hard, I'm sure," Jessica said sympathetically. "But necessary. Anyway, number two: as far as this Ivy Insider business is concerned . . . I think it's time to start playing dirty."

"Dirty *how*?" asked Callie.

Jessica smiled mischievously. "In order to beat Lexi at her own game, you're going to have to start thinking like her. No more Mrs. Innocent California Girl. It's time to bend a few rules before you get kicked out for violating ones you didn't even break in the first place."

"What exactly are you suggesting?" Callie asked slowly.

Grinning now, Jessica pulled something small and shiny out of her pocket, dangling it in front of Callie's face. "He would have given them to me," she said quietly, "but I didn't want him to get in any trouble in the event that you get caught. . . ."

Callie stared at the object suspended from her best friend's fingers. "Are you saying . . . what I think you're saying?"

"Uh-huh," said Jessica with a nod, pressing Matt's keys into Callie's hand. "You have to break into the *Crimson* building."

EIGHT

Breaking, Entering, and Pranking

A Day in the Life

At the *Harvard Crimson*

8:00 A.M.—All Staff Morning Meeting

Managing Editor: What super important stories are we going to break today, gang?
Staff Writer 1: Maa . . . Dunno.
Staff Writer 2: Dining halls smell sort of weird sometimes. Think there's a story in there?
Managing Editor: Hmm. Maybe. What were you thinking in terms of accompanying art? I'm thinking maybe we go big with this and make it our front page with my face, in close-up, as the photo.
Staff Writer 2: Um. Would that be a photo of you in the dining hall?
Managing Editor: What's a dining hall? I eat all my meals at Upstairs on the Square.

Staff Writer 1: Dining halls are things that smell like fish tacos. And I vote yes, because you're really pretty.
Managing Editor: Good, then it's settled.
COMPer: But . . . aren't Oprah and Lady Gaga visiting campus tomorrow for a forum on the new Born This Way Foundation?
Managing Editor: Drop and give me twenty, COMPling.

12:00 P.M.—Lunch Break

ME: Where's my super-duper, special, customized, named-after-me salad? Somebody bring it to me or I'll have you all castrated!
ME: I'm serious, people. I'm going to start with the freshmen. Then the sophomores. Then the business board. Then editorial. Art Board, you guys are safe for now—I still need somebody to take pictures of me.

3:00 P.M.—Departmental Meetings: Art Department

ME: Let's see how the new mock-up of *FM* mag looks with my face on the cover.
Photographer 1: You like?
ME: Hmm. Maybe. I'm thinking . . . it could be bigger.
Photographer 1: What, the title of the magazine?
ME: No. My face.
Photographer 2: But, er, well, ah . . . your face is already taking up the entire front and back covers.
ME: So what? Can't you make the magazine bigger?
Photographer 1: How much bigger?
ME: Hmm. How about one and a half times the size of the newspaper at the very least?

5:00 P.M.—Departmental Meetings:
Editorial Board ~CANCELED~

9:00 P.M.—Final Editorial Review~CANCELED~

Midnight—The *Crimson* goes to print.

The next day—BREAKING NEWS:

The Harvard Crimson

NEWS OPINION *FM* MAGAZINE SPORTS ARTS MEDIA

Breakfast At Tiffany's

Why I Have Never Set Foot in a Harvard Dining Hall

By LEXUS TEARDUCT,
SHODDY MANAGING EDITOR
and OCCASIONAL ADVICE COLUMNIST
at Really Really REALLY Prestigious Publications
For longer than you'd care to remember

This parody was brought to you by The Harvard Lampoon. http://harvardlampoon.com

Callie clicked off her flashlight several yards before she reached the bright red door to the *Harvard Crimson*. She glanced over both shoulders and then down across the street at Adams House to make sure the coast was clear. Luckily Plympton Street was completely deserted. Callie permitted herself a sigh. Even though it was three o'clock in the morning, there was no telling how late some students might be coming home from the library.

Her feet flitted across the pavement, covering the final steps in seconds. Then, without daring to look back, she slid the copy she'd made of Matt's key into the lock.

The hallway was cool and dark. Callie made sure to hug the right-hand wall, avoiding the stacks of newspapers she knew to be arranged against the left. Creeping along in total blackness, she tiptoed her way to the arch that opened into the first floor offices.

As anticipated, all the lights were off. Breathing deeply, she slipped inside. Wary of the computer desks, she edged over the floor one foot at a time, taking care not to bump into anything. When she had made it approximately halfway across the room, she reached into her back pocket, where she had folded the copy of her log-in records that the Administrative Board had requisitioned when the final Insider installment broke.

When she had been COMPing the *Crimson*, she had used one

of the two same computers every day, monitor #3 or monitor #4, sitting next to Matt as frequently as possible. The Insider articles had all been posted from different computers, and judging by the monitor numbers, the workstations in question were located elsewhere in the offices—either in the back or on the second floor.

Her plan was simple: determine where the Insider's computers of choice were located and then see if this triggered any visual memories of who had been sitting there around when the articles had been posted.

Of course, in order to look, she would need a little light. Her heart thrumming so loud it practically felt like someone on the street might hear, she clicked the flashlight on.

From somewhere in the back corner of the offices, she heard a soft distinctive whisper: *"Merde!"*

Dropping to the floor, Callie threw herself under the closest computer desk, setting the flashlight facedown to kill the beam.

Shit, she thought. Someone's here. But why hadn't they turned on the lights? Had she missed something? Holding her breath, she leaned against the side of the desk. Instead of supporting her shoulder, the hard wooden surface gave way. Callie only just managed to roll out from under it before the entire desk caved in, collapsing with a heart-stopping, definitive *thunk*.

A thin line of light scattered across the floor as her flashlight rolled away. Callie closed her eyes. This was it. Someone had stayed late to work in one of the conference rooms or managerial offices. Now she'd been caught, and if her fate hadn't been certain before, it was certainly inevitable now: she was going to be expelled. What other punishment could there possibly be for breaking and entering into an organization that the administration had explicitly banned her from ever setting foot in again?

The backs of her eyelids suddenly turned bright yellow. Blinking, she found herself momentarily blinded. The beam of another flashlight shone down on her, making it impossible to see anything but blackness behind the circle of light.

"*Qu'est-ce l'enfer . . . Callie?*" a familiar voice demanded.

"*Mimi?*" Callie replied in disbelief.

"Callie!" Mimi answered, finally pointing the flashlight elsewhere and bending down.

Callie allowed Mimi to help her to her feet. "What the—what are you doing in here?"

"*Shh!*" Mimi silenced her, scooping up Callie's flashlight and then pulling her down past the rows of computer desks. "In here," she continued, pushing Callie toward Grace's old office. *"Rapidement, s'il vous plaît!"*

Callie hurried through the door, closing it as Mimi clicked on the desk lamp. Dim light flooded the room. Callie could now see Mimi, clad in an all-black outfit quite similar to her own.

"What are you doing here?" Callie demanded in a whisper.

"What am *I* doing here?" Mimi repeated incredulously. "*Qu'est-ce que tu fais ici*?"

"Looking for answers," said Callie, unfolding the log-in records and holding them up. "I thought if I could come back here and get a sense of which computers the Insider used, then I might suddenly remember seeing Lexi—or whoever else—there that day."

Surveying the log-in records, Mimi nodded slowly.

"Now tell me why you're here," said Callie.

Mimi made a face. "It is technically the business of the *Harvard Lampoon* that must remain most top secret," she began. "May I trust that your loyalty to me is greater than to the *Harvard Crimson*?"

Callie almost smiled. "They did kick me out, you know. And I think you also know by now that you can trust me. Nothing you say will leave this room."

"I do know," Mimi replied with a grin. "But it never hurts to triple-check."

"Double-check?" asked Callie, smiling now.

"Why double when you can triple? *Tout cas*, I have come here *dans l'obscurité de la nuit* to make the *Crimson* full of loose screws."

"Huh?" said Callie. "You're trying to make everyone here crazy?"

"Not *crazy*." Mimi shook her head. "I am speaking literally of loose screws, *pas l'expression américaine*."

"You mean . . . you're in here"—Callie suddenly remembered the way that the desk had toppled over when she had leaned against it—"Loosening all the screws in the building?"

"*Exactement!*" affirmed Mimi.

Callie laughed, struggling to stay as quiet as possible.

"You will not tell, will you?" asked Mimi.

"No," said Callie, still laughing. "I won't. I wish I could be here to see the look on Lexi's face when . . ." Callie turned, realizing exactly whose office she stood in now. Framed issues of *FM* decorated the walls. Grace's old newspaper articles and photos of female journalists she admired had all been removed. A picture of Lexi and Clint stood on the desk; a Missoni scarf was strewn casually over the back of that familiar, ergonomic chair. Callie let forth an involuntary shiver.

"They stole our ibis again," Mimi implored, mistaking the meaning of Callie's anxious expression.

"Your *what*?"

"It is our . . . What is your word for *girouette*?"

Callie drew a blank.

"*C'est la* copper-colored bird *au sommet de notre* castle."

"The . . . weathervane with the bird on top of your castle?"

"*Oui!*" Mimi looked relieved. "*Un* weather-vane *c'est la girouette, en français*."

"Got it," said Callie.

"Last time they stole it was in the year 1953," Mimi explained. "They presented it as a 'peace offering' to the Soviets during the Cold War for the newly constructed *Université de Moscou. Il a été un désastre!*"

"Yes," said Callie, "I can see how that would be a disaster."

"The Lampoon president and the treasurer are upstairs on the second floor looking for it now," Mimi confessed. "We doubt they would be so stupid as to keep it here in their offices, but even if we do not locate it . . ."

"You're still pranking them back," Callie finished.

"*Oui*," said Mimi. "So be *très, très* cautious not to touch any of the desks while you are checking the computers. Otherwise . . . *kaboom*!" she whispered gleefully, pounding her fist into her palm.

"Okay," said Callie.

"*Après réflexion*," Mimi started, "I had better take that," she pointed at the log-in records, "and examine *les ordinateurs* on your behalf."

"Why?" asked Callie, handing her the sheet of paper nonetheless.

"If the bosses upstairs were to catch you, there is no telling what they would do," Mimi said gravely. "Kidnapping, at the very least, I am thinking."

"All right," Callie consented.

"Returning momentarily," said Mimi, slipping out of the office.

Callie felt even more on edge now that she was alone in Lexi's lair.

Several hair-raising minutes passed until finally Mimi returned.

"Monitors seventeen, twenty, twenty-two, and twenty-five are all located in the back of the office on this floor," Mimi whispered, shutting the door behind her.

"Are you sure?" asked Callie, crestfallen. She had been praying that at least one of the computer stations would be located upstairs on the second floor offices that housed *FM*, where Lexi had spent the majority of her time prior to her promotion.

"*Positif*." Mimi nodded.

"Crap," said Callie, frowning and chewing her lip. Closing her eyes, she struggled to picture what the office had looked like on a typical day during COMP. Try as she might, she could not call to mind any specific individual who spent the majority of his or her time in the back—especially since she and Matt had always done their work in the front, facing away from the rows and rows of computers behind them. And, while COMPers had been known to lie low at the rear computers so as to avoid marauding editors in search of an errand runner, Callie had never, not once, seen Lexi use a computer on the first floor.

Callie sighed heavily. "Is it safe to sneak out the front door?" she asked. "I mean, are the other two Lampoon people still upstairs?"

"*Pourquoi donc quitter maintenant?*" Mimi appeared puzzled. "Oh, *désolé*," she added in response to Callie's equally confused expression. "I have said, 'Why in your right mind would you leave *now*?'"

"Because breaking in was a total bust," said Callie. "I don't know why I thought being back here would help me." If anything, it had made things worse: reminding her of what she had lost—and everything else she still stood to lose.

"Have your screws come loose?" Mimi cried in hushed tones, grabbing Callie by the shoulders. "*Regarde ça!* Where better to find the proof you seek than in the office of your prime suspect?"

Callie stared at her. "I couldn't . . . I mean, I shouldn't . . . should I?"

"But of course you should!" Mimi replied. "Now, before we are discovered!"

Callie felt perspiration begin to form along her brow. Slowly she scanned the surface of Lexi's desk, from the photo of Clint to the telephone to the container full of pens. "But there's nothing here!" she whispered in a panic.

"*Ne sois pas une un idiote!*" Mimi admonished her. "Open the drawers!"

"Oh," said Callie. "Right." Cringing, she pulled open the top drawer of Lexi's desk. Inside she found more pens and what looked like a day planner. Seizing the little red leather-bound book, she opened it and began to read. It was, indeed, a day planner.

A tiny bead of sweat trickled down Callie's temple when she looked up at Mimi. "Do you know how to use a Xerox machine?"

"'Do I know how to'—yes, of course I do!" Mimi snapped. "*Dois-je ressembler à une idiote?*"

"Good," said Callie, gesturing at the copy machine in the corner. "Then can you please make copies of the entries for February third and nineteenth, March eighth, and April fourth?"

"It would be faster just to steal it," Mimi muttered.

"Yes, but then she'd notice that it was missing," said Callie.

"Fine," Mimi mumbled, taking the organizer and turning on the copy machine. "If you are insisting."

While the copy machine whirred to life, Callie busied herself with the other drawers.

"Any luck?" Mimi asked after a few minutes had passed, presenting Callie with the Xeroxed pages from Lexi's organizer.

"I can't seem to find anything else that looks relevant," Callie said, shutting one of the drawers a little more loudly than she had intended in frustration. "Although I'm sure this locked drawer must have something," she said, pointing to the bottom of the desk, "if only I had a key."

Mimi's eyes lit up. "Did somebody say . . . *keys*?" she asked, pulling a wrench out of a duffel bag that Callie hadn't noticed earlier in the corner.

"Uh, Mimi—"

"Hold on, hold on," Mimi insisted, taking several other items from the duffel, including a screwdriver, a pen knife, some rubber bands, a handful of nails, and an enormous plastic bag filled to the brim with screws. "Ah-ha!" she cried. "Voilà!" She dangled in the air a huge silver ring with an assortment of approximately thirty keys.

"Where did you get these?" Callie asked, accepting the key ring.

"Trust me: you are not wanting to know where, how, or when."

"Point taken," said Callie, trying to fit one of the smaller keys into the bottom drawer's lock. It refused to turn. "Do you really think that one of these is going to work?" she asked, trying the next one.

"We at the Lampoon have power you could not even begin to dream of," said Mimi. Callie, as always, had no idea if she was kidding.

"Well, if there's any proof at all," said Callie, still bent by the desk trying key after key, "then it's going to be here in this drawer. I've seen it open once before when her desk was still upstairs, that day she gave me a copy of the old sex tape in exchange for my breaking up with Clint—"

"*Hush*!" Mimi cried, looking stricken. "Did you hear—"

There was no need for her to finish her sentence: the footsteps were now audible, rapidly approaching the office of the managing editor.

"Under the desk, now," Mimi hissed at Callie, who dived under as the door creaked open.

"What's taking you so long in here, Clément?" a male voice asked.

The muscles in Callie's shoulders relaxed just the teensiest bit: from the sound of it, the intruders were the Lampoon members who had been upstairs and not the administration, the *Crimson* staff—or the police.

"I thought I might stop and pick some daisies," Mimi deadpanned.

A second voice followed the sound of the initial speaker chuckling. "Pack up your bag. It's time to go."

Callie listened to Mimi throw the items she'd removed back into her duffel.

"Did you finish loosening all the screws in here?" the first guy asked.

A pause.

"*En fait*," said Mimi slowly, "I have had an even better idea."

"Oh yeah?" asked the second guy.

"*Oui*," said Mimi. "I am thinking that we should steal her chair instead. Special treatment for a very special editor."

The silence seemed to drag on forever.

"Brilliant. I love it."

"Please, allow me," Mimi insisted, intercepting footsteps that appeared to have been headed for the desk.

Callie spotted Mimi's ankles move into view. Bending, Mimi pretended to grip the bottom of the chair. Now face to face with Callie, she widened her eyes, staring at the keys.

"But," Callie mouthed, *"I haven't . . ."*

Lips pressed together, Mimi shook her head and held out her hand.

In desperation, Callie mimed sliding one of the smaller keys off the ring.

Mimi nodded, grabbing the ring and doing it for her. Then, tossing the key at Callie, she straightened. "Whoopsie-daisy," she said, holding up the ring. "Almost forgot these."

"Come on," said one of the guys. "We need to leave, now."

"*Je comprends, je comprends*," said Mimi, dragging the chair behind her.

Craning her neck, Callie saw Mimi grin and throw the Missoni scarf over her shoulder. "*Un souvenir*."

"Great," said a voice. From the sound of it, the owner was retreating toward the door. "Go time."

Someone switched off the desk light, and then a few seconds later Callie heard the door to the office click shut. She forced herself to count to thirty before crawling out from under the desk. Her hand that held the flashlight was shaking, but she didn't dare turn on the desk lamp again. Wiping the sweat from her brow, she picked up the key and inserted it into the lock.

It slid in easily.

Then it turned.

"Gottcha," Callie murmured, yanking open the drawer.

There were only two items inside.

The first was a USB thumb drive labeled C, A—INSURANCE.

"You bitch," Callie said, pocketing it. Months ago Lexi had mentioned having another copy of the tape, but until now Callie hadn't known whether or not to believe her.

The second was a photo of a girl Callie didn't recognize.

With mousy brown hair and nondescript features, the girl, who appeared to be around Callie's age, was incredibly overweight, her eyes averted shyly from the camera.

Callie froze, clicking off the flashlight. Tilting her head, she listened.

Silence.

Probably just my imagination, she decided, though she could have sworn she'd heard a sound. She waited another full minute just to be sure and then clicked the flashlight back on. She stared at the drawer for several seconds but then stuck the picture into her pocket along with the copies of her log-in records and Lexi's day planner pages. Then she locked the drawer, praying that Lexi wouldn't be struck with the urge to blackmail anyone, or store any other contraband inside of it, soon.

In less than three minutes Callie had found her way back into the hall. Pulling the front door open just a crack, she peered outside into the darkness. Plympton Street was deserted.

Tiptoeing onto the stone steps, she pulled the door shut gently behind her. Then, with one final glance over her shoulder, she sprinted the entire way home.

"Fancy meeting the likes of you here," said Mimi from the overstuffed armchair in the common room, where she was midway through removing her shoes.

Callie grinned, leaning against the wall to catch her breath. "I take it you made it back to the castle undetected?"

Mimi solemnly raised a finger to her lips. "I have not the

faintest of hints as to what you are speaking of. And where were *you*, out so late?"

"Just doing a little laundry."

"*Vraiment*?" said Mimi, feigning disbelief. "*Moi aussi!* Our clothes are going to be so very clean."

Callie laughed. "Good night, Mimi," she called softly, heading for her room.

"Bon soir!"

Even though it was after 4 A.M., Callie had too much adrenaline pumping through her veins to even consider sleeping.

She spread the copies of Lexi's day planner pages out across her desk. Then she pulled printouts of the Insider articles from a drawer and studied them one by one.

The first, "Behind the Ivy-Covered Walls," had been submitted to FlyBy for publication (pending Grace's approval) at 6:49 P.M. on February 3. Eagerly Callie scanned the photocopy of Lexi's planner denoting details of her day on February 3.

Feb 3

8am–9:30am–FM morning meeting

11am–1pm–Government 1061

1pm–Lunch with G.B.

3pm–4pm–Economics 1011b Section

5pm–6pm–Pudding Board meeting

6pm–Dinner with the Roomies @ Dali

9pm–Pudding punch drinks with A.C., P.V. and A.G. @ Grafton

Callie reread the entry three times, struggling to stifle the rush of emotion that accompanied the 1 P.M. appointment. "Focus," she muttered aloud. How could Lexi have posted the article and simultaneously dined at Dalí? Maybe it had been a quick dinner, though the service at the tapas place had seemed deliberately slow the one time Callie had eaten there with Clint—plus, the restaurant wasn't exactly close to campus.

Callie flipped to the next Insider article, "Behind the Ivy-Covered Walls, Part II," submitted at 11:13 A.M. on February 19. Then she checked it against the day planner.

Feb 19

10am–11am: Yoga @ Karma Studios

12pm: Final FM mock-up meeting

2pm: Lunch with C.W.

6pm: Dinner with A.G.

8 pm: Black Tie Gala Fundraiser @ The Kennedy School

Don't forget to

-Confirm the limo for Pudding brunch tomorrow AM

-Confirm the venue for Uncle Joe's visit (Faculty Club?)

Yoga? thought Callie, trying, and failing, to picture Lexi relaxing and letting all the light fall into her spine—or whatever those yoga instructors preached. However, this entry did more than just confirm Callie's long-standing suspicion (that yoga was of the devil)—it placed Lexi, in all likelihood, at the *Crimson* around the time the second Insider article was published. Granted, she would have needed to draft the installment in advance to post it so soon after yoga (not to mention appearing in public in workout clothes, which, according to Lexi's columns, was a grave taboo). But still, this was promising. Lexi had clearly been at the *Crimson* for hours, even if she did eventually leave to have lunch with Callie's then-boyfriend at the time, Clint.

Callie frowned, trying to stop wondering what they had talked about and continue examining the evidence. "Okay, 'Behind the Ivy-Covered Walls, Part III,'" she mumbled aloud. "March eighth, at four oh two . . . What were you up to then, Ms. Thorndike?"

Mar 8

10am–11:30am: Art History 1214

12pm: Lunch with A.C.

*Remember to print your Gov Paper

2pm–4pm: Government 1061 Section

4pm: *GOVERNMENT PAPER DUE*

5pm–6pm: Study Group @ Lamont Library

7pm: Sign off on FM mock-ups @ the *Crimson*

<u>8pm</u>–C.W. @ Adam's House (!!!)

Ah yes, 8 P.M. on the eighth of March: the night Clint had hooked up with Lexi (unless you counted their kiss at Gatsby a few days earlier after Callie had left the party with Vanessa). Not that Callie needed any further proof of Clint's douchebaggery—

after all, he'd confessed to everything over spring break shortly after Gregory had given him a black eye—but it was strangely satisfying to see his lies documented in black and white. It made her miss having a boyfriend that much less.

Callie yawned, reading the entry again, but nothing in particular stood out. Lunch with Alessandra at noon seemed perfectly normal, given how hard Lexi had been wooing her to join the Pudding. And again, so long as she had already written and saved a draft of the third installment, Lexi could have arguably made it to the *Crimson* by 4:02 P.M.to submit it.

Callie's eyes lingered on the 8 P.M. entry, the double underline stinging ever so slightly. Earlier that day Clint had lied to her face, insisting that he had to miss dinner to make a meeting at the Pudding that evening. By "meeting" he had clearly meant "sex date" and by "Pudding," "my bedroom." Oh, well, thought Callie. No use crying over—

She bolted up in her chair. Clint hadn't just lied to her face that day—he had lied to her face in the *Crimson*. He'd brought her coffee and then excused himself in order to make his *four o'clock* squash practice!

"Oh my god," said Callie as the memories continued to return. That was also when she had discovered, shortly before Clint had arrived, that Lexi and Grace used to be roommates during their freshman year. And that sometime before the end of the semester, most likely after Grace had made the *Crimson* and Lexi had been cut, Lexi had mysteriously transferred out of their room. Midway through her search that day, Callie had had to log back into the *Crimson*'s website. Callie closed her eyes, recalling the conversation she'd had with Matt who, as usual, had been sitting next to her.

"Huh . . . that's strange," she had muttered.

"What?" Matt had asked.

"Oh, nothing," she'd replied. "It just says that it logged me out of our internal server because I was logged in at another location."

Matt had shrugged it off, blaming a buggy system or a session timeout. But he'd been wrong. Because, as Callie realized, the Insider had been there in that room on that very day, shortly before 4 P.M. readying to post the latest article. Using Callie's username and password, the Insider had logged into Callie's account from somewhere else in the room—at computer station 17, 20, 22 or 25, to be specific.

Callie held her breath, sensing she was on the verge of a major discovery. But no moment of clarity came. There had been plenty of students, COMPers and staff alike, in the first floor offices working that day, but no one stood out in particular as having acted suspiciously. And—there was no way around it—Callie felt fairly certain that Lexi had not been anywhere in the vicinity, since Callie had checked several times before stalking her former COMP directors on the internet.

"*Fuuughhidditybug*." Callie groaned, throwing her head down on her desk. She kept her forehead pressed against the cool wood for a minute or two before straightening. Maybe the final day planner entry, when compared to the final insider installment,

"Behind the Ivy-Covered Walls Part IV," published at 6:32 A.M. on April 4, would have some answers.

Apr 4

~~11am–1pm–Social Studies 226~~

~~1pm–Lunch with C.W.~~

~~5pm–C.W. Squash Match @ Malkin Athletics~~

EMERGENCY MEETING AT THE PUDDING

10am

"Dammit!" cried Callie. "Shit, shit, *shit!*"

A faint cough sounded from Vanessa's room next door.

"Crap," Callie muttered, succumbing to another yawn. Exhaustion hit her like a sack of bricks. Head pounding, she slowly stacked all the papers on her desk and then returned them to the bottom drawer.

Standing, she stretched. Spotting the log-in records, USB thumb drive, and photograph where she had tossed them on her bed, Callie grabbed them. She was about to throw the photograph into the drawer along with the other two items when she paused, reexamining the face of the girl in the picture. In this light it looked oddly familiar.

"Or you're just delirious," Callie muttered. Nonetheless, before she crawled, fully clothed, underneath her covers, she tacked the photo onto the right-hand side of the bulletin board, where it would remain, all but forgotten, long after sleep obliterated her consciousness.

NINE

And the Plot Thickens

The Harvard Crimson

NEWS OPINION *FM* MAGAZINE SPORTS ARTS MEDIA

Have You Seen THE CHAIR?

Managing Editor's essentials still missing, among other things, in the wake of Lampoon break-in

By ALESSANDRA CONSTANTINE, CRIMSON STAFF WRITER

Published: Thursday, April 21

Sometime between late last Tuesday night and early Wednesday morning, the *Crimson* suffered a massive break-in. In the downstairs offices the culprits loosened every screw. In the upstairs offices they superglued every chair and trash can, and various other typically mobile itmes to the floor. Needless to say, all work at the paper came to a grinding halt on Wednesday as editors stopped working in order to repair the damage.

The Harvard Lampoon, a semi-secret Sorrento Square social organization that used to occasionally publish a so-called humor magazine, has now publicly claimed responsibility for these atrocities, confirming widespread rumors proliferating all over campus.

The Administrative Board has declined to respond to the paper's formal request that disciplinary action be taken against the pranksters. "Former Harvard Provost Paul H. Buck set a very clear precedent for how to handle these so-called 'Pranking Wars,'" a high-ranking administrator commented Wednesday night. "As he said back in 1953 when the *Crimson* presented the Russian embassy with the Lampoon's ibis as a symbolic peace offering, 'Everyone's taking it as a big joke.'"

In this case the joke may yet be on the Lampoon, and perhaps the *Crimson*ites will, as they did back in 1953, be the ones to have the last laugh. The Lampoon's ibis is still missing, and its sudden disappearance, or so the Pooners claim, amounted to the *Crimson* having "fired the first shot."

Crimson managing editor and author of *FM*'s exceedingly popular advice column, Alexis Thorndike, is reported to be in negotiations for a trade: the ibis, a copper-colored weathervane that normally decorates the top of the Pooner's castle, for her chair. The chair is a custom-made ergonomic work of art by Eames for the Herman Miller company, designed specifically for Ms. Thorndike and presented as a gift upon her acceptance onto *FM* magazine during her very first semester at Harvard—a rare incidence of a freshman making the magazine on her first attempt in the fall. It features black fabric and a rosewood trim and is mounted on wheels for maximum movement and flexibility. Fortunately, it appears that no other items were taken from Ms. Thorndike's office.

If you've seen the chair or have any other pertinent information, please contact tips@FMmag immediately.

Grace threw the paper down onto a rickety metal table outside Café Pamplona, a tiny little coffee shop on Bow Street a mere block from the *Crimson* offices. Callie jumped back as the table wobbled and her tea sloshed over the sides of her cup, filling the saucer below.

"Er, everything okay there?" Callie asked Grace, grabbing a napkin.

"Frankly, no," Grace said shortly, sinking into her chair. "Have you *seen* this sloppy excuse for a newspaper?"

"Um, yes," said Callie slowly. "I . . . *read* about that break-in. Seems like people are saying that the Lampoon was responsible? It's really too bad—"

"Not *that*." Grace shook her head. "The break-in is a minor blip compared to the travesty that has become our copyediting department. Under *my* administration stories like these never would have gone to print!" She jabbed her finger on that Thursday's cover story, a follow-up piece about the escalating prank war between the *Crimson* and the Lampoon.

Callie squinted at the byline: *by Alessandra Constantine*.

"I thought new staff members weren't allowed to publish so early?" said Callie, taking a sip of her tea.

"They weren't." Grace frowned. "Not until the Devil Wears Prada, as you like to call her, started playing favorites. Now the only requirement for landing a cover story is her liking you."

"I'm guessing all of your articles have been printed in size four-point font on the back of the so-called 'Sports Section'?"

"You joke," said Grace, grimacing, "but it hits just a little too close to home."

Callie skimmed the opening paragraph of Alessandra's article. "Oops," she said, smiling in spite of herself. "Major typo alert! I guess it's true what they say: supermodels don't make the best spellers."

"It's actually probably not her fault," said Grace. "Those typos were likely added by someone else when the article was transcribed. And as for the choice of subject matter . . . Well, let's just say that in a week when students staged another walkout in an economics lecture, Obama visited the Kennedy School, and even that Asian basketball player scored a lot of goals—or baskets or whatever—the most important thing happening on campus was *clearly* determining the location of Alexis Thorndike's missing chair."

"Mm-hmm." Callie nodded absentmindedly, now engrossed in the article. Grace continued to prattle on, criticizing Alexis and making a mild case in Alessandra's defense, insisting that all novices are a little sloppy when they get started, even including the Insider, whose initial installments had required a fair amount of general editing.

"Andrews!" Grace barked. "Andrews, are you listening to me?"

"No," Callie confessed. "Did you see this?" she asked, holding up Alessandra's article and pointing to the final paragraph.

"Utterly ridiculous, right?" said Grace. "'Custom-made ergonomic work of art by Eames' my ass—"

"No." Callie shook her head. "I'm talking about the part claiming that Lexi joined *FM* Magazine during her first semester freshman year."

"What about it?" Grace asked, narrowing her eyes.

"Well, I mean—it's not true, is it?"

"How do you know that?" Grace demanded.

"I, er . . ." Callie winced. "Sort of kind of might have stalked you a little bit on the internet and the *Crimson*'s internal server?"

"Why?" Grace asked, appearing amused.

"I was curious about why you and Lexi hate each other so much. It seemed to go beyond a mere rivalry between the paper and the magazine."

"I see," said Grace. "And did 'stalking me,' as you say, turn up any answers?"

"I have a very . . . tentative theory," said Callie.

"By all means," said Grace, setting down her coffee, "let's hear it."

"Well," Callie began, "using that website where you can check who used to live in which dorm, I figured out that you and Lexi used to be roommates during your freshman year. You lived in a double in Thayer, but . . ."

Grace nodded. "Go on."

"She transferred out of the room midway through the semester. Now, I don't really know why, but I suspect it might have something to do with the fact that you both COMPed the *Crimson* during your first semester and that she got cut."

"Whereas I made it," Grace supplied in a murmur.

"Yes, exactly," said Callie. "So she gets mad and transfers out, and then once she makes the magazine, she starts trying to undermine you at every turn for, like, revenge—or something."

"That *is* a very tentative theory," Grace remarked.

"It's a little too thin for print," Callie agreed, borrowing an expression that Grace often used to describe an unconfirmed story that relied too heavily on anonymous sources.

Grace smiled.

Callie felt warmed and not just from her latest gulp of tea or the April sun peeking through the gray clouds above them. Earning Grace's trust back hadn't been easy, but now, after several meetings to discuss their progress on catching the Insider, it seemed like Callie had regained not only an ally but her old mentor, too.

"There's more to the story, isn't there?" Callie ventured, smiling in return. "Care to enlighten me?"

Grace appeared to be thinking it over. "Okay," she finally agreed. "Why not? But you'd better make yourself comfortable, because this could take a while."

Callie shifted in her tiny metal chair to indicate that she was settled in for the long haul.

Clearing her throat, Grace began, "As you know, Alexis and I were assigned to live together freshman year. Based on the stereotypes associated with her hometown, Greenwich, I assumed I would dislike her immensely. But I was wrong. In her e-mails over the summer before college started she seemed smart, sarcastic, and driven. All of this proved true in person, too. What's more, *she* was aware of the typical Connecticut boarding school stereotypes and was eager to overcome them: to establish a new self in college distinct from the Thorndike name.

"We bonded instantly over our mutual aspiration to join the *Crimson*, and over similar career goals beyond that. I'd always had my heart set on the *New York Times*, and she'd wanted to become the next major media mogul with her very own blogging empire or news conglomerate—two industries in which her complete and utter disregard for journalistic ethics might actually help her get ahead."

Grace paused to sip her coffee before continuing. "Anyway, like I said, during that first month we became fast friends. Yes, it was obvious from the start that in some ways we couldn't be more opposite. She's always cared about fashion and status and other nonsense that struck me as trivial. But that didn't change the fact that deep down we wanted the same things: to redefine ourselves and then ultimately become, via the *Crimson*, the Next Big Thing in journalism.

"When we started COMPing, we lived and breathed the newspaper. Our class schedules were nearly identical, and so naturally we ended up doing everything together: we woke up at the same time every morning and then ate together, wrote together, edited each other's pieces, and on one or two occasions after some particularly late nights at the *Crimson* offices, cried together. You know how it is." Grace nodded at Callie.

Callie murmured her assent, gripping her teacup and willing Grace to go on.

"This lasted for about two months, but in that short time it felt like almost two years had passed in terms of how close we had grown. And so I decided to share with her a secret I'd been keeping from everyone—myself included—for a very long time. That I was gay."

Grace let the statement hang in the air ever so briefly before resuming. "I told her and she reacted . . . well, better than I could have hoped for. She even did some online research about Harvard's LGBT resources and suggested I check out a place called the Queer Center, where I first met Marcus and essentially found the support system I needed until I was ready to come to terms with my sexuality and, eventually, come out to society. Back then though, I was still afraid. Afraid that who I was would affect my chances at everything—making it onto the *Crimson*, a future career in journalism, and even my overall happiness in life. The center really saved me. It showed me that I wasn't alone and that there's a place for people like me here, on this campus and in the larger world beyond.

"Around that same time two other things happened. Lexi started dating—a guy, as you know, named Clint—and a little white envelope showed up under our door. Of course the Pudding wanted her: she fit the pedigree in absolutely every sense. And I didn't fault her when it became clear that it was something she wanted, too. In fact, these two events had almost no impact on our relationship other than that she suddenly had less time.

"Having less time did, however, affect the quality of her work at the *Crimson*. Her pieces started coming back with more and more red pen marking the pages. We both made it through to the final round, but our COMP director warned her that she had just barely scraped by and would need to step up her game if she ultimately wanted to make the cut. One day he held up one of her pieces as an example of the kind of work that he wanted to see more of—a piece that *I* had edited heavily after she'd begged me to help her because she was 'just so busy' with Punch that week.

"Neither of us ever said anything about it after, but looking back, I think that's when the rift started to form. And yet, at the same time, she started relying on me—and my edits—more and more. Sometimes it felt like I was doing double the amount of work while she was out on a date or at a party "networking for our future," as she liked to put it. Then again, on only four hours of sleep a night over many months, it's easy to feel like you're drowning. And, as I reminded myself, she was doing even more than I was, in a sense—trying to balance the social in addition to the academic and extracurricular."

Callie nodded grimly. This account of COMPing, and the inevitable impossibility of "doing it all" at Harvard, certainly struck a chord.

"Only a few days before our final portfolios were due, our COMP director let it slip to me that they were only planning to take one freshman—meaning it was either me or Lexi, since we were the only two left. I went home and immediately told Lexi. Her reaction was to console me: the quality of our work being equal, she said, it was clearly going to come down to which one of us had the most connections. And since at least one Pudding member and two of her high school alums wrote for the paper, the spot would almost certainly go to Lexi."

Callie rolled her eyes. "That sounds a lot more like the Lexi I know."

Grace shrugged. "I think she believed she was being sincere, but given how much slack I'd been picking up for her, it was . . . irritating, to say the least. And besides, even before she got distracted by boys and social clubs, my writing was superior. She knew it and I knew it, and yet she still had an advantage over me, due to where she was born and to which clubs she belonged.

"To this day, I still don't know if the bitterness that I had come to feel played a part in what happened next. I continue to think that I never intended to 'sabotage' her, as she put it—but maybe, subconsciously, on some level . . ."

Grace stared off into the distance, her typically tough exterior seeming to melt away.

"What happened?" Callie finally dared to whisper, perching precariously on the edge of her seat.

"Our final portfolios were due on a Saturday at eight o'clock in the morning, sharp. The Friday before, we were holed up in our room finishing our final edits. Then Lexi's phone rang. It was the Pudding. They demanded her immediate presence at a top secret location somewhere in the Yard—she wouldn't tell me where—presumably so they could perform an initiation ritual."

The John Harvard statue, thought Callie, remembering the night during her first semester when she had received a similar summons.

"Lexi could barely contain her excitement as she changed out of her sweatpants and into the sort of outfit she seemed to be wearing more and more those days. While she rushed to get ready, she said something along the lines of, 'If I'm not back in time, would you?' and then gestured at her computer.

"She was already halfway out the door when I called to her, saying that surely she'd be back in a few hours. She laughed and said there was no telling how late she and Clint might be celebrating. Then she was gone. Off to get drunk and make out with her boyfriend while I stayed home seeing both us of through to the end.

"I sat down in front of her computer, determined that one quick proofread would be the last favor I ever did for her. Except, as I realized when I started, it wasn't going to be a *quick* final review: her latest articles still needed hours and hours of editing!

"Something inside me snapped. I stopped reading and hit Print. For the rest of the night I lay awake, half expecting her to come home and salvage her pieces before the deadline—but she never did. I waited and waited until, at seven fifty-seven the next morning—I remember because I was staring at the clock, watching it tick—I grabbed both of our portfolios, and I left.

"In between Pudding parties and spending the night at Clint's, Lexi barely noticed my frosty demeanor over the following weeks. Competing for the same spot had made things awkward, and she suddenly had a new set of friends—friends more like her high school clique, friends who all came from New York or Connecticut and dressed up for dinner in the dining hall. But when we were both at home in the room, we did still hang out. And that's exactly what we were doing two weeks later when we heard the *thunk* of somebody depositing two large manila folders into the metal drop-box on our front door.

"Lexi raced to grab them but then lingered, alone for several minutes in the hall. When she finally came back, I knew immediately what had happened. She threw my portfolio to the floor and then shoved hers, which contained the unedited pieces, in front of my face. 'How do you explain this?' she demanded, to which I replied that I didn't have to explain anything since her portfolio had been her responsibility."

Grace sighed heavily. "Things got even uglier after that. She yelled a lot about how I had sabotaged her and ruined her future, and I'm sure I said plenty of nasty things, too. In the end she demanded that I 'make things right' by resigning from the paper and giving her my spot."

"What'd you do?" asked Callie, realizing her tea had gone cold and setting down her cup.

"I refused, of course," said Grace. "And that's when she threatened . . . to out me—to the entire school—if I didn't do it."

Callie sucked in her breath. "Wow," she muttered, shaking her head. "Just . . . wow. The sex tape situation was bad, but *that* is just a whole new level of low."

Grace nodded. "I wish I could say that I told her to go ahead and, while she was at it, to go fuck herself, but instead . . ."

"*No*," Callie whispered.

"I'm afraid so," said Grace. "I went to our COMP director and told him I thought that Lexi rightfully deserved my spot."

"And what did he say?"

"He laughed and told me that I was crazy and that even if I quit, they wouldn't accept Lexi in my place. As a senior, he knew a thing or two about roommate troubles and tried to give me some advice that I wasn't really in the proper frame of mind to hear. All I could think about was that my secret would soon be revealed and that there was nothing I could do to stop it."

"Jeez," said Callie, dragging her hands down her face. "That's some seriously messed up stuff."

"I know," Grace agreed. "But she never did go through with it. She's a terrible person—and has only gotten worse over the years—but back then I guess there were still some lines that even she wouldn't cross. She did, however, tell the administration that I had created a 'hostile living environment' by hitting on her, and who knows what else. That's how she managed to transfer to another room. And then, after that, she told everyone who would listen that I had 'sabotaged' her at the *Crimson* and 'stolen' her spot.

"A few weeks later when she started COMPing *FM*, her story changed slightly: she had never really wanted to belong to the paper, since the magazine was 'obviously so much cooler' and way more her 'style.' But she did continue to stick to the overall I-stole-her-life theme, accusing me of kleptomania regarding her shoes, her clothes, her boyfriend—ironic, yes, I know. But I didn't dare refute her for fear that she still might tell everyone I was gay. And so for the next year I lived with the rumors, which had spread through the *Crimson* and my dorm. Fortunately, as soon as the other editors came to know me, they showed me nothing but respect. And eventually everyone else moved on to more interesting scandals and forgot all about it, too."

"Everyone except Lexi," Callie pointed out.

"I don't know," said Grace. "I used to think she was content with running the magazine. She's the perfect fit for *FM*, and everyone seems to love—or loves to hate—her column. But if she did orchestrate this entire Insider business for the purpose of having me demoted and you expelled, then it's probably safe to say that she never got over it."

Callie drank her cold tea while Grace sipped her coffee, letting it all sink in. Grace's story seemed like further evidence that Lexi was—and absolutely *had to be*—the Insider. Then again, the day planner Xeroxes that Callie carried in her bag indicated otherwise.

"Before I forget," said Callie. "One of the reasons I asked you to meet me here today was to show you these." Pulling out the day planner pages, she handed them to Grace.

"Andrews," said Grace, staring at the documents, "how the hell did you get these?"

Callie coughed. "Uh, let's just say that there was more than one item of misinformation in Alessandra's article," she started. "You see, I—"

"Not another word," Grace silenced her. "I've got enough problems as it is," she muttered, scanning the pages.

"So . . . what do you think?" Callie asked Grace after a few minutes had passed.

"I think," said Grace, handing the Xeroxes back to Callie, "that this is very bad news."

"What!" said Callie. "Why?"

"She appears to have a solid alibi on more than one occasion."

"She *appears* to," Callie conceded, "but just because she wrote an appointment down doesn't mean that she actually attended or—"

Grace was shaking her head. "There's something else that you should know. It didn't seem relevant earlier, but now . . ."

"What?" Callie demanded. "Tell me!"

Grace sighed. "There was a fifth Ivy Insider article. Well, really, it would have been the third if I had approved its publication."

"What?" Callie repeated. "When? Why didn't you—"

"Slow down, Andrews," said Grace. "And I will explain." Her voice had nearly gone hoarse from all the talking. She sipped her coffee and then said, "I was at home working late one night, a Saturday, I believe, last March, when a FlyBy submission notification popped up in my in-box. Curious, I logged on to FlyBy to review the article. One of the first things I noticed was the byline: it was signed by 'the Ivy Insider.' But as I continued reading, several things struck me as odd. It seemed unusual that anyone would be posting from the *Crimson* offices so late at night—I think it was after eleven, maybe even eleven thirty? And, even stranger, the event described was *still taking place* at the time that the article had been submitted for publication."

"What event?" asked Callie.

"That Gatsby party at the Fly," said Grace. "I knew it was that Saturday because I'd overheard you and Robinson discussing your weekend plans earlier—when you were supposed to be working." Grace grinned at Callie's sheepish expression. Clearly you could take the girl out of the managing editor's office, but you couldn't take the managing editor out of the girl.

"Saturday, did you say?" asked Callie. "That was March fifth. I remember because I saved the invitation. . . ." And then threw it away, in a rage, right before spring break. "What's weird about that? I mean, it wasn't a Pudding party, but Gatsby still seems like the sort of event that the Insider would love to cover."

Looking impatient, Grace shook her head. "How could the Insider write about the events of a party that wasn't even over yet and claim to have attended, while simultaneously typing and submitting the article from the offices of the *Crimson*?"

"Huh?"

"Do you know anyone who can be in two places at once, Andrews?"

"*Ohhh.*" Callie nodded. "I see your point."

"Let's not forget that at the time I still believed that *you* were behind the articles and figured that *you* could not manage to be at the *Crimson* while also attending the party. So I concluded that we had a copycat on our hands. Some COMPer, most likely, who saw all the attention the Insider was getting on FlyBy and wanted a taste of the action, so he or she fabricated the details of one of campus's most historically exclusive events. And, other lapses in judgment aside, I wasn't about to approve a news story that I had strong reason to suspect was a complete work of fiction."

"But now," Callie started, connecting the dots, "you think that the article might have been authentic?"

Grace furrowed her brow. "It's possible. But that would just be further evidence that Alexis is *not* involved . . . unless there's any chance that she was *not* at the party that night?"

"Oh, she was at the party," Callie said darkly.

"Well, if the article was authentic, then the Insider definitely wasn't there," said Grace, "and he or she must have made up all the details about the party."

"I don't know," said Callie, feeling hopelessly confused. "All the other installments were disturbingly true. I mean, the Insider knew things that only a real—well, *insider* would know! Maybe whoever it is found a way to leave the party early?"

"Maybe," said Grace. "Did you notice anyone leave sometime around eleven?"

"Uh," said Callie, "*I* probably left around that time, with my roommate Vanessa. I was not having . . . a lot of fun."

"Well, your roommate can't have been behind it, could she?" said Grace. "She didn't have access to the *Crimson* offices."

"Two days ago I would have agreed," said Callie. "But today . . ." She gestured down at Alessandra's article detailing the break-in. "Who knows who might have been able to get their hands on a set of keys?" Swallowing, she pictured Mimi and her large silver key ring.

"I don't know, Andrews," said Grace. "It seems highly unlikely that the Insider wasn't at least COMPing the *Crimson*, if not already a member of the staff and possibly the Pudding, too. If that *isn't* the case, then—"

"Then everyone's a suspect and it's *highly unlikely* that I'll ever figure out who the hell did it!" Callie finished. "*Gah!*" she groaned, burying her forehead in her hands. "Shit, shit, *shit!*"

Grace said nothing, allowing her a moment to freak out in peace, for which Callie felt grateful. That is until Grace murmured, "Hmm. Don't look now, but—"

"What?" said Callie, immediately turning. "Oh. Fuuuck."

Clint had just traversed the intersections of Bow and Arrow Streets, making his way toward them with what looked like two containers of frozen yogurt from BerryLine.

"Could this day get any worse?" Callie said, turning back to Grace. "Quick, hide me!"

If it'd been Vanessa sitting there, she would've thrown Callie the paper and then set about creating a diversion. Grace, however, merely raised an eyebrow as if to say, *Seriously?*

Callie grabbed the strap of her bag, eyeing the door that led inside the coffee shop, but before she could get up—it was too late.

"Hi there," said Clint, stopping and pretending to be—as he had successfully done for so long—a gentleman.

"*Grrhi,*" Callie muttered, letting the strap fall to the ground.

Grace nodded curtly.

"So," said Clint, lingering on the sidewalk near their table, "how's it going?"

"Uh . . . fine?" The cup in Clint's left hand was filled with plain frozen yogurt topped with strawberries and gummy bears. Callie had hand delivered enough frozen yogurt back in the good old days (of being blackmailed) to know who it was for.

Alexis Thorndike.

Callie craned her neck, squinting at the *Crimson* offices, but didn't see Lexi anywhere.

"So I heard the strangest rumor," Clint was saying.

"What?" Callie's head snapped back to attention.

"Apparently, according to some people, I am a 'poopy pants.'"

Grace looked like she was about to throw up. Callie blushed. "Whoever said that must be pretty immature, huh?" she blurted, trying to be blasé in naming one of the reasons he had cited for breaking up with her.

"Yeah, well." Clint broke into his signature grin, the corners around his green eyes crinkling. "That was always one of the things that I liked best about you."

Before Callie could even begin to fathom how to respond, Clint's phone beeped loudly.

"Uh-oh," he said, reading the text. "The old ball and chain's come a-calling."

"Is that any way to refer to your girlfriend?" Grace demanded.

"Who said it was my girlfriend?" Clint replied, winking rakishly at Callie. "Bye, now."

Stunned into silence, the two girls watched him walk away, headed for the *Crimson*.

"Straight people have never made any sense to me," Grace finally said.

"That's right," Callie agreed. "Men. Do not. Make. Sense! Especially on this campus. I'm starting to think they're all a bunch of douche bags, each and every o—"

"What?" asked Grace, staring at Callie, whose lips had frozen midway through forming the word *one.*

"I just remembered something," Callie whispered.

"What?" Grace repeated.

"It's—nothing. . . ." Callie stated, still looking stricken. "I was just—confused."

"If you say so," said Grace.

Callie nodded slowly. "Really, it was nothing."

But it wasn't nothing. Because, as Callie had just remembered, there was somebody else who'd left Gatsby early that evening on Saturday, the fifth of March. And that somebody's name was Gregory.

TEN

The Wigglesworth Walruses

www.facebook.com/profile/gregory.b.bolton

Welcome Back! We're glad you've decided to reactivate your profile. Please fill out this brief survey or, to see what your friends have been up to, skip straight to your Newsfeed.

OK Zeyna is listening to **Secret Lovers** by **Atlantic Starr** on **Spotify**.

Adam Nichols added a photo: "Don't Wake the Sleeping Dragon"—with **Dana Gray** at **Lamont Library**.

> **Mimi Clement:** *Enfin*, somebody else sleeping *en public* for once...Just do not let her drool on that book or *la bibliotheque* WILL charge a fine.

Bryan Jacobs:
Mmm, pizza!—with **Callie Andrews** at C**ambridge, 1 Restaurant.**

Bryan Jacobs was with **Callie Andrews** at **Brattle Street Theatre**.
Tyler Green, **Marcus Taylor** and **2 others** like this.

> **Vanessa Von Vorhees:** Fiiiinallly...Took you long enough.
> **Tyler Green** liked this.

> **Jessica Marie Stanley**: WHAT?!?!? My bestie and my ex??? J/K, love that you guys have been hangin out. Catch up sesh soon, BJakes?
> **Bryan Jacobs** liked this.

> **Vanessa Von Vorhees**: Tyler Green I thought I told you to STOP LIKING MY POSTS!!!
> **Tyler Green** liked this.

Clint Weber and 6 others were tagged in T**he Harvard Squash Team**'s album—End of Season Dinner + Award Ceremony at **The Murr Center.**

Alexis Thorndike was with **Alessandra Constantine** at **Starbucks, Harvard Square**.

Jessica Marie Stanley > **Matt Robinson**: The link for that internship I was telling you about...Don't be a stranger!

Vanessa Von Vorhees, **Mimi Clement**, **Dana Gray** and **3 others** became friends with **Jessica Marie Stanley**.

Mimi Clement via Twitter
Splish splash I's taking a bath! #Money$$$Tub #LaVieEnRose #OhHiVanessa

---

Callie Andrews is **In a Relationship**.
Vanessa Von Vorhees, **Mimi Clement**, **OK Zeyna**, and **3 others** like this.

> **Vanessa Von Vorhees**: Ahahahaha. Ha ha. HA!

> **OK Zeyna**: Jenga>Grand Theft Auto???

> **Mimi Clement**: Jenga! P.S. Personally it is my belief that you will be very happy together. Does this mean we all receive the As?

> **Jessica Marie Stanley**: When's the wedding? Cambridge or California? I'll mark my calendar. Or should we wait for *him* to confirm the status with a hyperlink first ;)

Are you SURE you want to DEACTIVATE your profile?

> **No**, take me back to my newsfeed

> **Yes**, I'll reactive it later

"Whatchya doin', roomie?"

"Hi, Vanessa," said Callie, her hands hovering over her laptop's keyboard. "Please—do come in," she added, suffusing her voice with irony since Vanessa had already sprawled across Callie's bed, propping herself up on some pillows.

"You working?" asked Vanessa.

"Not really," said Callie, swiveling in her chair.

"What are you writing, then?" asked Vanessa, peering at Callie's computer screen. "Is that—"

"It's nothing!" Callie insisted, minimizing the Microsoft Word document.

"It is!" Vanessa declared, clapping her hands. "You're finally writing that short story!"

"Trying to write," Callie corrected her. "So far I haven't gotten past the first sentence."

"Well, certainly not for lack of material," said Vanessa, spreading her arms out as if she was utterly exhausted. "I hereby officially authorize you to use my crazy life for inspiration."

"Oh?" said Callie, trying not to smile. "Shall I ghostwrite your memoir, then? And should we call it *Eat, Party, Love*? Or how about *Vanessa's Strangelove: How I Learned to Stop Worrying* and *Ask the Hipster*—"

"Agh!" Vanessa silenced her with a scream. "I thought. We agreed. To never. Speak of that. Again!"

Callie laughed. "But it would make such a great short story: *The Mystery of the Missing Suspenders.*"

Vanessa sighed dramatically. "All right," she said. "As long as you finish it and turn it in—which you have to do, as promised, because technically I did—sort of—ask him out."

"Yes," said Callie. "If only you'd listened to me and written him a poem like I'd suggested, we could be playing with your 'miniature Hipster babies' right now."

"Somebody needs to take sex ed again." Vanessa laughed. "Well," she went on, eyeing Callie's computer, "I don't want to interrupt you. . . ."

"Yes you do," said Callie. "So what is it?"

"Well," said Vanessa. "I guess I was sort of wondering . . . When dealing with the Big D, did you ever have to decide which parent you wanted to live with?"

"The Big D?" Callie echoed. "Is that what we're calling . . . divorce these days?"

Vanessa nodded. "I'm trying to put a human face on it."

"More like another anatomy part," Callie said. She would have laughed if Vanessa hadn't suddenly looked so glum. "Um . . . no, I never had to choose. I was young enough when it happened that I didn't get a say in the matter, and my parents were still on good terms—relatively speaking—so there weren't any custody battles or anything. Everyone just agreed on a fifty-fifty split, and that was that."

"Hmm." Vanessa chewed her lip, seeming to think things over. "I mean, it's not like I have to choose who to *live* with—thank god," she said finally. "My home is technically here now, at Harvard, and I'm sure I'll get my own apartment and everything after we graduate. But summer vacation is coming soon, and my dad is supposedly setting up a bedroom for me in the new place that he's getting with . . . *ugh* . . . The Secretary."

Callie grimaced sympathetically. "That's still a thing, huh?"

"Yes," said Vanessa, "they are still in lust. I had been hoping that her attraction to him might have faded what with the recent downward trends of the markets—especially with the whole—oops."

"That's okay," said Callie. "You can say it. Hedge fund scandal. See? It's not so bad. Or how about, 'that boy who used to occasionally say hi to me in the halls might be a white-collar criminal'?"

"I'm sure that Gregory had no idea even if his dad did use his trust fund to pay off bad investments," said Vanessa.

"I'm not," said Callie, remembering all the mysterious, angry phone calls that Gregory had made that semester, presumably to his father. "But I'm not sure whether I would think it was wrong to have helped his dad in that scenario either. I mean, obviously it would be wrong if he knew the money was being used to defraud investors, but if he just thought he was doing his father a favor . . ." Callie shrugged. "Then again, who knows *what* he's capable of?" she muttered, swiveling back to her computer and absentmindedly opening a browser. There was no way that, on top of everything else, he could be the Ivy Insider—right?

"I thought you swore off Facebook this week!" said Vanessa, watching Callie log in to her account.

"Yes, but—like all serious drug addictions—it's not. So easy. To quit!"

"You do realize," Vanessa said, starting to giggle, "that you're still listed as 'in a relationship,' right?"

"What?" shrieked Callie, navigating to her profile page. "Goddammit," she said, clicking the button to change her status.

"Yeah, whoops." Vanessa laughed. "Did he—what's it you call your heavily accented econ TF? Oh yeah—the Rouski actually flat out deny your request?"

"Luckily," said Callie, investigating his profile, "he does not appear particularly Facebook literate. And based on the lack of weirdness in class this week, I'd say he didn't even notice my invite to romantically hyperlink—thank god! Otherwise I could never show my face in econ section again." Callie shuddered, closing her browser. "Enough Facebook. Let's change the subject, please."

"Okay," said Vanessa. "What are *you* going to do over the summer?"

Callie sighed. "At this point," she said, "it doesn't make much sense to plan past May. I mean, if I get kicked out or asked to take a year off, I imagine I might need to . . . figure out . . . a new life . . . strategy or something."

Vanessa made a face. "You're going to catch whoever did it," she promised. "Just look at how much new stuff you've added to the board!" she exclaimed, jumping up to examine it. Her eyes roved over all the notes and index cards and recently tacked-on day planner pages. "Hey," she said suddenly, pointing at a picture on the right. "Who's this?"

"Beats me," said Callie. "I found it in Lexi's desk when I . . . um—"

"You don't think—I mean, it couldn't be—is it *Lexi*?" Vanessa cut her off, staring at the photo.

"The thought occurred to me," said Callie. "But I don't think vampires can get that tan."

Vanessa sighed, plopping back on Callie's bed. "You know who it actually sort of does look like?" she said, grinning wickedly. "A fat Alessandra!"

"Vanessa!"

"Come on," said Vanessa, "don't tell me you can't see it. A little dark hair dye and a couple months of fat camp, some collagen for the lips and some plastic for the boobs, because I hear those things shrink when you go to 'rehab' for the summer, and—"

"Stop," said Callie. "Just stop."

"Actually," Vanessa continued, "if you really want to see what a fat Alessandra might look like, Google 'Constantine family photos.'"

"God," said Callie, "you really *are* a psycho stalker."

"Nah-uh," said Vanessa, "it was homework, I swear! I had to write a paper for one of my art history classes on fashion in the nineteen seventies featuring some of the top trendsetters of the time, one of which included Alessandra's mom."

"Her mom," Callie repeated, wondering where this was going in spite of herself. "Isn't she, like, some Brazilian model or something?"

"Luciana Garcia, former *super*model," Vanessa corrected. "And yes. But anyway, I needed to find photos of some of her old signature outfits, so naturally I'm on image search, typing away. The first hundred or so hits turned up some of Alessandra's recent modelesque photos, but if you dig a little deeper, as only I and the top engineers at Google know how, you can find old family photos, and let me tell you, Alessandra's younger sister, Allison—not very creative naming by the way, if you ask me—is a porker. I mean, they don't *really* look alike, but it still helps facilitate a very . . . satisfying mental image."

"I didn't know Alessandra has a sister," Callie remarked.

Vanessa nodded. "There are a lot of things that you don't know and that you would never know without me here to guide you. Gee, maybe I should start a private detective agency so I can spy on people having secret love affairs or—"

"*Qu'est ce-que vous dires sur des amours secrétes*?" Mimi poked her head around the door to Callie's bedroom.

"I have no idea," said Callie. "She lost me a few minutes ago."

"I'm just trying to give Callie material," Vanessa said indignantly, "for the short story that she's writing about my life!"

"How boring," said Mimi.

"Hey!" Vanessa snapped.

"I mean . . . I am bored." Mimi grinned, flinging herself on the bed next to Vanessa. "And oh—so—sleeeepy," she said between yawns.

"Maybe if you hadn't been staying out all night so much recently," Dana called from the common room.

"I cannot understand you if you are yelling at me," Mimi called back, tucking her hands behind her head and staring at the ceiling.

Dana appeared in the doorway, hands on her hips.

"You know the D-meister makes a good point," Vanessa said slowly.

"Yeah," said Callie, "where *have* you been before you come sneaking back in the mornings?"

Mimi looked at Dana. *"Je suis désolé, mais je vais avoir de la difficulté à vous comprendre. Pourriez-vous répéter, lentement?"*

"Really?" asked Vanessa. "You're going to play the I-don't-understand-your-English card?"

"*I* think she has a secret boyfriend," said Callie. "Why else wouldn't we have seen any strange men in the common room recently?"

"Obviously," Vanessa interjected, "it has to do with the Lampoon. I hear their parties are, like, the most insane events at this entire school, only no one can get in other than members until their senior year. Hey!" she said suddenly, turning to Callie. "You're funny. Why don't you try COMP—"

"No!" said Callie. "Don't! I'm not COMPing any more editorial boards ever again! And now if I could just have a moment to try to work on this short story. . . ."

Instead of moving, Mimi and Vanessa seemed to settle in, rearranging the pillows on Callie's bed. From where she still stood in the doorway, Dana cleared her throat.

Callie sighed. "Was there something that you wanted, Dana?"

"Actually, yes," she replied, stepping into the room. "I seem to have found myself with some free time on my hands, and I was wondering if I might borrow a book. A, er, fiction book."

"Of course," said Callie, making a *help yourself* gesture at the shelves.

"Is this one any good?" Dana asked, picking up the copy of *Persuasion* off the nightstand and squishing next to Vanessa on Callie's bed.

"Uh—yes," said Callie. "It's the last book that Austen ever wrote, and it just so happens to be my favorite."

"What's it about?" asked Dana, flipping to the page marked by Callie's bookmark.

"Well," said Callie, "it's been criticized by some as a 'simple' love story or Cinderella tale, but it's really so much more complicated than that. Austen was ill when she wrote it—in fact, it was first published after she died—and so some say it was written hastily, but I think that just makes it more honest and raw, having never been carefully revised."

"But what is it *about*?" said Vanessa as Dana skimmed the pages.

"A girl—woman, I should say—named Anne who was very much in love with a naval captain, Wentworth, but was forced by her family to break off the engagement because he was too poor. But eight years later he returns a rich man, having made something of himself in the navy. Only now, to Anne's bitter disappointment, he seems far more smitten with a pair of young ladies called 'the Musgrove girls.' So then she starts seeing this other guy, Mr. Elliot, who is her cousin—"

"Her cousin?" Vanessa repeated. "Ew!"

"*Ce sont les* times," said Mimi with a shrug. "*Continuer.*"

"So Mr. Elliot is extremely good looking and charming and seems to really like Anne, who's on the verge of marrying him when she learns about his hidden past. Of course, she decides *not* to marry him, only Wentworth gets the false impression that she is still with Elliot, just as Anne had the false impression that he would marry one of the Musgrove girls. But then Wentworth decides to write Anne this secret love letter anyway, pouring out his heart and saying things like 'you pierce my soul' and 'I am half hope, half agony.' Here," said Callie reaching for the book, "if you want I can find that passage and read it to you. It's the best part."

"*No*," said Vanessa. "I think we got it."

"Yes, thank you for the thorough explanation," said Dana, setting the book back on the nightstand. "I can see you really love it from all the margin notes everywhere, but it doesn't sound like it's for me. I think I'll go with this one instead," she added, standing and pulling a copy of Dostoyevsky's *Crime and Punishment* off the shelf.

Callie cringed at the mention of the margin notes—which Gregory had scrawled on nearly every page. Rereading the book, whenever she could bear to pick it up, almost made it feel like they were together again, their heads bent close as they switched off turning the pages in the New Haven hospital. *Almost.*

"Tell me another fairy story, *Caliente*," said Mimi, stretching her arms toward the ceiling. "There are still two hours to go before dinner. . . ."

"Wait," said Callie, "what time is it?"

"A quarter to four," said Vanessa, checking her phone.

"Uh-oh, time to go," said Callie, flinging open her closet.

"*Où?*" asked Mimi.

"IM soccer," said Callie, grinning as she pulled on a bright blue T-shirt over her sports bra and stepped into some shorts. Bending, she reached for her trusty shin guards, socks, and her favorite pair of cleats.

"Since when do you play IM soccer?" Vanessa demanded.

"Twice a week since the beginning of this month," Callie answered, lacing up her shoes.

"*Mais oui*, have you not noticed?" Mimi asked Vanessa.

"I thought those were special treadmill shoes!" said Vanessa.

"Wow," said Callie, "you really have never been inside a gym."

"Harsh!" said Vanessa. "But true."

"I didn't realize you were playing again either," said Dana. "Why haven't you invited us to any of your games?"

"Um . . . I can't imagine it'd be very interesting to watch: we just play the other freshman dorms and upperclassman houses, which each have their own teams—but we never practice or anything. It's nothing like . . ." High school, she silently completed the thought. No point in saying it out loud, since none of them could appreciate what it had been like to play at that level, anyway. "Did you guys, uh . . . want to come?"

"Are there boys on the team?" Vanessa asked.

"Yes." Callie smiled. "The teams are coed. In fact, OK is our team captain."

"Now that is something I am needing to see," said Mimi, her eyes gleaming.

"He's good—you'd be surprised," Callie defended him. "Actually, our whole team is surprisingly . . . adequate. If we win this game, we get to go to the play-offs."

"Impressive," said Dana.

"It's really not—" Callie started.

"I'll get my coat," Dana finished.

"Fetch mine, too, please, thank you!" Mimi called after her. "Vanessa?"

"Attend . . . a sporting event?" Vanessa wrinkled her nose. "I mean, it's not like I have anything better to do, but . . ."

"There only need to be three girls out of eleven total on the field per team at any given time," said Callie.

"Sold!" said Vanessa. "Let's do this!"

As they all made their way out the door, she added, "What do we cheer when we're in the stands? Does your team have a name?"

"Yes," said Callie, pointing at her T-shirt and then spinning around so Vanessa could read the words on the back.

"The Wigglesworth . . . Walruses?"

"Uh-huh," said Callie. "The Wigglesworth Walruses."

Nothing could compare to the way that cleats felt when they first bit into grass. Callie breathed deeply, inhaling the scents of dirt and spring. A perfect calm settled over her as she jogged out onto the field.

That tranquility lasted all of thirty seconds.

"What are *you*—guys doing here?" she asked, stopping en route on the opposing team's side of the field.

"We play IM soccer, and basketball, every spring," Clint answered. "Coach says it's the best form of cross-training to stay fit during the off-season."

"I do it to work off the old potbelly that comes with one too many beers," said Tyler.

"And *I* play," Bryan finished, "because the Adams House Honey Badgers need someone who's actually talented to be on the team."

Grinning, Clint punched him on the arm.

"What?" asked Bryan. "I can't help it if water polo is a *real* sport."

Clint raised his eyebrows. "As opposed to squash, which is . . . ?"

"A type of vegetable?" offered Tyler.

"Blondie!" Callie heard OK calling to her from the other side of the field, where the rest of her team stood warming up.

"Gotta go," said Callie, ready to sprint once she realized that, in addition to Mimi, Dana, and Vanessa, Alexis Thorndike probably sat behind her in the stands.

"Can't wait to see your moves out there, Andrews!" Clint called after her retreating back.

"Sorry," Callie muttered when she reached her team.

"All right, Blondie?" asked OK.

"Never better," she said, bouncing on the balls of her feet. Grabbing her right ankle with her right hand, she stretched her quad the way her physical therapist back in California had recommended.

"Good," said OK, lowering his voice, "because I was worried for a second there that we were going to have to play one of the real girls."

"Am I not a real girl?" asked Callie, following his eyes over to where some of their second-string alternates stood on the sidelines, one of whom was reading a magazine.

"No," said OK, grinning. "What you are is the best damn forward this football team's ever seen! Now huddle up, people!" he cried, summoning the rest of the players into a circle. "Men," he began, "and obligatory women—"

"Hey!" said one of the girls, Elizabeth, who lived on the third floor of entryway C.

"And mandatory lady guests," he corrected himself. "Now, I'd be lying if I said this afternoon's game was going to be easy. The Honey Badgers may look like a pack of sweater-vest-wearing sissies, but I've been watching their game tapes—"

"What tapes?" asked Bobby, who played forward alongside Callie.

OK rolled his eyes. "It's a metaphor." He cleared his throat. "As I was saying, in reality, much like their namesake, they are some of the most vicious, maniacal, bloodsucking creatures ever to crawl the face of this field."

Callie laughed.

"No laughing in football!" OK barked at her. "This is the last match standing between us and the play-offs, us and infinite glory, us and gift certificates to Ben and Jerry's. So what is it, men, and obligatory—"

"Just 'women' will be fine," said Elizabeth, looking weary of the huddle.

"Will you fight?"

"Uh . . . go, Walruses?" their center midfielder cheered halfheartedly.

"That's right," said OK, "because, though they may take our lives, they may never—take—our FREEDOM!"

"Let's just keep it mellow and play, man," said Bobby.

"Sounds good," OK said with a shrug.

The referee's whistle tweeted.

"Heads or tails," he asked Callie who, along with Bobby, would be facing off against Bryan and a tall girl from Adams House.

"Tails," she said.

"Heads," the ref declared after flipping the coin.

"Tough luck, Andrews," said Bryan, giving her a smile. "We'll try not to go too hard on you."

"This is one area where I *don't* need your charity, Jacobs!" Callie called, retreating out of the center circle. The ref placed the ball in front of Bryan on the halfway line and then backed away, blowing his whistle twice.

Game on, thought Callie.

Suddenly, as it had always been when she was on the field, everything around her seemed to be happening half a second slower. Bryan took the kick, passing to the female forward. Before Callie's brain could respond, her legs had carried her all the way there. She stole the ball from the other girl with ease, dribbling past Tyler, who played left midfielder. Sprinting, she took the ball up the side, tangling only briefly with one of the defenders before she saw an opportunity to center it. She placed the ball directly in front of Bobby, who, after two touches, flew past the final defender to take a shot on goal—

The ball hit Clint's hands with an audible smack as he caught it.

He grinned at Callie as he ambled forward, almost lazily, and then drop-kicked the ball clear across to the other side of the field.

Callie cursed under her breath. Their defense may have had a few holes—or were maybe just off to a slow start—but Clint appeared to be an irritatingly competent goalie.

Callie hustled to the halfway line, waiting for the Walruses to take back possession.

A few minutes later their defenders had cleared it, with Elizabeth chipping the ball to OK in a manner that might just inspire him to stop referring to her as an "obligatory" member of the team. He trapped the ball with his chest and then took it back onto the Honey Badgers' half. Callie crisscrossed behind him in an overlap as the other forward followed up from the side.

"Man on!" Callie yelled as Tyler started gaining on OK.

Looking up, OK kicked the ball to Callie. Attacking once again from the left, she waited until OK was in position and then passed it back. He fired it toward the goal.

The ball ricocheted off the goalpost (which, as far as Callie was concerned, was the most frustrating sound in the world). Callie raced for it, but Clint beat her there, scooping up the ball and then throwing it to one of his defenders.

After twenty more minutes of solid, even play back and forth, Callie was coated with a fine layer of sweat. This, she thought, running for the ball, is better than anything. Better than getting an A on a test, better than any of her favorite foods, and way better than hooking up with a certain goalkeeper—

"Dammit," Callie muttered under her breath. Clint had just blocked her first shot on goal. Granted she had kicked it as hard as she could directly at his head, making the ball much easier to catch than if she'd aimed anywhere else, but still.

Only a few minutes left before the halftime whistle would sound. The score remained zero-zero.

Callie fell back as the ball soared onto their side of the field. Performing some fancy footwork, Bryan outmaneuvered Elizabeth. Callie stared in horror, watching the ball soar into the upper left-hand corner of the—

"GOAL!" Tyler screamed, enveloping Bryan in a hug along with some of their other teammates.

OK looked just as awful as she felt, screaming at their team to get back in position. It paid off—in a matter of seconds, Callie and Bobby were back inside the Honey Badgers' penalty box. Dribbling toward the center, Callie found herself facing two oncoming defenders. At the last second she back passed to OK, who stood just outside the box.

"YES!" she screamed a moment later, running over to OK and jumping into his arms.

Clint stooped to retrieve the ball from inside the goal net.

The halftime whistle cut through the air.

"Wow," said Vanessa breathlessly after running over to the sidelines from the bleachers. "You guys are good."

"Really good," Dana agreed, handing Callie a bottle of water.

"Thanks," said Callie, drinking some and squirting a little over her forehead.

"You are *ohh-kaay*," Mimi informed OK, laughing. "But Callie is better."

"Ha!" said Callie, redoing her ponytail. "I guess all of that running I've been doing hasn't hurt."

"I'll say," remarked Vanessa. "You know, I was nervous at first because a lot of those boys out there . . ." She watched one of said boys pour water all over his head and then shake out his hair like a shaggy dog. "Um . . . oh yeah! A lot of those boys are—bigger than you—but you just seemed so much *faster*. You really were like one of the guys!"

OK's head shot forward. "See!" he said to Callie. *"See?"*

Mimi pouted, looking at Callie. "I only wish," she started, speaking softly, "that you had hit you-are-knowing-who in the face!"

"You mean scored," said OK. "You wish she had scored."

"*Non*," said Mimi. "I mean what I have said. I want to see a face-SMACK!"

"I'll keep that in mind," said Callie, laughing.

"Um," Dana piped up. "I wouldn't do anything . . . *untoward* if I were you. Some sports reporters from the *Harvard Crimson* are sitting directly behind us, and they brought cameras."

"For IM soccer?" asked Callie. "Really? Are our varsity teams that bad this year?"

Dana shrugged.

"I told you, Blondie," said OK. "I told you that this was an important match!"

"Yeah," echoed Vanessa, "don't you want to beat Cli—the Honey Badgers?"

"Oh, hell yeah," said Callie, taking one final sip of water.

The players started to take the field.

"Let's go, Walruses!" Mimi and Dana cheered.

"And see if you can't knock Tyler down for me," Vanessa whispered in Callie's ear.

Callie giggled. "Thanks for being here, you guys!" she called over her shoulder, running back to the center circle.

Twenty-five minutes into the second half, the score was still tied, one to one, and Callie started to hit a wall. Her knee felt fine, but her quads ached as she dribbled the ball time and time again up the side, only to find herself blocked and forced to center it to Bobby or one of the attacking midfielders, who could not seem to get past Clint.

Groaning in frustration, Callie watched the other team's offense regain possession. From way outside the box Bryan took a speculative shot that soared about ten feet wide of the goal. The Wigglesworth goalie drop-kicked the ball, and it flew through the air toward Callie, who jumped—but Bryan, far taller, beat her there, trapping the ball with his head.

"Oh, no you don't," Callie mumbled, looping around him to face off from the front. Bryan tried to fake left, but Callie saw it coming, throwing all her weight toward the ball as it went right.

Suddenly she was flat on her back, pain shooting through her shin. Bryan must have accidentally kicked her instead of the ball. She tried to stand, but the pain was too intense. The whistle shrieked as she rolled onto her side.

"Callie!" Bryan's face hovered above her, full of concern. "Callie, are you okay? I'm so sorry! I was trying for the ball and . . ."

Callie saw the ref hold up a yellow card over Bryan's shoulder. "I know—I'll be fine," she told him through gritted teeth.

"Are you sure?" he asked.

"Yes," she said. "Just give me another minute here."

Gripping her hand, Bryan continued to kneel next to her, waiting for her to recover. Clamping her teeth together, Callie placed her free hand on his arm and used it to pull herself to her feet.

Her teammates cheered, and Bryan wrapped her in a giant hug, apologizing profusely.

"Yeah, yeah," said Callie, breaking away. "We'll see if you still feel like hugging me when you lose."

"Seems like her mouth is still working fine," Tyler called as Callie limped aside to let somebody else handle the free kick. Clint, who had come nearly twenty yards out of the penalty box, ran back toward goal.

Wincing, Callie started a slow jog up the field. Her shin still hurt, but she felt fairly certain the injury wouldn't result in anything more major than a nasty bruise. Just a few more minutes, she prompted herself, trailing behind the midfielders as they passed the ball up the field. So move it!

She forced herself onward, her shin screaming in protest all the while. Bobby seemed on the verge of shooting, but at the last second one of the other team's defenders kicked the ball out behind the goal line.

The flag went up: corner kick.

OK volunteered, sprinting over to take it. With less than a minute to go, the final whistle could sound at any second.

Callie positioned herself in front of the goal along with the rest of the offense. Clint fidgeted near the front post, his eyes glued to OK. A tall, male defender planted himself directly in front of Callie. She watched OK wind his foot back, curling the ball in a perfect arc toward goal.

The defender in front of Callie lunged, and the ball collided with his shoulder. Callie saw it bounce up into the air and she jumped, thwacking her forehead against the slick black-and-white leather with all her might.

The ball was in the goal before her feet hit the ground.

Tweet, tweet, tweet!

"Blondie!" OK bellowed, lifting her onto his shoulders. "You did it!"

Callie beamed. For the first time in months her head felt completely clear, no room for anything save elation.

Vanessa, Mimi, and Dana streamed out onto the field with the rest of the spectators.

"Are you okay?" Dana screamed, motioning at OK to lower Callie immediately.

"A little ice and I'll be fine," said Callie, testing her leg out on the grass.

"I said to knock down *Tyler*, not fall down and hurt yourself, you crazy klutz," Vanessa lectured, throwing her arms around Callie.

"Seriously, I'm fine," said Callie. "Really," she added to Bryan, who had come over to double-check. *"Fine."*

"Good game, Andrews," Tyler called. "I can't believe we have to go back to the house and tell them we were beaten by a freshman g—"

"She's not a girl!" OK insisted angrily. "Don't call her that!"

"Nice kicking," Mimi said to OK.

"Thank you," he said civilly. "Nice . . . attendance."

"No shame in getting our asses kicked by a former high school superstar, Tyler." Clint had come over from the goal, extending his hand toward Callie.

Clasping Clint's hand, she shook it.

"You won," he said.

Callie smiled, letting go. "I know."

ELEVEN

Garden Party

Dear Freshies,

Well, it's finally here: my favorite time of year. Time to dust off those wedges, pull out the pastels from the back of your closet, pick up a new pair of designer shades, and kick back while you wait for the invitations to start slipping in under your suite's front door. That's right, folks: it's Garden Party season!

What is a garden party, you ask? Oh, children, children, children. A garden party is a late-afternoon, springtime soiree featuring casual, colorful dresses; cocktails; dancing; and live music, and a little light snacking and conversation, too. Still uncertain what is entailed at this some-would-say-antiquated-but-I-say-delightful event put on by your favorite social clubs? Then please refer to Emily Post's *Etiquette*, Chapter XIII, "Teas and Other Afternoon Parties," (a book in this advice columnist's opinion that will *never* go out of style), or my own set of slightly more modernized rules for one of the few types of gatherings on campus that hearken back to the olden days when decorum still mattered.

ALEXIS THORNDIKE'S GUIDE TO GARDEN PARTY ETIQUETTE

Proper Attire: Linens, light colors, bright colors, or even appropriate patterns. There's no such thing as dim lighting outside in spring, so ladies, please: don't be caught dead in that bottom-booty-baring outfit you'd wear to a 10 P.M. party at the Spee. Instead, dress as if you were meeting your future mother-in-law for afternoon tea shortly after she's asked you to start referring to her by her first name, Coco. Ladies, also note that shoes may be removed in the event that you are invited to play Ping-Pong or cornhole or even a pickup game of croquet. Large sunglasses and even larger hats: encouraged. Sandals: mandatory—grass and mud will prove fatal to your favorite stilettos.

Proper Conversational Topics: The weather—it's so gorgeous. Classes—they're almost over. Your dress—it's so fabulous. Your summer plans?—sound incredible. A stroll?—I'd love to.
Remember to KIL (that's "Keep It Light") lest you *kill* the conversation.

Proper Food and Drink: Fortunately, if your hosts are worth their weight in handwritten paper invitations, you needn't fret: all of the food offerings will be bite-sized, from tiny triangle cucumber sandwiches to mini macarons and tea cakes. Punch will be served in bowls and glasses (I personally find that real glassware always encourages better behavior), and please do not allow anyone to see you sipping anything stronger than white wine, champagne, or beer. Day drinking under the hot afternoon sun is nothing short of dangerous, and often—when not performed by seasoned experts—leads to egregious violations of the above, and below.

Proper Dance Moves: No grinding. No crumping. No moonwalking. No breaking, locking, or popping, and absolutely *no* preludes to the so-called "horizontal mambo."

Proper Plus Ones: Actually, it's perfectly acceptable to fly solo at these low-key events. The goals are mixing and mingling, after all, and you might do well to bring a girlfriend since oftentimes a date will only drag you down.

—Alexis Thorndike, Advice Columnist @ *FM* Magazine

"Can I interest you ladies in a cucumber sandwich?" a waiter asked, extending a silver platter.

"Thanks," said Callie, taking seven and piling them one after another on a cocktail napkin. "What?" she added at the expressions on Mimi and Vanessa's faces. "I'm hungry!"

Vanessa shook her head. "Food is supposed to be for show, not for eating!"

Callie shoved one of the tiny triangle sandwiches into her mouth. "That—is the most—ridiculous thing—I have ever heard," she said between bites. "According to who?"

Vanessa tilted her head toward the gazebo in the back of the Hasty Pudding's garden, next to the benches underneath the willow tree. "Who do you think?"

Callie turned.

Alexis Thorndike leaned against the gazebo's white wooden railing, presiding over the party as per usual.

"Whatever," said Callie, going to work on her last sandwich. "I'm so over all of this."

"Say it ain't so, Blondie," cried OK, coming over to where the girls stood in a group near the flower beds lining the brick pathway winding up to the rear entrance of 2 Garden Street. He wore a white linen suit over a pink shirt, pulling it off without a second thought. Callie eyed him jealously, feeling frillier than she ever had in her entire life, forced by Vanessa to wear a poufy pink dress covered in green bows that made her feel like an upside-down cupcake.

"Yes, cheer up," Vanessa insisted. "We couldn't have asked for better weather, and finals are still so f—"

Vanessa cringed, remembering that Callie might not make it that far. It was the second Sunday in May, and her hearing was only a week away.

"Where'd Matt go?" Callie asked OK grumpily.

"Last I saw him, he'd been unlawfully detained by a young lady over by the dance floor," said OK. "Ah yes, see? Right over there." Matt stood near the shiny wooden planks that had been laid out over the grass next to the gazebo, ready for the live band's arrival at six. Brittney, a sophomore in the club, appeared utterly fascinated by him. Callie watched her pluck his glasses off his face and put them on her own, striking a *so how do I look?* pose.

Callie smiled in spite of herself. Although there was zero chance of a love connection—even glasses couldn't change Brittney's belief that Africa was a country—Matt's confidence certainly seemed to have increased exponentially since Jessica's visit.

"This punch is delicious!" Dana declared, returning from one of the tables set up along the far wall of the garden with her second or third cup. "What's in it?"

"Uh . . ." Mimi looked at Vanessa. "Punch juice?"

"Delicious," Dana repeated, smacking her lips together. "You know, I must admit that I am pleasantly surprised. When I accepted your invitation, I expected the worst; but I was wrong to have prejudged all of your parties as hedonistic orgies. Tell me, are they always like this?"

"Oh yes," said Mimi, nodding vigorously. "And they only become more . . . *civilisé* with every extra glass of punch!"

"Wonderful," said Dana.

"It is, Dana," said Vanessa, snagging two glasses of prosecco from a passing waitress. "It really is."

"Fine," said Callie, accepting the champagne flute from Vanessa. "Might as well try to enjoy it."

"That's the spirit," said Vanessa.

"Uh-oh," said OK. Callie followed his gaze to Matt and Brittney, who seemed to be refusing to return his glasses. "Excuse me, ladies," he continued. "WonderPrince has some rescuing to do."

"What's that over there?" asked Dana, pointing at two large pieces of plywood arranged opposite each other on the lawn. Each had a small circular hole cut into one end and was elevated off the ground at a thirty-degree angle.

"Those are cornhole platforms," Vanessa explained.

"What is this 'cornhole'?" asked Mimi, wrinkling her nose.

"It's a beanbag tossing game," said Vanessa. "It's fun. Each team of two stands behind their plywood and tries to toss a bean—or corn—bag through the hole in the other team's platform. You get three points if you make it, and one if you land the bag on the platform."

Mimi started at the platforms. "And how does one win this baghole?"

"*Corn*hole," said Vanessa. "Whichever team reaches twenty-one first wins."

"Let us play!" declared Mimi. Squinting, she sized them up. "I choose Dana," she announced finally.

"Thank you," said Dana, looking pleased.

"What!" shrieked Vanessa. "I'm the only one here who actually knows how to play!" she called, following Dana and Mimi over to the platforms.

"Thanks a lot," said Callie, stooping to retrieve a beanbag.

"No offense," said Vanessa. "I know you're good with your feet on a soccer field and all, but I've seen your attempts at balance or aim in other scenarios and well . . ."

"Come on," said Callie, tossing the beanbag up and catching it. "This is Mimi and Dana we're talking about here. We can totally take—oops."

Vanessa bent over to retrieve the bag that Callie had just dropped.

"Don't say it!" Callie warned her.

"Wasn't going to," said Vanessa.

"Qu'est-ce qui prend tant de temps?" Mimi cried impatiently from behind the other platform. "Are you afraid?"

"Yeah," Dana yelled, looking unsure how to trash-talk. "Are you experiencing anxiety over the possibility of losing?"

Callie laughed.

"After you guys!" Vanessa shouted.

Three seconds later Mimi's beanbag soared straight through the hole in their platform.

"Beginner's luck!" Vanessa called, watching her own beanbag fall about a foot short.

Mimi and Dana celebrated with a double high five. Then, with an underhand toss, Dana lobbed her beanbag through the air.

It landed on Vanessa and Callie's platform, an inch away from the hole.

"What's that? Four-nothing?" called Matt, approaching with OK. Brittney trailed at their heels.

"Uh . . . wanna come over here and give Little Miss Hopeless some pointers, Matt?" asked Vanessa, handing Callie a beanbag.

"Sure," he said, looking grateful. "Now, Callie, just swing your arm back and then step forward as you throw—*oh*."

Her beanbag had landed on the grass, midway between the platforms.

"Next time, you might want to try keeping your eyes open," Matt suggested. "But not to worry, you guys can still catch—"

Mimi's beanbag plopped, for the second time, straight through the hole.

"Crap," said Vanessa.

OK had joined Mimi and Dana across the way, assuming the role—from the sound of it—of their coach.

Vanessa's next toss landed on the platform, but Dana's beanbag quickly flew back, striking the top of their platform and then sliding down through the hole.

"Ten to one!" OK announced loudly.

Keeping her eyes open wide, Callie threw her beanbag. This time, it fell about two-thirds of the way across.

"That was . . . better," Matt encouraged, clapping a hand on her back.

Vanessa groaned. Callie giggled, picking up her champagne flute and taking a sip. "That was terrible!"

"I'm glad you seem to finally be enjoying yourself," Vanessa muttered. "Oh, come on!" she yelled in disbelief as Mimi's beanbag soared through the hole in their platform for the third time in a row. "That's, like, statistically impossible!"

"I am *statistiquement impossible*!" Mimi screamed back when OK was done whooping and twirling her around.

Several other garden partygoers had gathered around to watch, including Tyler, who arrived just in time to make Vanessa miss her next shot.

"We call winner!" Tyler announced. Callie turned, but Tyler's usual partner in crime, Clint, appeared to be on the other side of the party near the gazebo, socializing with his girlfriend and her standard gaggle of junior girls. Instead, Tyler stood with a group of seniors.

"I'm afraid it doesn't look like they'll have to wait long," Matt muttered as Dana scored another point.

"Yeah!" OK yelled, hugging Dana. "That's my Dana! Boo-yah!"

"Enough!" cried Dana, though she looked moderately excited.

"Hey!" Matt said a moment later. "You actually hit the bottom of the platform this time!"

"Woo!" Callie cried, raising her hands over her head.

Vanessa finally cracked a smile, even as Mimi sank her fourth shot through the hole.

"Seventeen!" OK screamed, beside himself.

"I must admit," Tyler called, coming over to Callie, "after that soccer game, I am enjoying seeing you lose at something."

"Enjoy this," Vanessa muttered, sinking her first shot.

"Nice," said Tyler. "You've got a good arm on you. Though I should know, given the way you used to abuse me."

"Aw," said Vanessa as Dana readied for her next throw. "You miss me, don't you?"

"Not at all," said Tyler, taking a sip of his beer.

"Well, good," said Vanessa. Dana's beanbag teetered on the edge of the hole and then fell through. "Because I'm seeing someone else now."

"Oh yeah?" asked Tyler. "And who might that be?"

"Twenty points!" OK cried, running around in circles and trying to force Dana to do a victory dance. "Only one more and we win!"

"*We*?" Mimi asked. "When you have done nothing except to make me a headache?"

"I'd rather not say," Vanessa said to Tyler.

"More like he doesn't exist." Tyler smirked.

"Oh, he more than exists," said Vanessa. "In fact, he's here now—right, Callie?"

"Uh—yeah, totally," said Callie, trying to aim the beanbag.

"Is that so?" asked Tyler. "Where? Because I'd love to be introduced. After all, I'm technically the host."

"Uh . . ." Vanessa faltered. "Um . . .well . . ."

"It is I," Matt suddenly announced, throwing a stiff arm around Vanessa, "who is . . . her boyfriend."

Callie dropped the beanbag and it fell—through the hole . . .

in her own platform. "Score," she whispered awkwardly, picking it up.

"Tyler," said Tyler, holding his hand out to Matt.

"Matt—aka Matt of Vanessa and . . . Matt."

"That's right," said Vanessa, looking torn between relief and revulsion. "We have a nickname."

"Blondie, throw the beanbag!" yelled OK.

"Oh," said Callie, "right." Deciding to try her original strategy, she closed her eyes and threw. Opening one, she saw the beanbag jutting off the closest end of Dana and Mimi's platform.

"You did it!" Vanessa shrieked, breaking away from Matt.

"We won!" Callie screamed. "We won!"

"No you did not!" shouted Mimi from across the way as her beanbag soared through the air. It landed on the platform, missing the hole by a hair. "We did! C'est vingt-un, bitches!"

All of a sudden OK grabbed Mimi and kissed her on the lips.

"*Quoi*—what are you doing?" she cried, throwing him off with surprising strength for someone approximately one half of his weight.

OK froze for a split second, appearing panicked, before he seized Dana and kissed her on the lips, too. "Celebrating!" he cried. "Because I love—winning!"

Dana wiped her mouth with the back of her hand, looking livid. "Adam *will* hear about this," she threatened. "That is above and beyond what I ever—never . . ." Shaking her head, she stalked off.

"*Attends*!" Mimi cried after her. "Who will be my partner *pour le deuxième* match?"

“I will!” Vanessa volunteered, racing over to Mimi as fast as her wedges could carry her.

“Uh, hey, nice to meet you, man,” Tyler said to Matt, shaking his hand again before picking up the beanbags. “And good luck.”

“Er—thanks,” said Matt. “You know, she’s a real firecracker, I’ve always said—”

“Come on,” Callie interrupted, pulling Matt away. “We’ll be watching from over there,” she added to Tyler.

A few of the bystanders had set up some white folding chairs on the sidelines. “Here, take my seat,” one of the seniors, a guy who seemed vaguely familiar, said to Callie, standing.

“Oh no,” she said. “I couldn’t.”

“I insist,” he said, flashing her a smile that showed all of his teeth.

“But my friend—”

“I think I’ll go catch up with Dana, actually,” said Matt. “If you don’t mind, that is?”

“No,” said Callie, “of course not. See ya later,” she added, sinking into the seat at which the senior still expectantly gestured.

“Have we met before?” he asked, smiling again as the second game began.

“I do feel like maybe I’ve seen you somewhere. . . .” She tried to place his face, distracted by the sight of Lexi and Clint. It looked like they were fighting—again—especially when Lexi stormed off, headed indoors. Breaking away from a nearby group, Alessandra quickly followed her—to offer consolation, most likely, since these days it seemed those two were thick as thieves. "I'm Callie, by the way."

"Nice to meet you Callie, I'm J—"

"Jeffrey?" she interrupted, vaguely remembering seeing a senior of similar height and build slipping out of Vanessa's bedroom during the first week of school.

"Jeremy," he corrected her. "But don't worry: I get that all the time. My cousin Jeffrey goes here, too, and we're practically twins."

"*Oh*," said Callie, watching a beanbag fly through the air. "I think that must be it."

"So you've . . . met Jeffrey, huh?"

"Ye—*no*!" She laughed, realizing his implication. "I mean, yes, but only through my roommate."

"Good," he said.

They watched for a few more minutes in silence, during which neither team scored any points. Callie yawned.

"Bored?" asked Jeremy.

"No, just tired," said Callie. "You know: reading period, finals, internships—life?"

"Sounds like someone's a little more stressed than she should be on a gorgeous day like today."

Callie smiled ruefully. "For some reason I never seem to find these types of parties relaxing."

"Well, then, how about we get out of here, I buy you a real drink, and we can go relax somewhere else—like back at my place?"

Callie burst out laughing.

"It was worth a try," he said, laughing, too.

"God, does that ever actually work?" she asked.

"You'd be surprised," he answered. "And now, if you would answer a few simple questions for a feedback survey," he went on, miming holding a clipboard. "You: a) have a boyfriend, b) don't find me attractive—"

"I have a boyfriend," Callie said quickly, opting for the Vanessa way out. Option B would have also been a lie anyway, since he *was* attractive—in a tan, blond, distinctly not-Gregory kind of a way. Callie sighed. Would there ever come a time when she might stop inadvertently comparing every guy that flirted with her to *him*? Stop hallucinating his face in a crowd? Stop clinging to that final shred of hope and accept the inevitable: that Gregory would most likely never, ever, be—

"Oh yeah," Jeremy was saying, examining her face. "You're that IM soccer chick who's dating Bryan what's-his-face, you know, from the Fly?"

"Uh . . . what?" asked Callie.

"Yeah," he said, "I just saw a picture of you two on the front page of the sports section last week about to go at it on the field!"

"*What?*"

"You didn't see it?" he asked. "Aw, you need to get your hands on a paper because it's actually totally cute—you're on the ground and he's holding you and there's some clever caption like 'Lovers Face Off for Playoffs' or something—"

"Uh—yes," said Callie, just to shut him up. "That's us." It appeared that Grace had not been exaggerating two days ago when she'd announced that the editorial board was now "officially in shambles." Apparently Lexi's regime no longer required basic fact-checking. One simple phone call to Callie and she could have confirmed that she was *not* dating Bryan, as Jeremy—and who knows who else—had assumed. . . .

Callie gasped.

"Hey—where are you going?"

Callie ignored him, racing over to where Vanessa stood, readying to toss her beanbag. "Vanessa!"

"What?" asked Vanessa, irritated at the interruption.

"That article—the one about the date auction—did it imply that Bryan and I were, like, romantically involved?"

"What article . . . Oh." Vanessa made a face. "*That* article. Yeah. I think it did. But it was also very clear that almost everything in the article was totally made up. Pure—gossipy—trash. I mean, I think it even misattributed and misquoted some of the things that *I* said about Gregory. . . . What? Why do you look like you have to pee and there's no bathroom?"

"Just—give me your iPhone for a second, would you?"

"Don't you have a new phone now?"

"Yeah, but it doesn't have the internet!"

"Okay, god, calm down," said Vanessa, handing over her phone. "That applies to you guys, too!" she yelled at Tyler and his teammate, who had been signaling at her to throw the beanbag, and Mimi, who was tapping her foot impatiently.

It didn't take long for Callie to find the article she was looking for. There it was: the caption about her and Bryan being "lovers," just like Jeremy had said, underneath a photograph that actually kind of made it look like they were. "Oh my god," said Callie, her fingers flying across the screen as she searched for the Society Pages article.

"I know, right?" asked Vanessa. "We are totally about to win."

"Oh . . . my . . . god . . ." Callie repeated, reading the words on the screen.

"*Quoi*?" asked Mimi. *"Ce qui s'est passé?"*

"I gotta go," said Callie, thrusting the phone at Vanessa.

"Where—hey—why?"

"I'll explain later!" Callie called, racing toward the back gate. Bursting out onto Garden Street, she ran without stopping until she reached Wigglesworth.

"What are you doing home so soon?" asked Dana, looking up when the door to the common room flew open.

Callie leaned against the wall, struggling to regain her breath. "Had to—just realized—need to talk—to Gregory."

"Gregory?" Dana repeated. "Is he back?"

Clutching a stitch in her side, Callie shook her head. "Have to find—a way to get—a message through."

"How?" asked Dana. "Did he reactivate his phone line? Or his e-mail?" She suddenly looked sheepish. "I overhear things . . . through the walls sometimes—without meaning to."

Callie shook her head. "No," she said. "And I don't know how I'm going to get through to him. I already tried *everything*, and none of it worked. I guess . . ." Her eyes grew wide. "I guess I'll just have to go to New York!"

"New York?" Dana echoed, following Callie into her bedroom.

"Yes!" said Callie, flinging open her closet and reaching for her gym bag. "I'll go to New York. Now what should I pack?" she muttered, turning to her dresser.

"Is that—such a good idea?" asked Dana, hovering near her bed. "How are you even going to get there?"

"I don't know. Bus?" said Callie, tossing a sweatshirt into the bag. "I think they leave every hour from South Station. . . ."

"But where will you stay?"

"I don't need a place to stay," Callie insisted. "I just need to find Gregory and then everything else will . . . work out. Somehow."

Slowly Dana shook her head. "It doesn't sound like you've thought this through."

"Maybe not," said Callie, "but there isn't any time!"

"Why not?"

"Because there just—isn't!"

"Stop," said Dana, her tone shifting from gentle to forceful. "Drop the bag, sit down, and look at me."

Callie obeyed, sinking onto her bed.

Dana sat next to her. "Now what, pray tell, is the rush?"

"I think Gregory thinks that I started dating someone else the second he left—and that I told a reporter for the school magazine that I don't want him now that he's poor! That's why he suddenly stopped trying to reach me! That and because my phone broke. But all those calls from the restricted line to Vanessa's phone afterward were from before that article about the date auction, too! And of course, the soccer photos appeared, and—well, who knows what else!" Callie cried, trying to explain. Dana listened patiently, but her demeanor somewhat resembled a nurse listening to the rants of a feverish patient.

"So don't you see?" Callie pleaded. "I have to go to New York so I can explain it all and then he can finally break up with Alessandra and we can . . . finally . . ."

Dana rested a hand on Callie's back. "Gregory left in a huge hurry," she said finally. "He didn't have time to break up with his lady friend or leave you anything more than that Post-it note. I—understand how hard that must have been, how hard it must still be. So it's only natural to want to believe that there must have been something more, some great misunderstanding, perhaps, with an equally grand *deus ex machina* type of explanation."

Dana cleared her throat. "But things don't always turn out the way they do in stories. Sometimes real life and real troubles like Gregory's get in the way, and real people just don't have time to write secret love letters confessing everything. Like that character in your book you like so much." Dana nodded at the volume on the nightstand before continuing, insisting that God had a plan and that waiting patiently was actually the fastest way to a resolution.

But Callie was no longer listening. Reaching for the copy of *Persuasion*, she flipped through the pages until she found the section that she had volunteered to read not one week earlier. Her bookmark had only been a chapter away. In a few days she would have found it—although it might have been many weeks earlier if she'd been smarter, or less preoccupied.

"What are you doing?" asked Dana. "Are you okay?"

Tears were pouring down Callie's face. "Read it," she said, handing the book to Dana with trembling fingers.

Callie—You pierce my soul. I am half agony, half hope, wondering if you will still want me after everything I have done, everything I have lost, and everything you may learn in my absence. I wish I could explain,

306 PERSUASION

sentence; her heart was too full, her breath too much oppressed.

"You are a good soul," cried Captain Harville, putting his hand on her arm, quite affectionately. "There is no quarrelling with you. And when I think of Benwick, my tongue is tied."

Their attention was called towards the others. Mrs Croft was taking leave.

"Here, Frederick, you and I part company, I believe," said she. "I am going home, and you have an engagement with your friend. To-night we may have the pleasure of all meeting again at your party," (turning to Anne.) "We had your sister's card yesterday, and I understood Frederick had a card too, though I did not see it; and you are disengaged, Frederick, are you not, as well as ourselves?"

[Captain Wentworth was folding up a letter in great haste, and either could not or would not answer fully.]

"Yes," said he, "very true; here we separate, but Harville and I shall soon be after you; that is, Harville, if you are ready, I am in half a minute. I know you will not be sorry to be off. I shall be at your service in half a minute."

Mrs Croft left them, and Captain Wentworth, having sealed his letter with great rapidity, was indeed ready, and had even a hurried, agitated air, which shewed impatience to be gone. Anne knew not how to understand it. She had the kindest "Good morning, God bless you!" from Captain Harville, but from him not a word, nor a look! He had passed out of the room without a look!

but like our old friend Wentworth, for now I must speak to you by such means as are within my reach. I will call as soon as I can, but writing me at the following address may be your only way to reach me for a while. Tell me that you will wait and I will promise to tell

"What—"

"Just read it," Callie insisted.

you everything. Tell me it doesn't matter that I no longer have anything to offer except myself and I will return: yours for as

PERSUASION **307**

She had only time, however, to move closer to the table where he had been writing, when footsteps were heard returning; the door opened, it was himself. He begged their pardon, but he had forgotten his gloves, and instantly crossing the room to the writing table, he drew out a letter from under the scattered paper, placed it before Anne with eyes of glowing entreaty fixed on her for a time, and hastily collecting his gloves, was again out of the room, almost before Mrs Musgrove was aware of his being in it: the work of an instant!

The revolution which one instant had made in Anne, was almost beyond expression. The letter, with a direction hardly legible, to "Miss A. E.--," was evidently the one which he had been folding so hastily. While supposed to be writing only to Captain Benwick, he had been also addressing her! On the contents of that letter depended all which this world could do for her. Anything was possible, anything might be defied rather than suspense. Mrs Musgrove had little arrangements of her own at her own table; to their protection she must trust, and sinking into the chair which he had occupied, succeeding to the very spot where he had leaned and written, her eyes devoured the following words:

"I can listen no longer in silence. I must speak to you by such means as are within my reach. You pierce my soul. I am half agony, half hope. Tell me not that I am too late, that such precious feelings are gone for ever. I offer myself to you again with a heart even more your own than when you almost broke

long as you will have me. In haste, Gregory Brentworth Bolton
P.O. Box #28376 229 E 85th St. New York, NY 10028

"Fine," Dana conceded, spreading the book across her lap.

"Wow," Dana said softly, setting down the book. Grabbing a tissue from the nightstand, she blew her nose loudly. "Allergies," she muttered, wiping her eyes.

"I knew it," Callie whispered. "I knew it all along! Dana," she cried, leaping to her feet, "I could kiss you!"

"Please—don't," said Dana. "One from OK was already bad enough as it is."

"All right," said Callie, giggling deliriously and slinging her bag over her shoulder. "Well, then—wish me luck!"

"Good lu—*wait*. You're not still entertaining the idea of going to New York, are you? When your hearing's less than a week away? And, last I checked, you still don't have any idea who . . ." She gestured at the bulletin board, which had started to look like the work of a conspiracy-theory-driven madman.

Callie opened her mouth to protest, but Dana pressed on. "What about finals? Reading period is supposed to be for studying, not spontaneous trips to— Well, do you even *know* exactly where it is that you're going?"

"No." Callie froze in her doorway. "But it can't be too far from that PO Box address. . . ."

"Why not just write to him," Dana pleaded, "like his note suggests?"

"Because I can't bear to wait another minute knowing that he thinks—that I think—when I know—that he doesn't know— I just need to clear it all up and *now*!" Callie cried. "I'm sorry, but I'll just have to explain it better when I get back! Please tell Mimi and Vanessa—"

"Tell us what?" Vanessa called from the common room. She and Mimi had just returned from the party.

"Oh, thank goodness," Dana muttered. "I never thought I would say this but—I need you two to talk some sense into her!"

"*Qu'est qui ce passe*?" asked Mimi, starting for Callie's bedroom. "Why did you quit the party *très rapidement*?"

"Yes, and why does it look like you're about to run away from home," Vanessa asked, "wearing *my* Tory Burch dress?"

Too flustered to speak, Callie handed Vanessa *Persuasion* while Dana summarized what had transpired.

"But why should she not go to New York *maintenant*?" asked Mimi. "Even if you do not locate him, you can return within a day or two—*je sais, je sais*," she added grumpily to Dana. "*Mais un ou deux jours sans* studying never killed anyone's grandma, and perhaps *un petit voyage c'est exactement* what she needs for the brain clearing to *attraper* the Insider!"

Slowly Vanessa shook her head. "Believe it or not, I agree with Dana. Even if you didn't have less than a week left until your hearing, not to mention finals, and even if you did know where to find Gregory, I still don't think now is a good time to go to New York." Setting down *Persuasion*, she sighed. "It'll probably be all over the papers later tonight, but according to the latest update from that tireless gossip-whore otherwise known as my mother, the SEC hearings start tomorrow.

"Essentially," Vanessa continued, placing a hand on Callie's shoulder, "it's like being on trial except without the handcuffs. The proceedings could entail"—she cringed—"months of testifying, all day every day, and given certain confidentiality issues, you can bet the lawyers have Gregory and his dad locked in a hotel somewhere not even the most ruthless reporters could find them."

Wailing, Callie flung herself onto the bed. Every ounce of adrenaline-induced energy evaporated instantaneously. She resolved never to move again.

"There, there," said Dana after a beat. "'Those who hope in the Lord will renew their strength.'"

"Um . . . yeah," said Vanessa. "Like Journey and the D-meister said, 'Don't stop believin'.' You just need to be patient, get through your hearing, and let Gregory and his dad get through theirs. And in the meantime you could still try writing him that letter. . . ." She stood, digging through the desk until she found paper and pens.

"*Oooh, c'est romantique!*" exclaimed Mimi. "Let us hope that he has not ceased to check *le bureau le poste* because you have been having *des relations sexuelles avec* Bryan."

"What?" Callie shrieked, sitting up. "I have *not* been having *des relations*—I mean, *sexual relations* with Bryan!"

"Oh," said Mimi. "*Pourquoi pas*? And *why,* then, have you been checking in all over the Facebook?"

"What are you—*ohdearaghgghwww*!" Callie groaned, covering her eyes. "You don't think—there's any way that—I mean, his profile's been deactivated, right?"

"Here," said Dana, handing Callie the envelope and stamp she'd just retrieved from her room. "Explain the mix-up, mail the letter, and then pray."

"Amen," said Vanessa. "Hopefully then you can stop obsessing."

"And *start* obsessing *sur votre* upcoming expulsion!"

"MIMI!" Vanessa and Dana yelled at her.

"Désolé."

"No," said Callie. "Mimi's right. You guys are, too. Send the letter—then focus on staying in school," she muttered, sitting at her desk and starting to write: about how she was never involved with Bryan or anyone else, and had never said those things at the date auction that the magazine had printed. Finally, on her third page now, she finished with an account of how she might have only one more week left at school.

Then she stuck the pages in the envelope and kissed the back for good luck. "So, um . . . how exactly does one go about sending snail mail these days?"

"Uh . . ." said Vanessa.

Mimi shrugged.

"Seriously?" Dana blinked. Shaking her head, she said, "Come on. I'll take you to the nearest mailbox."

TWELVE

The Birkin List

THE BIRKIN LIST

- ~~Attend a Crew race~~
- ~~Go to at least ONE Harved museum~~
- Go to freshman formal <u>with an actual freshman</u>
- Pee on the John Harvard statue
- Jump off Weeks Bridge into the Charles River
- ~~Sit in on at least THREE classes taught by famous professors~~
- ~~Turn in Callie's short story~~
- ~~Use all the money left on Harvard ID to buy candy from Greenhouse Café~~
- ~~Eat in every house dining hall~~
- Have a slumber party in the common room
- ~~One last scorpion bowl at the Kong~~
- Run spring Primal Scream?
- Sex in Widener (with . . . ???)
-
-
-
-
-

"Well, there's another thing we can cross off the list," said Vanessa, getting up off the grass by the Charles River and stretching. "I cannot believe it took me this long to learn about the glory of these so-called sporting events!"

"*C'est magnifique*," Mimi agreed, watching the men's eight row back toward the boathouse from the finish line, their oars cutting through the water in perfect unison.

"You're not going to jump off the bridge right now, are you?" asked Dana, skeptically eyeing the setting sun.

"No," Callie answered. "It's too cold today. And besides, you guys have to start getting ready for Freshman Formal."

"Are you quite *sure* you will not be joining us?" asked Mimi, pouting as they started to walk home to Wigglesworth.

"Yes," said Callie. "I don't have a date, and I still don't really have any idea what I'm going to say tomorrow morning at the hearing." She stared down JFK Street, all the way to the end where it terminated at Harvard Yard. The large brick and white columned buildings seemed to grow larger with every step. Would she even be a student here by this time tomorrow?

"Mimi and I don't have dates either," Vanessa pleaded.

"Then what would you call OK and Matthew graciously volunteering to escort you at the suggestion of Adam and me?" asked Dana.

"Uh . . . how about 'my worst nightmare'?" said Vanessa.

"You may have OK," said Mimi. "I prefer Monsieur Robinson's dance moves in a party scenario. Much more entertaining."

Callie laughed.

"Are you sure?" Vanessa wheedled. "Please, please, pretty please—come?"

"Not tonight," said Callie, her eyes flicking up to read the inscription above Dexter Gate. *Enter to Grow in Wisdom.* She remembered passing under it on her very first day of school, awed by the majestic beauty of the Yard.

"But you will be there when we return *pour la soirée pyjama, mais non*?" asked Mimi.

"Yes," said Callie, "I'll be home for the slumber party so Vanessa can cross another thing off her precious list."

"The Birkin List is *our* list," Vanessa insisted. "And I think we can all agree that it has made this last week—I mean, this *past* week," she corrected herself with a sidelong look at Callie, "a lot more fun for . . . everyone."

Callie nodded. She wanted to tell them all how much the week had meant to her—and how grateful she was to have had them in her lives as roommates, however briefly—but a lump had formed in her throat.

"Remind me again why it's called the Birkin List," Dana asked while they trudged up the stairs in entryway C.

Vanessa sighed. "When I was little, I did not understand the concept of a 'Bucket List.' Even when I was older and saw a bucket for the first time—"

"Wait," said Callie, stopping outside the door to C 24. "How old?"

"It still didn't make any sense," Vanessa continued, ignoring her. "What *did* make sense was the long waiting list at Barneys for the latest Hermes Birkin bag. I lusted after that bag for my entire freshman year of high school until I finally realized: why waste so much time waiting for just one bag while life is totally passing you by? There were so many other purses out there, yet here I was missing out on my best years to accessorize. And so I made a list of everything I wanted to do before I got the Birkin."

"Ah," said Dana. "Now, that makes perfect sense."

"Was that—*sarcasm*?" Vanessa asked, whirling around to face Dana. "Is our little D-meister finally all grown up?"

"Don't," said Dana, smacking away the hands that were reaching out to pinch her cheeks.

"Fine," said Vanessa, lowering her arms. "But still—I'm just *so* proud!"

"And but still just *so* annoying," said Mimi, mimicking Vanessa's tone.

Vanessa made a face.

"Now would the other half of Team Best Ever at Baghole," Mimi continued, "care to join me in my chambers? I will allow you to go into great detail regarding *la* length *inapproprié de mon formelle* dresses."

"Okay," Dana agreed. "If you'll show me how to do that hair thing again, I will gladly help you pick an *appropriate* formal dress."

"Deal," said Mimi, grinning and offering Dana her arm.

Now alone with Callie in the common room, Vanessa turned to her. "Are you *sure*—"

"Yes," Callie reassured her. "I need to stay and go over everything again from the beginning.

"I'll be *fine*," she added, wishing Vanessa would stop looking at her the way a new wife might when seeing her husband off to war. "Really. I'm sure I'll think of something at the last minute. . . ."

"Okay," said Vanessa. "I'm going to go change, but we'll all be back before midnight, and if you think of anything that you need between now and then, just call Brad—"

"Go!" Callie cried. "Change! Get ready! Seriously! It's fine!"

"All right!" Vanessa disappeared into her bedroom.

Callie stayed in the common room for a few minutes, taking everything in. Finally, with a sigh, she returned to her own room to mull over, for the millionth time, the bulletin board.

Three hours had passed since everyone left, and during that time Callie had grown almost dizzy from pacing around the tiny stretch of floor by her bed. No answers had come; no revelations dawned; no epiphanies suddenly lit metaphorical lightbulbs above her head.

She stared at Matt's list of "facts" about the Ivy Insider. But no matter how many times she read them, the pieces of the puzzle refused to come together. "Fact: I'm totally screwed," she muttered aloud.

Absentmindedly she lifted the picture of Gregory from Harvard-Yale off her bookshelf. In the past week she had spent an embarrassing amount of time staring at it, and rereading his note—the most incredible, inspired secret love letter of all time, in her humble opinion—handwritten on the pages of *Persuasion.*

How long did snail mail take these days, anyway? She couldn't remember the last time that she had mailed or received an actual letter. And was he even still checking that post office box? Frowning, she flung herself backward onto her bed, still holding the photo.

Maybe he'd received her letter—and was on his way back right now! In a minute he'd pull up front in a taxi, wearing a tuxedo, and ask her—better late than never—to Freshman Formal. Then they'd stay up dancing all night—and spend the entire next day in bed.

She sighed. If only it were real, he might have even made her forget it was probably her last night at Harvard. In fact, being around him made her forget a lot of things—like that one time when she'd accidently caught him in nothing more than a towel on his way out of the shower and she had temporarily forgotten how to speak. Or that other time, right as he'd first kissed her on the balcony of their hotel in New Haven, when she'd have been hard-pressed to remember her own name.

Come back, she willed him, staring at his image. Please. "Come back," she whispered.

A strange thwacking noise sounded against her window.

Callie shot straight up. What the—

There it was again: someone appeared to be throwing rocks.

Diving over her desk, Callie yanked up the shade just in time to see another pebble crack against the pane. She threw the window open, stuck her head out into the cool night air, and looked down.

"Calleeeee!"

"Clint?" she screamed back, ready to kill him for having just become literally the biggest disappointment of her entire life. "What the hell are you doing here?"

"Let me up!" he shouted by way of response, stumbling a little. "My ID card—can't—seem to find . . ."

"Have you been drinking?" Callie called, staying where she was.

"Need to talk . . . I need to talk to you!" he insisted, slurring.

Thank god most of the freshmen in her dorm were probably at the dance.

"Go home, Clint!" she said, starting to shut her window. "Sleep it off!"

"Wait!" he cried. "You were right—about Alexis . . . whole time . . . I HAVE—information. . . ."

Callie froze, chewing on her lip. Were these the drunken ramblings of a jackass (likely), or was she about to hear an earnest, alcohol-induced confession that might somehow pertain to the Insider? Worth a try, she decided, poking her head back out the window. "I'll be right down!" she called. "Stay there, and stop shouting!"

"I'm sorry for shouting!" Clint shouted, heading over to entryway C.

"Just get in," she said, letting the bright green door slam behind him.

"Callie," he said, grabbing her elbow, "so glad you could come over tonight—I mean, me—let *me* . . ."

"Okay," said Callie, shaking off his hand. "No more talking." Inside C 24 she guided him over to the couch. "Sit," she said, watching him flop down. "Good. Now drink," she instructed, handing him a Nalgene full of water.

"You'rrrreallyprrretty," he slurred, peering at her through half-closed eyes. A little water dribbled down his chin.

"Or you're just really drunk," Callie remarked, perching a safe distance away on the edge of the armchair.

"S'not sodrunk," he protested, trying to set the water on the table and missing by a few inches. "Huh. S'funny."

"Finish it," Callie said. "Okay. Now what is it that you wanted to tell me?"

"Wha?" Clint blinked. "But I already told you."

"Told me what?"

"That you'rrrpretty!"

"Oh god," said Callie. "Give me your phone."

"'E.T. phone home,'" said Clint. "Wait—he can't—she burned it."

"This was a mistake," Callie muttered, going into her bedroom to retrieve her new cell. Quickly she dialed Tyler's number. "Tyler?" she said when he picked up.

"Callie?" his voice came over the line. "Please tell me you are with Clint."

"Unfortunately, yes I am," she said.

"Oh, good . . . *She found him!*" he called, presumably speaking to someone else. "Sorry," Tyler apologized. "A bunch of us guys were just chillin' at the Fly, and Clint had a *liiittle* too much to drink—"

"You think?" asked Callie.

"And then he somehow escaped. Right out from under my watchful eyes."

"How shocking," said Callie. "Would you mind maybe coming to pick him up?" she asked, glancing at Clint, who had slumped over one of the couch pillows and started to snore.

"No problem," said Tyler, "just give me twenty minutes."

"Ten would be better," said Callie, hanging up.

She grabbed *Persuasion* and settled into the armchair so she could make sure Clint didn't wake up and do something stupid. She'd been reading for a solid fifteen minutes when she heard him speak.

"You were right, you know."

"Right about what?" she asked. He was still slumped across the couch, his chin propped up by the pillow, but his eyes seemed ever so slightly more focused now.

"Uhlexus," he said on the exhale. "She's a . . . evil . . . witch."

"I'm sorry you feel that way," said Callie, actually meaning it a little. He just looked so pathetic at the moment. "But I'm sure you'll have made up by morning."

"No." He shook his head vehemently. "She's still . . . the same. Hasn't changed . . . at all."

Callie nodded. "I can't say I'm surprised."

"She's still . . . blackmailing . . . found out—this morning . . ."

"Blackmailing *who*?" Callie said sharply, remembering the thumb drive labeled C, A that she'd stolen out of Lexi's office. Was there still *another* copy of the sex tape out there?

"S'not you." Clint shook his head. "S'someone else . . ."

Callie relaxed. "Again, I'm not sure why any of this should be surprising."

Clint seemed to shrug from where he lay. "Shouldnaever brokenup withchu."

Callie propped her cheek in her hand. "Actually, I'm so glad you did."

"Dunts'pose . . . ?"

"No way," said Callie. "Finally!" she cried a moment later, standing to get the door.

"I'm so sorry," said Tyler, striding over to the couch. "He and Lexi are going through sort of a rough patch at the moment, if you hadn't already guessed—"

"Wicked witch," Clint muttered petulantly.

"Come on, buddy," said Tyler, throwing his arm around Clint and helping him to his feet. "That's it," he encouraged, still supporting almost all of Clint's weight and inching slowly toward the door. "Pick up those feet—one after the other. . . . There ya go. . . . See ya later, Callie—and thanks for calling me."

"No problem," she said, making sure they at least made it to the end of the hall.

Less than two minutes later the door to the common room flew open again.

Fortunately this time it was Mimi, Dana, and Vanessa, all clad in formal attire. "Did we just see what I think we saw?" asked Vanessa.

"What—Tyler and Clint?"

"Yuh-huh," said Vanessa. "What on earth was that about?"

So Callie told them.

"Where are the boys?" Callie asked when she was done recounting Clint's strange visit.

"We decided to do the ditching," said Mimi, stifling a yawn. "The formal was rather boring, and we would prefer to spend this time with you."

Dana nodded.

"Slumber party?" Vanessa proposed, her eyes widening maniacally.

"*Oui!*" said Mimi.

"I'll get the marshmallows," said Vanessa.

"I'm going to go put on my pajamas," said Dana.

"Let's all change," Callie suggested, "and then bring our mattresses out here?"

"Brilliant!" said Vanessa, tossing the marshmallows onto the couch and dragging the coffee table over to one side of the room to clear space.

A few minutes later they had successfully combined their four twin mattresses on the floor to create one gigantic super mattress. Clad in pj's, they watched Vanessa make s'mores, roasting the marshmallows over a scented candle. Then, in between bites of graham crackers and melted chocolate, they reminisced about the highlights of the dance, from Vanessa's renewed hunt for a freshman "fish" whom she could train over the course of the next three years and raise into the perfect boyfriend to OK's epic freestyle rap battle with DJ Damien Zhang.

"It all started to go downhill after he rhymed 'royalty' with 'bow to me,'" Vanessa explained, sending Callie into another spasm of sidesplitting giggles.

"Ah," said Callie finally, wiping her eyes. "I should have just gone with you guys."

"I take it you did not make any progress?" asked Dana gently.

Callie shook her head, then lay back on one of the mattresses and stared at the ceiling. "Unless you count Clint's 'revelation' about how Alexis is still evil . . ."

Vanessa shrugged, climbing under the covers next to her. "Well, at the very least I think it's safe to say that when your ex shows up blitzed out of his mind, trash-talking his current girlfriend, and—sort of—asking for you back, you definitely won the breakup."

"Tsk, tsk, tsk," Mimi clucked. "Callie is already winning after he restarted dating Lexi."

"True," said Vanessa.

"But what are you going to do, then—about tomorrow?" Dana asked quietly after standing to dim the lights.

Callie sighed, watching the flame of the candle flicker.

"If it were me," said Mimi, hopping into bed, "I would simply not show. How will they manage to have the hearing if you do not attend? Trust me. *J'ai été expulsé de nombreuses institutions dans ma carrière académique.*"

"Your less-than-exemplary record with boarding schools is exactly why she should *not* listen to you!" said Dana. "Now, what you need is a plan, even if it's just a backup—"

"Matt already volunteered to come in and 'testify' that I was sitting next to him at the *Crimson* when the third Insider article was posted from a computer all the way on the other side of the offices," said Callie. "So maybe if I don't think of"—she yawned—"something before tomorrow morning then I can ask him to come with me. . . . But I don't want to drag him into this—especially since, if Lexi *is* one of the students on the judiciary board, she'll probably just accuse him of lying or colluding and find a way to have him kicked off the paper, too."

"And you're *sure* she didn't do it?" asked Vanessa.

"I'm not sure," said Callie, "but Grace seems to be, and since all the evidence we could find just seemed to exonerate Lexi . . ." She shook her head, pulling the covers up to her chin. "Maybe Matt was right. Maybe if I hadn't wasted so much time obsessing about how Lexi had to be the Insider, I wouldn't have been so blind to other possibilities."

"*What* other possibilities?" asked Vanessa. "Who's more conniving than Alexis Thorndike? Who else is a member of the *Crimson and* was a veteran member of the Pudding?"

"Maybe whoever did it was only one or the other—or neither," said Callie, her eyelids feeling heavy. "There are ways of getting into the *Crimson* without being a staff member or a COMPer. . . ."

"*Oui*," Mimi murmured.

"And maybe even ways to find out what happened at private Pudding proceedings without actually being there."

"Hey," said Dana. "Didn't Clint used to bring you coffee at the *Crimson* a lot?"

"What are you saying?" Callie asked.

"He's in the Pudding," said Dana, "and he spent a fair amount of time in the offices, right? *And* he showed up here the night before your hearing clearly feeling guilty about something—from the sound of it."

Mimi gasped, throwing off her covers. "What if—he and Alexis—were conspiring together for the entire duration!"

Callie giggled.

"*Quoi*?" Mimi demanded.

"I've just never heard you sound so excitable," Callie explained.

Mimi rolled over onto her stomach. "I am not eager to see you gone," she said, propping her chin in her hands.

"None of us are," Dana agreed. "You can't leave school now—not when I was finally getting used to you three."

"Aw, D-meister!" said Vanessa.

"I still don't approve of most of your lifestyle choices," Dana insisted, "but somebody needs to keep you all in line, and I guess I . . . don't really *mind* being the one to do it."

"I will try to take you not *minding* me as a compliment," said Vanessa.

Callie was glad it was dark save for the light of the candle. Undetected, she rubbed her damp cheeks on the side of her pillow. She hoped they knew how much she had come to love them this year, because there was no way she could manage to say it out loud without breaking down completely. "I . . . don't think it could have been Clint," Callie said finally, trying to stay focused. "The whole reason Lexi hates me in the first place is because we started dating—why would she do all those things to keep us apart if they were secretly together the whole time?"

"Meh," said Mimi, sounding sleepy. "It was worth a pondering."

"What about . . ." Vanessa started. "You're not going to like this, but— Oh, never mind."

"What?" asked Callie.

"Okay, don't freak out," said Vanessa, "but have you considered the remote possibility that it might be . . . well . . . Gregory?"

"I *considered* everyone," said Callie. "But I refuse to believe that he was involved."

"Yes," said Dana, "why would he ever do anything bad to Callie when he—seems to have a great deal of affection for her? I may not be an English major, but even I could tell that was a very—moving letter that he wrote to her before he left."

"But in the letter he also asked for her forgiveness," said Vanessa. "For things that she might *learn* he had done during his absence."

"Clearly he was talking about his dad," said Callie. "And his history with other women."

"I still cannot believe that Alessandra turns out to be such a sneaky little liar," said Mimi. "Though what did we really know about her, anyway? She just appeared—*poof*—out of nowhere. Kind of like this zit on my forehead. *Pop pop!*"

"All that stuff with his dad," Vanessa pressed on, speaking over Mimi, "meant he knew he was going to be poor soon, right? Meaning he might have had a reason to suddenly resent the Pudding! He never seemed to really like being there, anyway."

"If only he'd gotten my letter and come back," Callie mused, "we could have asked him."

"And what about that fifth Ivy Insider article?" Vanessa continued, refusing to drop it. "Didn't you say he left Gatsby early that night, too?"

"So did you," said Callie, yawning again.

"Yeah, with *you*," said Vanessa, finally lying back down.

The room was quiet for a few minutes except for the sound of their breathing. The candle burned lower and lower until eventually the flame snuffed out.

"There is one more thing," Vanessa murmured. Dana and Mimi were silent and had probably already drifted off.

"What?" Callie whispered, rolling onto her side.

"Remember when we snuck into his bedroom after the date auction," said Vanessa, "because you wanted to prove that Alessandra was lying about how he had never even read a single Insider article? And then we saw what looked like an old installment in the trash?"

"So?" said Callie. "I was correct, wasn't I? Alessandra is a liar. In fact, I bet he never even called her and she just made up that entire conversation."

"You're probably right." Vanessa sighed. "I was just wondering if maybe she said all that to protect him because, after hanging around with him a lot, she discovered that he'd written the articles—that *he* was the Ivy Insider. . . ."

"Mmm," said Callie. "Mm-hmm . . ." She shut her eyes, overcome by that familiar falling sensation that often precedes sleep. Down, down, down, she drifted until, all of a sudden, her body gave a tremendous jolt.

"Hey—" Vanessa called in hushed tones. "Where are you going?"

Instead of answering, Callie sprang to her feet, slipped out into the hall, and then pushed open the door to C 23.

All the lights were off; it looked as if Adam, Matt, and OK had returned from the dance and retired for the evening. Callie headed straight for Gregory's bedroom, flipping on the light. Everything appeared to be in its place, including the large perforated, metal wastebasket next to his desk.

Callie stared at the crumpled piece of paper at the very bottom of the basket. Through the crisscrossing metal only part of a headline was visible: "Behind the Ivy-Covered Walls, Part—." Callie hesitated for only a moment before she dumped the entire contents of the basket onto the floor—previous assignments, tissues smeared with lipstick, tests, old receipts dating back months before he left, and all. Reaching for the article where it had fallen facedown, she flipped it over and read:

Behind the Ivy-Covered Walls: Part III (DRAFT)
On the evening of March fifth, a privileged few gathered inside the Fly Club for Gentleman for one of the oldest, elitist, and most exclusive affairs on campus: a party whimsically entitled The Great Gatsby . . .

THIRTEEN

The Hearing

http://www.nytimes.com/pages/business/index.html

The New York Times

May 14

Business

Bolton Teen Exonerated in Hedge Fund Scandal

Pierce Bolton Testifies Before the SEC That Son Gregory Had No Involvement Though His Trust Fund Was Depleted to Pay Off Investors

By ROB DUNBARTON

Published: May 14

MANHATTAN – For weeks the hedge fund industry has remained in turmoil following the declaration of personal bankruptcy by Pierce Bolton, founding partner at Bolton and Stamford Enterprises. This week Bolton finally testified in front of the Securities and Exchange Commission, which has in conjunction with the State of New York been conducting an ongoing investigation of his fund. Three unnamed sources who attended the proceedings confirmed on the condition of anonymity that Bolton admitted to paying off investors with personal funds.

Over the course of the past two years Bolton failed to inform investors regarding the perilous state of their assets after a series of bad investments, instead paying out withdrawals from his own accounts. "It was easy enough to see after we started examining the books," said one SEC official, who also wished to remain anonymous. "[Bolton's] set showed severe losses, but the numbers released publicly to investors told quite a different story—of growth unparalleled by almost any other firm. [The fund] claimed a unique trading algorithm, when in reality the only magic ingredient, so to speak, was Bolton's immense personal wealth."

"We cannot comment on the actual proceedings," said Eliza Chapham, director of the hedge funds division at the Securities and Exchange Commission. "But criminal charges are highly unlikely to follow given Bolton's cooperation and the apparent overall financial health of the firm. I cannot speak to the ramifications this might have in the civil courts," she added, "but since no one is actually owed any money and Bolton no longer has any to award in a settlement, civil action seems, again, unlikely."

Widespread speculation among insiders in the financial services industry and various news outlets in the city indicated that Bolton's son, Gregory, a freshman currently enrolled at Harvard University, might be implicated in the ongoing investigation. A former summer intern at Bolton and Stamford, Gregory was rumored to have authorized his father, Pierce, to access his trust fund (once estimated at upward of 88 million, rendering him by far the richest teen in Manhattan) for the purposes of defrauding investors.

Late this afternoon the Bolton family attorneys issued a statement alleging that this is not the case. "As our client will soon testify," Noel Rubenstein wrote in an e-mail to the *Times*, "his son, Gregory, had no involvement in these events. While [Gregory] did realize that his trust fund had been accessed without his consent a month prior to the bankruptcy filings, he did not authorize the transactions."

An employee of the firm who worked closely with Gregory during his summer there spoke with the paper, again on the condition of anonymity. "If I had to guess, I would say that Gregory knew to what end his father was using his inheritance. Ethics may not run in the family, but mathematical gifts and economic savvy certainly do. But it's also probable that by the time he figured it out, the investigation was already underway, so who's to say what action, if any, he might have taken against his father."

Gregory Bolton came into possession of the trust fund (now estimated at less than the tuition cost of a Harvard education) following his eighteenth birthday last summer, left to him by the late Mrs. Bolton, who passed away after a long battle with breast cancer in 2005. Neither Gregory nor his stepmother, Trisha Bolton, could be reached for comment.

Mr. Rubenstein echoed Ms. Chapham's previous remarks, insisting that, due to recent large investments, "the fiscal health of the firm is quite robust." He added: "Pierce Bolton has cooperated and taken responsibility for his actions to the fullest extent and, in spite of this minor lapse in judgment that has yielded no consequences for anyone other than his family, will remain a pillar of the financial services industry. The media has certainly been relentless—particularly with regard to his son—but we hope that this statement and account of the SEC proceedings will pave the way for the teenager to soon resume his normal life."

The conference room in University Hall was cold and sterile, same as it had been the Monday after spring break when Callie and Grace initially appeared before Dean Benedict and two other administrators. All three had returned for her Student-Faculty Judicial Board disciplinary hearing today, in addition to another female faculty member and three students, one of whom was—to Callie's great dismay—Alexis Thorndike. They all sat along one side of a large rectangular table. A single empty chair waited on the other.

Callie swallowed, clutching a folder containing several papers and what would have been the third Ivy Insider installment. She almost would have preferred to have arrived with nothing.

"Ms. Andrews, please, be seated," Dean Benedict instructed from the center of the table. The male and female faculty members on either side of him remained expressionless, as did the two male students, whom Callie had never met, but a faint smile flickered across Alexis Thorndike's face.

"We have established this Student-Faculty Judicial Board," the dean continued, "including a representative from the school newspaper, the *Harvard Crimson*, and an English professor from your intended major's department, to allow you the chance to speak to the strong evidence that you are responsible for authoring a series of anonymous articles published to the newspaper's former

FlyBy blog and signed by the 'Ivy Insider.' You have received copies of relevant materials identical to those distributed to this board, featuring documentation of your log-in records on the computers at the *Crimson* offices. Six weeks ago in this very room, you maintained your innocence in these matters, even though yours was the only password-protected username online during every instance of an Insider posting. Is that still the case?"

"Yes," Callie murmured.

"What was that?" he asked.

"Yes," she repeated, forcing herself to look up and face the board. Several of them had started taking notes or were reexamining the "relevant materials" from manila folders similar to her own. Lexi, however, reclined in her chair as if she were settling in for the series finale of her all-time favorite television show.

"After we have heard your arguments," Dean Benedict explained, "we will determine what—if any—disciplinary action ought to be taken."

Lexi beamed. Callie imagined that the older girl was using every ounce of strength she had not to scream, *"EXPULSION!"*

"Needless to say," the dean continued, "this is an incredibly grave matter, given that a private document went public containing harmful comments that could even be construed as harassment targeting individual students."

Callie nodded.

"And you acknowledge, for the record," piped up one of the female faculty members, "that you are a current member of the organization the Hasty Pudding Social Club, which authored this document, and that you were in possession of the password needed to access the so-called Punch Book?"

Callie nodded again.

"Well, then," said Dean Benedict. "By all means, the floor is yours."

Callie set her folder on the table and opened it, staring unseeingly at the papers inside. In all her life her throat had never felt so dry. She wished she had thought to bring a water bottle. Or, better yet, that she had taken Mimi's advice and elected to skip the hearing altogether.

Seven sets of eyes honed in on her. Each second felt like an hour. "Um . . ." Callie shuffled the pages in front of her, finding the unpublished draft of "Behind the Ivy-Covered Walls: Part III." It was supposed to be her trump card, and yet, in her possession, it proved nothing. In fact, just displaying it without any evidence of the true author might make the case against her, since the first question out of their mouths would be: "Where did you get that?" And if she replied, "I found it," they would follow with, "If you didn't write it, then who did?"

Even if she told them, it would sound like a lie: the final, desperate diversion of a girl who clearly only had an unpublished draft because she was in fact the Ivy Insider.

And in the next-to-impossible event that they *did* believe her, what then? Expulsion, probably, for the very person she'd spent weeks praying would return.

Callie flushed, furious that she could even consider defending him after what he'd done. No explanation—on a Post-it, or in the pages of a book, or even in person—could possibly account for *this*.

The faculty member who'd questioned her a moment ago coughed pointedly. "Ms. Andrews, as I'm sure you can imagine, we're all busy people who don't have the whole day to sit—"

"What," Lexi suddenly said shrilly, staring at the door, "are *you* doing here?"

"Callie—" said a voice, deep and serious, at the exact same second she turned.

Her lips formed the shape of his name, but no sound came out. She inhaled sharply, wanting to cry—to scream—to throw her arms around him and hold him—no, *hit* him until he admitted *why* he'd done the things he'd done—

"Young man," said the faculty member Lexi had interrupted, "these are private proceedings that you're interrupting—"

"I know," he said, his eyes never leaving Callie's face and looking—to her horror—like he was on the verge of smiling.

Was he actually . . . enjoying this?

"But I have some new—crucial—information to these proceedings. You see, Callie"—his smile faltered—"is *not* the author of the Insider articles. In fact, *I*—"

"STOP!" Callie screamed suddenly, leaping to her feet. Her heart, which felt as if it had ceased beating the moment he entered the room, began to beat violently.

"I couldn't agree more." Lexi's clear, high voice cut through the air. "I'm sorry, Gregory—I'm sure we can all appreciate that you've been through a lot—but this interruption is simply unacceptable. Disciplinary hearings are supposed to be private proceedings between the accused student and the board."

"Now, wait just a moment, Ms. Thorndike," Dean Benedict intervened. "If, ah—Mr. Bolton, isn't it?—has uncovered some new piece of evidence, then perhaps it would behoove us to hear what the young man has to say?"

"Actually," Gregory started slowly, appearing confused at the expression on Callie's face, "I would like to . . . er . . . formally request that this board reconvene tomorrow."

"Reconvene tomorrow?" a faculty member repeated. "When she's already had six weeks to build her case? Forgive me, but I fail to see how allowing her a little more time could possibly contribute to anything other than to waste our own."

Callie turned back and saw Lexi nodding fervently.

The professor from the English Department cleared her throat. "Actually, I don't see the harm in granting what you point out to be simply a *little* more time," she said. "Especially if, as this Mr. Bolton seems to be saying, new information has come to light."

Callie stared at the manila folder in front of her, paralyzed by indecision. Slowly she reached to open it as the students and faculty members continued debating, painfully aware of Gregory, who stood only a few inches away. What if this was all a trick? What if he had only pretended to be on the verge of confessing in order to prevent her from showing them her solitary piece of proof?

"Ms. Andrews?"

Her hand froze, hovering over the unpublished draft of the Insider installment.

"If we vote to reconvene here tomorrow," Dean Benedict continued, "can you affirm that you will attend, ready to argue your case and accept our judgment as final even if you and Mr. Bolton fail to present any compelling additional evidence in the interim?"

She grabbed the article. But what if, a tiny voice pleaded in the back of her head, Gregory had never meant to frame her and had returned, with a plan, to somehow make it right? Meeting the dean's eyes, Callie started to nod. "Yes," she managed, her voice barely above a whisper.

"Then it's settled," the dean announced a moment later, counting four hands including his own. "You are all free to go, but we will expect you to return again this time tomorrow."

Much shuffling of papers and scraping of chairs could be heard as the members of the board stood and started gathering their things.

Alexis was the first one out of the room, brushing past Gregory without a word.

After the last faculty member had left, Gregory double-checked the hall and then quickly shut the door. Crossing over to where she still stood, leaning against the table and clutching the Insider installment, he cupped her face in his hands.

He looked too good to be real. His cheeks were flushed; his dark brown hair tousled as if he'd just taken the stairs up to University Hall two at time. Or as if she'd just run her fingers through it. Those blue eyes sparked like an electric current as they held her gaze, refusing to let go; that tiny crescent-moon-shaped scar stood out white against the line of his jaw, right below his lips.

A full thirty seconds passed as he continued just to stare at her, his smile gradually expanding into a delirious grin.

It was almost enough to make a girl forget all of the terrible things he'd done.

And then he kissed her.

She was melting. The hand that held the article fell limply to her side. Nothing mattered anymore—not the hearing, or his absence, or even that he had been behind the entire mess to begin with. As long as he kept kissing her, she could go on giving in to the impossible fantasy: that in spite of everything, it would all work out in the end.

Breaking away, Gregory started to laugh. "Hi," he said eventually, still laughing—presumably at her inability to speak.

"Hi?" she echoed, finally finding her voice and pushing him away. "'Hi'? Is that all you have to say—AFTER EVERYTHING?"

"I'm sorry," he said, instantly somber. He reached for her hands, but before he could grab the article, she yanked it out of reach.

"What's the matter?" he asked, dropping his arms in alarm.

"What's the matter?" she cried. "Are you KIDDING ME? HOW COULD YOU DO THIS?"

"I'm sorry," he repeated. "But it's not like I had much of a choice."

"Of course you had a choice!" said Callie. "You didn't have to do any of it! You do realize that I almost got expelled today?"

"Yes, I do." He stared at her with a funny look on his face. "I got your letter. And clearly you got mine. So then why . . . ?"

"You got my letter?" she blurted.

"Yes." He continued to watch her closely. "I never stopped checking the PO Box."

How dare he look like *he* was the one who'd been hurt in all of this? "Well, obviously," she said, her fists clenching around the article, "things have changed since then."

"What do you mean, 'things have changed'?" he demanded. "Are you saying that you *are* with that Bryan guy now—"

"I was never *with* Bryan!" she exploded. "In fact, if you knew how many hours—entire nights, even—I *wasted* thinking about you"—she flushed, silently cursing her phrasing before continuing—"wondering *when* you were coming back, *why* you didn't bother to leave me with more than a Post-it note, how you still seemed to have a *girlfriend*—"

"I said I was sorry!" he bellowed. "The Post-it—the way I left—that I believed the rumors—that I ever gave up trying to contact you—*I apologize for all of it*! What more do you want?"

"I want to know why," she said after a beat, her voice deadly quiet. "*Why* did you do it?"

Exhaling angrily, Gregory ran a hand through his hair. "Look," he started. "By the time I realized the potential ramifications of what I'd done—it was already too late anyway. And then the paper went to press and I had to leave before I had a chance to explain. Again—I'm sorry Callie, okay? *I'm sorry.* I never thought anyone was going to get hurt. And, in the end, I think I'm the only one who really lost anything—"

"What do you mean you're the only one who really *lost*

anything?" Callie practically screamed. "How can you act like what you did doesn't affect me? *I* almost lost everything—my position, my—"

"Wow," Gregory interrupted. His expression had turned to stone. "You're the last person I thought I'd hear that from. Who knew that the trust fund—and the *position*—meant so much to you?"

"What," said Callie through gritted teeth, "does your stupid *trust fund* have to do with the fact that you *framed me*, cost me my position at the paper, and might still get me kicked out of school?"

"What are you—you don't think . . . Oh no—you do! You think I'm the one who . . . wrote the Insider articles?" His eyes twinkled, almost like he was amused.

Callie's head was spinning. "Yes," she said, though she felt far from certain now, "and I have proof." She held up the article. "Last night I found *this* at the bottom of your trash."

"What is it?" asked Gregory, reaching for it.

"The unpublished draft of an article that *you* wrote," snapped Callie, refusing to yield the piece of paper, "but never had a chance to publish like the rest of the Insider installments that you posted using my log-in name and password."

"I see," said Gregory. "And you say you found that in my . . . oh. Yes. That makes sense."

Callie watched—stunned and infuriated as he, once again, began to laugh. Doubling over, he grabbed his side, saying in between gasps, "If that's the only reason you're upset right now—then everything—us—*we*—are going to be—okay!"

"How is everything possibly going to be okay?" Callie cried, hopelessly confused. "I'm about to be expelled!" Either he was more evil than Lexi—hence the laughter—or Callie had seriously missed something. "Are you prepared to tell the judicial board that *you're* the Ivy Insider?"

"No," said Gregory, straightening and wiping his eyes. "I'm not."

"But—"

"I'm not going to tell them it was me," he continued, "because I didn't write that or any of the articles."

"But . . ." Callie sputtered as he seized her hands, still grinning like this was the best day of his life. "If you didn't write them—then who did?"

Alessandra was waiting in the common room of C 23 by the time they returned, having responded immediately to Gregory's text. Her face fell when she saw Callie walk in after him, her arms frozen in midair. "You're back," she said after a beat, continuing on course as if to give him a hug.

He held up his hand to stop her. "Alessandra," he said, "I owe you an apology. Because my father's lawyers have had me on lockdown, I was unable to do what I should have done, in person, long before I left." He took a breath. "It's over," he said on the exhale. "I think you already knew that, but I'm sorry just the same that it got dragged out under the circumstances."

Alessandra seemed less surprised and more hand-caught-in-the-cookie-jar, avoiding Callie's eyes.

"Now I believe it's your turn to apologize," he said, "to Callie."

"Why should I apologize to *her*?" Alessandra demanded, looking half-indignant, half-afraid.

"How about for framing me and trying to have me expelled?" asked Callie. "Or lying to make me believe that Gregory had called you? Or pretending to be nice to me and Matt so that you could steal my password when I helped you set up your account on the first day of COMP?"

"I—you . . ." Alessandra appeared stricken. "Can't—prove anything . . ."

"Actually, Alessandra, we can," said Gregory. "I can't believe I never gave a second thought to the way you were pumping me for information after every Pudding event. I assumed it must have been because you wanted to belong so badly or were genuinely interested in how I'd spent my day. But that wasn't the real reason, was it?" he asked. "Just like you never really cared about me either."

"I do care about you!" Alessandra cried, bursting into tears. "I completely fell for you! I wasn't supposed to, but I did!"

Gregory seemed stunned into silence. Callie couldn't help but wonder exactly how many teary love confessions he'd endured in his eighteen years. No doubt this wasn't the first.

Practically sobbing now, Alessandra sank onto the couch. Eventually Gregory sat down next to her, keeping about a foot of space between them. Callie stayed where she was by the door, regretting that her mission for a quick confession had somehow landed her smack in the middle of a nasty breakup.

But not all of Alessandra's tears were for Gregory. "I didn't know," she managed between cries, "that you were—could have been—expelled!"

Callie stared at her. "Yes . . . you did!" she declared, suddenly remembering something. "That's why you told me—at the Spee—that I should enjoy my time here while I still could!"

Alessandra shook her head. "Didn't know—at first—when I agreed . . ." She let out a wail. "She *made* me!"

"*Who* made you?" Callie asked. "What? Are you saying that somebody else was involved?"

Alessandra continued to shake her head, dissolving into hysterics.

Callie looked at Gregory. Wordlessly he got up and went to the bathroom, returning momentarily with a box of Kleenex.

"Alessandra," he said, handing her several tissues, "we need you to calm down."

"Yes—stop crying," said Callie. "Please." Alessandra's tears were only making Callie feel sorry for her and feeling sorry for the girl who had gone to such great lengths to ruin her life was, in turn, only making her more furious.

They waited in silence while Alessandra tried to get a hold of herself. She seemed to go through at least half of the tissues before the steady stream of water leaking from her eyes gradually slowed to a drip.

Callie came and perched on the other couch opposite Alessandra and Gregory. "Why me?" she asked quietly.

"It wasn't personal," Alessandra murmured. "Not at first, anyway. I needed someone who was in the Pudding and had access to the *Crimson* just in case . . . well, something like this happened."

"And you saw an easy way to learn my password on the first day of COMP by pretending to be late and then asking for my help getting set up on the computers?" Callie prompted.

"I *was* late that day," Alessandra replied. "You typing in your password right in front of me was just luck—or stupidity, depending on how you look at it."

Callie bristled. "So when exactly did you decide that instead of just impersonating me you would try to have me expelled, too?"

"It was never . . . a decision," said Alessandra. "When I started writing the articles, I didn't think that I would get caught, meaning that you would never get in trouble. I actually did like you, that is until I found out that you'd lied to my face about—" She blushed. No point in stating the obvious, since he was currently sitting next to her.

Callie glanced at him, wondering if she would ever go to such insane lengths—like trying to have someone expelled—just to eliminate the competition. Immediately answering no would be a lot easier if he would just stop smiling every time he caught her staring.

"Why target the Pudding?" asked Callie, shaking herself. "Maybe you didn't have anything against me in the beginning, but it seems like you definitely had it out for the club."

Alessandra scoffed. "If you read the articles, then you should know why."

"I'm well aware of the negative aspects of the social clubs on campus," said Callie. "And in a lot of ways, I agree with your objections: to elitism, exclusivity, or choosing members based on superficial reasons like looks or wealth or athletic ability or private jet ownership or whatever. But that's a stereotype, too, and it doesn't apply to everyone in the Pudding or a Final Club." Callie narrowed her eyes. "Why do I get the feeling like you're avoiding my question?"

Alessandra pursed her lips.

"Fine," said Callie, leaning back and folding her arms. "Save it for when it's time to explain everything to the Ad Board tomorrow morning."

Alessandra's panicked expression returned in an instant. "I can't go," she whispered.

"You can and you will," said Callie. "One way or another, they need to know the truth, and I think it'd be better if they hear it from you rather than Gregory, who can confirm that you've been using him for information all semester and that you threw away that unpublished draft in his . . . bedroom"—Callie flinched—"while studying one Sunday afternoon."

Alessandra was shaking her head.

"And," Callie pressed on, "if that's still not enough, I can call Matt, who was there that day at the *Crimson* when my computer at the front of the offices suddenly logged me out—right after you arrived and said hello and then went to work in the back of the offices and at the same time that the Insider article about the Freshman Fifteen party at the Pudding was posted."

"What if they vote to have me expelled?" Alessandra asked in a tiny voice.

Callie frowned. "I guess you should've thought of that before you published the last article."

"But I didn't—"

"Didn't what?" asked Callie.

Alessandra clapped her hands over her mouth. She looked terrified.

"What is it?" Callie demanded. "What are you not telling us?"

The tears had started to flow again. "I'm not the one who—can't tell you or—" Alessandra broke down, burying her face in a handful of Kleenex.

"What can't you tell us?" asked Gregory, in a voice that could have coaxed honey from a bear or the corset from Queen Victoria.

Alessandra blew her nose loudly, still shaking her head.

Callie leaned forward suddenly. "Gregory—I know you were the source for all the Pudding articles, but what did you tell her about Gatsby? Did you see her after you left early, or were you texting her while it was happening?"

Gregory thought for a minute. "No," he eventually said. "She told me she had to work late that night. I didn't see her until the next day when she came over to study and edit her pieces for COMP. And the only person I communicated with over the phone at that party was . . . my dad. I'd caught him using my trust fund. And I'd guessed what he was up to. So I confronted him—and that's when you walked in. Or *fell* in, I should say."

Callie nodded slowly, racking her brain. A memory seemed to be struggling to surface, like a voice calling to her through the fog on the other side of a soccer field. "I remember wondering why you didn't bring Alessandra as your date for the evening. But you were busy helping Clint carry in the champagne, so I asked Lexi where she was instead. And she said—" Callie gasped. "She said that 'Alessandra had *Crimson* business that night'!" Callie turned to Alessandra. "How did she know? How did she know that you would be there?"

"Don't." Alessandra's voice was muffled through the tissues. "Please . . ."

But there was no stopping now. "How did you get the password to HPPunch dot com? Gregory: is there any way she could have found it by going through your bedroom or your phone?"

"I doubt it," he said. "I never wrote it down anywhere. In fact, I never even logged in to the site."

Callie nodded again, flooded with that half-satisfying, half-dreadful feeling: she'd been right all along. (Well, half right, in any event.) "It wasn't your idea to write the last Ivy Insider article, was it, Alessandra?" she stated flatly. "It was Lexi's."

Alessandra let out a wail. *"She blackmailed me!"*

Gregory looked at Callie, stunned. Even Callie felt her jaw drop a fraction of an inch, for hearing it out loud was a lot different than suspecting the entire time.

"She caught me in the act!" Alessandra continued, "and was going to turn me in and expose me to the club!" She raised her head, her face splotchy and red. "But then, when she found out I'd been using *your* username and password, she said she had a better idea."

"Of course," Callie muttered. "How could she pass up an opportunity to take down me and Grace in one fell swoop?"

Alessandra nodded. She seemed finally to be all cried out. "At first she just wanted you kicked out of the Pudding. That's why she called the cops on her own party for the Freshman Fifteen—so the members would later think you did it. But then . . . like you said, she saw an opportunity and she couldn't resist."

"She knew Grace would publish the Punch Book unedited, didn't she?" asked Callie, marveling at Lexi's mastery in spite of herself.

Alessandra nodded. "And she convinced me that you deserved to take the fall because you were a serial boyfriend stealer and were still after . . . you know . . . even though you were with Clint." Alessandra swallowed. Gregory sat perfectly still.

"But I didn't realize until later that you could be expelled—I swear," said Alessandra. "And when I found out what had happened a few weeks after the Ad Board first called you in, I went to her and told her I couldn't go through with it." Alessandra clasped her hands together and stared at her fingers. "That's when she explicitly threatened me. Turns out, she recorded our conversation in which I confessed to being the Insider and saved it to a flash drive. If I tried to tell the Ad Board that you didn't do it, I would go down instead."

Callie gaped. "But didn't you have similar proof of her involvement? Text messages? E-mails? Anything?"

"She's too smart for that." Alessandra sighed. "Even her texts from Gatsby giving me the blow by blow for that unpublished article just sound like updates from a friend who subbed in as my . . . boyfriend's plus-one for the night."

"But—" Callie sputtered. "But what about the final article?"

"She didn't write it." Alessandra shook her head. "She just gave me her password and told me what to do. I had my reservations, but . . ."

"But you did it because . . ." Callie said slowly, "you were mad at me?"

"Not just that." Alessandra hesitated. "I also did it because I was mad . . . at the Pudding."

Clearly, thought Callie. But *why*?

"I didn't transfer here from USC," Alessandra said finally.

"What?" said Callie.

"I took last semester off, but the year before that I was enrolled at Harvard . . . as a freshman."

Callie glanced at Gregory, who also seemed too shocked to speak. Alessandra went on. "My full name is Alessandra Garcia-Constantine. Growing up, I thought Alessandra was too flashy—too much of a 'hot girl' name—so I always went by Alessan instead. And shortly before I came to Harvard, my father made a rather large—rather public—donation; so I decided to drop the second half of the hyphenate in order to make a fresh start in college. Even though my mother—and her last name—had been the bane of my existence growing up, there were . . . reasons it was a lot less likely that people would put two and two together."

"Yes?" Callie encouraged, though she was starting to get a sense of where this was going.

"During the fall of my freshman year someone *did* put two and two together—and that someone was in the Pudding. They figured out that the famous supermodel had a daughter enrolled, and so, without ever having met me, they punched me.

"That first event was a disaster," Alessandra recalled, glancing at the now nearly empty box of tissues like she might need another one at any moment. "Even in a brand-new dress I stood out like a . . . whale in a wading pool. Literally. Nobody could figure out who I was, or why I was there, so I spent the second half of the evening hiding in the coatroom with a tray of cupcakes . . . which is where I was when I overheard two members laughing about me: saying how they wouldn't have 'enough room' to describe 'that mistake' in the Punch Book."

Callie stole a peek at Gregory, expecting him to look uncomfortable. "I remember you saying that in high school you used to be 'curvier,'" he prompted, ever so gently.

Alessandra nodded glumly. "As you probably both guessed by now—that was a major euphemism. I was the world's fattest, ugliest supermodel's daughter, and even though people weren't usually *mean* about it, everyone always looked at me—and my mother—like they were just *so* sorry I'd gotten the short end of the genetic stick."

She cleared her throat. "I spent the rest of my freshman year trying to stay as invisible as possible. And it worked: I made almost no friends—and no enemies to make soul-crushing comments about my weight either. But by the end of it I was seriously depressed. Something had to be done. So I asked my parents to send me away to one of those 'camps.' It took more than six months, but afterward I looked like—well, like I do today. I even started using 'Alessandra' again.

"Before coming back to school, I decided to test-drive the new me at a New Year's party at the Ritz—where we met," she said, turning to Gregory. "A bunch of other Pudding people were there that night, too. I couldn't believe it—not one of the upperclassmen recognized me, and they all couldn't stop gushing about how I 'just had to join' their club. So I told them I'd just transferred mid-semester—from USC, which was easy enough to post online along with recent photos—and that I would be *just thrilled* to consider their society. That's when the idea for the Insider articles first came to me. And from then on, everything went according to plan for a while . . . until I started falling for you," she murmured to Gregory.

"I guess I wasn't a very good boyfriend," he said. "If I'd been better, you might have felt like you could tell me more . . . about you."

Alessandra shrugged. "I could see that you were trying. And I knew you didn't have a lot of practice, so I was flattered that I was the one who'd finally inspired you to make an effort."

Callie tried to keep her expression neutral.

"But I also eventually figured out that you didn't love me—that you were in love with someone else. It was those texts on your phone that did it. 'I think about you every day. It's like I'm going crazy. I know you think I could never change but maybe, for you, I could.'" Alessandra frowned. "The fact that you never sent them only made it worse somehow. It made them seem more honest: obviously you weren't just using a line to coax some girl into bed. I'm talking about you, by the way," she said, grimacing at Callie.

"I'm sorry," Gregory said to Alessandra again. "I didn't know I—felt that way. Or maybe I did know but had given up and was trying to move on because I didn't think my feelings would ever be returned. . . ."

Callie wanted to throw her arms around him and tell him exactly how she felt—over and over and over again—but instead she sat on her hands.

"I forgive you," said Alessandra. "I only hope . . . that maybe one day you can forgive me?" She looked at Callie.

"I'm sorry that you had such a terrible experience at the Pudding, and about . . . everything else," Callie said eventually. "And as for the Insider thing: I'll forgive you in the morning if I'm still around to do it."

"You will be," Alessandra affirmed. "I'll tell the board everything—that it was all me."

"And let Lexi get away with it?" Callie yelped. "No way!"

"What choice do I have?" asked Alessandra. "I can't exactly prove her involvement, and if I implicate her, I'm positive she'll make good on her threats: to publish in the *Crimson* the whole story of who was *really* behind the Ivy Insider and why—complete with an old photo she managed to track down."

Callie's eyes went wide.

"What?" asked Alessandra.

"Stay here," Callie cried, leaping to her feet. "I'll be right back!" she yelled over her shoulder before dashing out into the hall. Running into her bedroom, she grabbed the photo that she'd tacked onto the right-hand side of the bulletin board. Then, she threw open the bottom drawer of her desk and pulled out the USB flash drive labeled C, A—INSURANCE. In thirty seconds she was back inside the common room of C 23, panting, thankful that she didn't have to stop and explain anything to anyone since they were all out at various libraries, studying for exams.

"What is it?" Alessandra asked again.

"Is this the photo, and is this the flash drive?" Callie said, shoving both onto Alessandra's lap.

"How did you—"

"*I* broke into her office during the Lampoon break-in and I took them," said Callie.

Gregory raised an eyebrow at her.

"What—like you never did anything wrong in your life?" she asked him.

"This is my 'impressed' face," he deadpanned.

Callie held back a smile.

"No wonder she didn't tell me that other items in her office were missing when I wrote that *Crimson* article," Alessandra mused. "What a sneaky little b—"

"Text her," Callie interrupted. "Find out where she is and tell her that you need to talk, right now."

"She's in her office at the *Crimson*," said Alessandra a moment later, looking up from her phone.

"Yeah, well, it won't be her office much longer," said Callie. "Come on," she added, compelling the other two to stand. "And Alessandra: make sure your iPhone has a working recording app."

FOURTEEN

Insider Ousted

CALLIE ANDREWS

Grace, where are you?!?

Callie, what's up?

Heading to the Crimson offices, can you be there in 5?

I think so. Why?

Time for Lexi to confess.

Seriously?

Yes!!!

I'll be there in two.

"I'm sorry, but I'm quite busy today—oh . . . it's you," said the clear, high voice from where its owner sat in a regulation wooden chair. Callie smiled, wondering where Mimi had so successfully hidden the coveted, ergonomic 'throne' of their campus's about-to-be-overthrown queen bee:

Alexis Thorndike.

"Both of you together," Lexi corrected herself, looking from Callie to Alessandra. Gregory was waiting just outside the offices so he could fill Grace in when she arrived. Lexi smirked. "I guess that means you think you've got it all figured out," she said, sounding altogether unconcerned. "And I guess *you*," she addressed Alessandra, "no longer care if the entire school learns that you're a lying, name-faking, former little fatty with a revenge streak and a flair for penning anonymous FlyBy blog posts.

"Then again," Lexi continued, kicking back in her chair, "I don't suppose you'll be here for much longer, so maybe you won't mind."

Alessandra glowered. "Is that so? What do you suppose the chances are of *me* getting kicked out for an article that was *your* idea in the first place?"

Callie's pulse thundered and she forced herself to avoid looking at Alessandra's purse.

"I have no idea what you're talking about," Lexi said sweetly.

"Sorry. I really wish I could have helped. But like I said, I do have a lot of things that need to get done today, so if you could please just see yourselves out—"

"No." Callie shook her head. "We're not going anywhere until you admit that you were responsible for the final two Ivy Insider installments. *You* called the cops on that Pudding party, and *you* leaked the club's password so that the Punch Book would be published. *And* you blackmailed Alessandra to force her to do your dirty work!"

Lexi laughed. "What a delightful little story!" She clapped her hands. "But I'm afraid I did no such things. Though that bit about the blackmail is especially creative. I wonder, whatever gave you that idea?"

"How about *these*?" said Alessandra, holing up the photo and the flash drive.

Lexi's expression momentarily darkened. But then she smiled. "If I was using those items to coerce you somehow, as you say, then why do you have them instead of me?" Her brown eyes danced. "Unless of course one of you admits to breaking into my office? I'd hate to think it was you," she said to Callie, "and while you were strictly banned from the building, too. I wonder if that's enough for the Ad Board to reconsider your expulsion even if Alessandra isn't just covering for you with regard to the Insider articles. Or maybe the two of you broke in together, just like you've been collaborating this entire time?"

"It's over, Alexis." Grace shut the door and smiled grimly at

Callie. "Too many people know too much for you to get away with it this time."

"As if it wasn't already crowded enough in here already," Alexis muttered, finally appearing, for the first time, unsettled. "Although I suppose being packed into a room full of girls is kind of like your dream come true?"

"That's right," Grace agreed. "Keep bullying me about my sexuality. It'll make a great addition to all of your e-mails from freshman year. You know the ones I'm talking about—where you told me to give up my seat on the *Crimson* or you'd out me to the student body?" Grace glanced at Alessandra. "She might not have any written documentation of your efforts to blackmail her," Grace continued to Lexi, "but you weren't always so careful, were you? Even up until last semester you still put a few things in writing that you maybe shouldn't have. . . ." Grace turned to Callie. "Isn't that right, Andrews?"

"Um . . . right!" said Callie. "She e-mailed me just before I left for Thanksgiving break with a certain video file in the attachment and then implied she'd see me *if* I ever came back!"

Grace nodded. "That sounds a lot like something that happened in a widely circulated article I read at the start of this semester. It was called 'Sex, Lies, and Videotape,' and in it an exceptionally brave freshman girl admitted not only to having her privacy violated when her ex-boyfriend filmed her in secret but that a certain unnamed upperclassman had been using knowledge of the tape to harass her all year and coerce her into doing various tasks."

"What's your point?" said Lexi icily.

"My point," said Grace, "is that the administration's main concern with the Punch Book going public and the final Insider installment is harassment. Bullying. Students picking on other students based on gender, physical appearance, socioeconomic status, and yes, sexuality."

"Isn't it too bad, then," Lexi replied, "that *you* were the one who published it."

"And yet you are the one with a proven record of harassment," Grace countered, "and a long history of forcing other students to do your bidding with threats—from giving up a rightfully earned spot on the *Crimson* to giving up a guy or giving up on staying in school."

Lexi stared Grace down for a full thirty seconds before declaring, "A few old e-mails taken out of context still won't prove that I had any involvement in the Ivy Insider articles. Now please leave my office immediately before I am forced to call Dean Benedict and tell him that you three are threatening *me*."

"By all means, make the call," said Callie. "We were going to suggest that anyway. And while you have the dean on the phone, you can tell him the truth. How you caught Alessandra working on an Insider article here at the *Crimson*. How you told her that instead of quitting, like she offered, she should keep on writing about the topics you gave her. How first you were plotting to have only me kicked out of the Pudding, but then you eventually decided to give Alessandra the password to HPPunch dot com and have her publish the Punch Book, knowing full well that both Grace and I would go down for it. Ready?" Callie finished, picking up the phone on Lexi's desk.

"It'll be her word against mine," said Lexi, looking from the landline to Alessandra.

"Actually," said Callie, "it'll be your word against Alessandra's—and Clint's." Callie swallowed. She had hoped it wouldn't come to this, but they needed that confession. "That's right," she continued. "Guess who had one too many drinks last night and came over to my place? He couldn't wait to tell me all about how he was through with you because he'd caught you blackmailing someone else and—figured out all the other things that you'd been up to. . . . Oh—my bad!" Callie cringed, pressing her advantage. "Did he forget to let *you* know that it was over before he started hitting on me? That does kind of sound like him, though, doesn't it?"

Lexi finally cracked. "Clint would—*never* betray me to the Ad Board! He doesn't have a clue why I was blackmailing Alessandra or that it was my idea to publish the Punch Book, and even if he did sense that something was up, he'd never turn me in because he'd be too afraid of losing his summer internship with my uncle!"

"Gotcha!" Alessandra exclaimed, pulling her iPhone out of her purse and hitting Pause. "Just in time, too," she muttered, noticing that the available recording space had almost maxed out. "In some ways you really were a great mentor," Alessandra said to Lexi, quickly saving the recorded file and e-mailing it to

Callie and Grace. "I learned a lot of things from you. Like how to record a conversation without the other person noticing. And how it's always so important to back up your work," she finished, tossing her cell into her bag as Grace's and Callie's beeped with the incoming message.

Lexi stared from one girl to the other, speechless. Finally her eyes settled on Callie. "Clint didn't actually—"

"He did," said Callie. "But you'll have to get him to tell you exactly what happened—if he can remember. I hope you'll manage to work things out," she added wryly. "You two really do deserve each other."

"You seem confused," Grace jumped in, surveying Lexi's stupefied expression. "So why don't I tell you how it's going to go down from here. First you're going to recuse yourself from the Student-Faculty Judicial Board. Then you're going to propose to Dean Benedict that, based on my exemplary behavior while on probation, he ought to restore me to my position as managing editor."

Callie nodded. "You will go to the hearing tomorrow morning with Alessandra and explain that the final Insider installment was never her idea. And if you don't—well, now we have our own 'insurance.' You can quietly tell the Ad Board what you did or we can publish the whole story publicly, so everyone at the paper will know how you achieved your hostile *temporary* takeover and everyone in the Pudding will know that you betrayed them. The choice is yours," she finished before Lexi could protest.

"And," said Alessandra, "just in case you ever get the urge

to blackmail someone else again, we're going to be hanging on to this." She patted her purse. "We hope it will inspire you to remember to be nice to COMPers in the future."

"So—you're letting me stay on the magazine?" Lexi asked, recovering her powers of speech.

"That's not up to us," said Grace. "It's up to the administration. My guess is that the punishment will be less severe, though, because no one individual was responsible: it took all of us, with the obvious exception of Callie, to make this mess."

"What about the Pudding?" Lexi turned to Callie.

"What about it?" asked Callie.

"Will you tell them that I was responsible for the publication of the Punch Book?"

"You can tell them yourself," said Callie. "Or don't. It doesn't matter to me, because I'm not a member anymore. I quit."

"You *what*?" said Lexi sharply.

"I quit," Callie repeated. "I finally realized Alessandra was right: I *don't* want to belong to a club with people like you in it, even if not everyone in it is like you."

Alessandra smiled.

Lexi seemed to be biting back the urge to inform Alessandra that the only club that would accept her when Lexi got through telling everyone about the Insider articles was Weight Watchers.

In the meantime Grace had been eyeing all the new décor on the desk and walls. "Right," she said, clearing her throat. "Well, then, since the hearing is tomorrow morning, I'll expect all of your stuff to be out of here by noon. Feel free to take the chair, too, since I seem to recall hearing something about how your Eames is missing." Grace smirked, opening the door to the office. "Shall we?" she asked the other two.

Callie trailed after her and Alessandra and was almost out of the office when Lexi called to her, "I don't get it."

"Don't get what?" asked Callie, turning to face her.

"Why not expose me to the Pudding or try to have me expelled?" Lexi seemed genuinely confused. "I would destroy you with half as much."

Callie shrugged and stepped out of the office. "Because I'm not you."

"We won!" Callie screamed, leaping into Gregory's arms.

"She confessed?" he murmured, twirling Callie through the air once before breaking away, glancing pointedly at Alessandra.

"She did," said Grace, offering him her hand. "Thanks for hanging around out here and filling me in."

"Absolutely," he said, shaking her hand. "I'll see you . . . around?" he added to Alessandra, who looked exhausted and eager to leave.

"Probably not at the Pudding," she said ruefully. "Until tomorrow?" she added to Grace.

"University Hall at nine o'clock sharp," said Grace, turning in the direction of her upperclassman house.

"I'll be there," Alessandra confirmed for Callie's benefit before walking away, too.

"So," said Gregory, turning back to Callie, "what now?"

"I was thinking of heading back to Wigglesworth," she said, struggling to keep a straight face. "I've got a *lot* of catching up to do—you know, on studying? Like, for finals?"

"That's funny," he said. "So do I."

"You do?" said Callie. "What a coincidence."

"Come to think of it," he said, taking her hand effortlessly and starting to walk, "I imagine your econ grade has suffered drastically during my absence. And how are you surviving Literary Theory now that you no longer have my notes to copy?"

Stopping, Callie smacked him on the arm. "*You're* the one who just missed like six weeks of school—

"Didn't miss it as much as *you* missed *me*, apparently," he shot back, seizing her and tickling her sides. "If only I'd known how many *hours*—nights, even—that you wasted—"

Shrieking with laughter, she broke away, sprinting toward their dorm.

"Wait," he cried, catching up and grabbing her hand to keep her from opening the bright green door to Wigglesworth, entryway C—the very place where she had first laid eyes on him at the beginning of the year on Move-in Day.

"What?" asked Callie, alarmed. Had they forgotten something? Overlooked some loophole that would allow Lexi to worm her way out of everything before tomorrow?

Gregory was looking very grave indeed as he leaned in until he was less than an inch away from her face. But at the last second his lips curved into a smile, right before they brushed her own.

"Oh," she said, moments—or was it hours?—later when they broke away. "*That.*"

"Whoo-hoo!" a voice suddenly screamed from above.

Mimi and Vanessa were hanging out Callie's bedroom window, whistling and applauding. "Your highness!" Mimi screamed over her shoulder. "You are missing the performance!"

"Yes, don't let us interrupt," Vanessa yelled down. "We're not, like, *dying* to know how your hearing went. What's it to us if you've been expelled? We haven't been losing sleep over it for weeks—"

"Oi!" OK screamed, jamming his upper body out the window of Vanessa's bedroom next door. "HE'S BACK! What gives, mate? You don't write? You don't call? Not even to warn me of your imminent return? You know: I've half a mind to give you a good pummeling with Mr. and Mrs. Fist," he finished, waving his arms in the air.

Gregory flashed OK his impossible-not-to-forgive-instantly grin. "Sorry, bud. I had to go see about a girl."

Callie beamed.

Dana's bedroom window flew open. "Welcome home!" Matt and Adam yelled at Gregory. "What are you waiting for?" Matt added to Callie. "Get up here and tell us how it went!"

Callie looked at Gregory. He shrugged. "We could always just run away," he murmured, his lips brushing her ear. "Hitchhike back to New York, steal a boat and sail to Vieques, or hide out somewhere closer to campus . . . I happen to know of a certain conference room in University Hall that ought to be vacant until tomorrow morning."

"You have thirty seconds to get up here," OK bellowed, "or Mr. and Mrs. Fist will be down for a chat."

Callie laughed. Tempting as the offer was—to escape and enjoy a few more precious moments alone—she owed her friends, who had sacrificed so much of their time and effort to ensure that she stayed in school, an explanation.

"All right," Gregory conceded, surveying her face. He opened the bright green door. "After you."

Half an hour later their roommates finally appeared to have run out of questions.

"Hey," Vanessa said to Callie, pulling her aside while OK demanded, for the seventh time, why Gregory hadn't hidden a note for *him* in a copy of *his* favorite book ("But wouldn't that have ruined all the pictures?" Gregory asked, earning him a 'good pummeling' from 'Mr. and Mrs. Fist'). "Before I forget," Vanessa continued, "this was delivered to our room earlier today."

It was a copy of the *Harvard Advocate.* Swallowing, Callie took the magazine and opened to the table of contents.

THE HARVARD ADVOCATE

SPRING

FEATURES

Commencement: A Senior Reflects

Jeremy C. Holden

Is It Really an Economic "Crisis"?
Hedge Funds, Harvard, and Wall Street

Andrea F. Wilson

FICTION

The Bottom of the Well

Akiko Keido

Roommates

Callie I. Andrews

ART

"I painted this for you"

Oil on canvas

Shelby Samuel

Reflections: IV

Metal, glass, & wood

T. M. Boyle

POETRY

Shallow Depths

Maxwell W. D. Morrison

This is not a "Poem"

Julian P. James

"Oh my god!" she screamed, hugging Vanessa and jumping up and down.

"What?" asked Dana, looking alarmed.

"Have I misunderstood?" Mimi rushed over. "*Tu n'es pas vraiment expulsé?*"

"No," said Callie, letting go of Vanessa. "Everything's fine. More than fine," she added, as Gregory came to read over her shoulder.

"Callie wrote a story about four insane—*ly* awesome—roommates, clearly largely inspired by yours truly," Vanessa explained. "You guys are in there, too, 'Mini' and 'Davina.'" She giggled, grabbing the magazine from Callie. "But mostly me. I'm going to be *famous*!"

"Not so fast," said Gregory, lifting the magazine high above Vanessa's head. "I think this first printing belongs with its rightful owner."

"Thank y—" Callie started, yelping as she watched Gregory tuck it into his back pocket. "Hey!" she cried, sliding her arms around his waist in an attempt to retrieve the magazine. He grabbed her wrists, holding them close to his chest and staring down at her, overcome with silent laughter.

"*Ahem.*" Matt cleared his throat loudly. "Isn't it time that we were on our way . . . to the, uh, library?"

"Huh?" asked OK.

"Oh, *riiight.*" Vanessa nodded. "I completely forgot about how we all agreed to spend *the entire afternoon* studying in the library."

"What?" said OK. "When did that happen?"

Shaking her head, Mimi started pushing him toward the door.

"But I don't have any books!" he cried.

"Dana and I have got you covered," said Adam, making his way for the door.

"Excellent idea, Matthew," Dana agreed, grabbing her textbooks off the coffee table.

"But," OK sputtered, resisting Mimi's shoves, "you can't possibly expect Callie and Gregory to want to study at a time like this—"

"They—are not—invited," Matt said very slowly, arching his eyebrows.

"Wh—oh!" OK grinned. "I get it."

"*Tu prenait une éternité*," Mimi muttered.

"Might I suggest," said Dana as the others filed out into the hall, "that you *do* join us at the library—if not today then perhaps tomorrow? If you don't pass economics, Callie, then all of this will have been for nothing, and Gregory, I can't imagine how far behind—"

"Actually," said Gregory, "I watched all the lectures online and my lawyer contacted my professors, who sent along my assignments. And since there wasn't much else to do . . ." He grinned at Callie.

"Still," said Dana. "Reading period is nearly halfway over and—"

"Dana, I apologize but I'm going to have to cut you off," he said, taking Callie's hands, "because whether you leave or not, I cannot last a single second longer without"—he looked at Callie—"doing"—he leaned in—"this."

Their lips met, and neither one noticed as a very disgruntled Dana pulled the door shut behind her, leaving them alone at last.

FIFTEEN

Yardfest

Dear Soon-to-be Sophomores:

Here's a little SAT vocab word you may or may not remember: *sophomoric*, meaning "pretentious but juvenile" or "conceited and overconfident of knowledge but poorly informed and immature." Of course it also means "of, relating to, or characteristic of a *sophomore*."

Goodness—was a better word ever invented?

No need to stress too much about the "poorly informed part" (after all, this advice columnist will still be here next year to try to cure your incurable immaturity) or even the inevitable "sophomore slump" (an expression that refers to the depression and academic apathy of second-year students after an often unforgettable freshman year). Why? Because first it's time for summer!

FIVE TIPS FOR A STRESS-FREE SUMMER

Don't stress too much about your internship. People, it's called *unpaid* "work" for a reason. Junior year is when you're supposed to start obsessing about the big old J-O-B problem lurking postcollege, but for now just try to enjoy dipping your toe into the professional world. Try to explore whatever (hopefully new) city you've found yourself inhabiting, and try to learn something in addition to what your new boss likes in his or her coffee.

Don't stress too much about your relationship. Whether you and your honey are meant to be (even though he applied to and accepted that j-o-b on the opposite end of the country) or decide, like many do, to take a break during the steamy summer months, try to remember that regardless, he or she will always be here when you get back. And in the meantime . . . tennis instructors, anyone?

***Do* stress about your emotional and physical well-being.** Harvard is *hard*. Now more than ever, you need to relax, rejuvenate, and refresh before buckling down over the next three years. Join a gym. Meditate. Let that zombie skin tone brave the light of day. See what the inside of a spa looks like for the first time. Try electroshock therapy or whatever else you can do to eliminate the necessity for real therapy later in life. (Though nothing wrong with a little old-fashioned Talking Cure right now if necessary: you can always bill it to health services!)

Don't stress about your grades or other disappointments (major disasters?) of the year. Guess what? You still have six more semesters of grades–at the very least!–to spend endless sleepless nights agonizing over, just as I doubt all of life's major disasters are behind you. So move on and buck up because I can guarantee that later you will look back on your time as a freshman as one of the happiest, healthiest, most carefree, fun, and exciting years of your life.

***Do* take advantage of the final days of school.** Even if you haven't left the library in weeks–oops, too soon!–you'd have to be blind *and* have a sensory processing disorder not to realize that summer, insofar as the weather, is already upon us. So go out and get some ice cream. Run barefoot through the grass in Harvard Yard. Learn to throw a ball–of any kind–so Dad will finally stop calling you his little NerdDork. Go to Yardfest: everyone will be there, along with food, sunshine, and live music–plus, it's free. And finally, tell your friends and roommates–or that special someone–that you love them, even if you think you already do it every day.

Until next year,
Alexis Thorndike, Advice Columnist
Fifteen Minutes Magazine
Harvard University's Authority on Campus Life since 1873

"Where *were* you guys last night?" Vanessa demanded of Callie and Gregory, setting down her half-eaten hot dog. "You missed the last Pudding party of our freshman year!"

"I quit, remember?" said Callie. All three, along with Matt, Mimi, Dana, Adam, and OK, were sitting on the grass in the middle of Harvard Yard next to a giant tree with a tire swing hanging from its branches. Nearly the entire student body surrounded them. Exam period had finally ended, meaning that it was time for Harvard's last organized event of the year: Yardfest, a huge outdoor barbecue followed by a live concert on the stage that had been erected on the steps of Memorial Church.

"I quit, too," said Gregory, popping a potato chip into his mouth. "No more money for dues."

"I'll spot you, mate," said OK, clapping a hand on Gregory's shoulder. He'd been acting considerably less moody following the return of his 'top mate.' However, even Gregory had proved so far unsuccessful at determining the identity of OK's secret lover, who, according to Matt, was the only logical explanation for OK's recent mercurial temperament.

"Yeah, you guys can't quit!" said Vanessa while Adam and Dana—rather audaciously—sipped Coke from one can using two straws, and OK returned to sharing Mimi's copy of *Tatler*. Vanessa lowered her voice. "Especially not after what happened last night!"

"*Ce qui s'est passé?*" Mimi demanded, lowering the tabloid. Even Matt momentarily stopped chewing his hamburger.

"Lexi was going around telling everyone who would listen that because she's starting a new magazine over the summer and going to be applying for jobs next year on top of running *FM*, she'll hardly have time for the Pudding anymore. She's also up for president of her Final Club, the Bee, in the fall so she said she might even be forced to choose between the two—though, according to her, 'Obviously the Bee is *so* much more prestigious than the Pudding'—or at the very least resign as one of the members of the Pudding's board!"

"Oh," said Mimi, yawning. "*That.*"

"But that's not all," Vanessa insisted. "Later after Lexi left, I overheard Clint thanking Tyler for 'letting her go so gracefully' and Tyler thanking Clint for 'coming to him with what he knew'!" Vanessa eyed them, one after another, clearly disappointed for lack of a bigger reaction. Finally Vanessa turned to Callie. "You're not even a little bit upset that she didn't get tossed out kicking and screaming? I mean, after what she did to you?"

Callie shrugged. "Not really. I expected something like what you described might happen after Lexi came clean to the Administrative Board and Alessandra quit the Pudding and got put on academic probation for a year. Although I *am* surprised that, from the sound of it, Clint is the one who turned her in to Tyler."

"Speak of the devil," Vanessa whispered suddenly, pointing at the nearest grill. Clint and Tyler stood in line waiting for food.

Alexis Thorndike was nowhere to be seen.

Spotting Callie and Gregory, Clint nodded cordially, raising his hand.

Callie waved back, smiling at Tyler. "We *did* date them," Callie reminded Vanessa. "And I actually really like Tyler."

"So, ladies," Tyler called, coming over while Clint finished filling his plate, "any special plans this summer?"

"Callie just so happens to have recently landed a *very* prestigious internship in New York City," Vanessa announced.

"Really?" Tyler asked her. "That's awesome!"

"Yep," said Callie. "I got a phone call from someone who works in hiring at *The New Yorker* two days ago. One of their editorial interns backed out at the last minute and, after seeing my story in the *Harvard Advocate*, they asked me if I'd like to fill her spot!"

"What spot?" asked Clint, joining Tyler.

Gregory's arm tightened around Callie's shoulders. She smiled, resting a hand on his knee.

"Callie got a job after writing a story based on my life, my mantras, and my teachings," said Vanessa. "It's in the *Advocate*. You should read—asap. It's probably going to win, like, a lot of awards. And did I mention that it's mostly about me?"

Callie thought she heard Mimi snickering behind her magazine. "It's not really a *job*," Callie explained. "I'm interning at *The New Yorker*, and I'm sure it will be mostly fetching coffee or doing other peoples' research. And of course they're not actually paying me—though I will have a living stipend and housing in the dorms at NYU."

She looked at Gregory, who had already declared his intention of sharing said dorm room while he figured out what he wanted to do now that he'd lost interest in finance.

"And you're, uh, still planning to intern for Governor Hamilton in Washington, DC?" Callie asked Clint.

"Yes," he said, looking somewhat grim. Callie neither asked—nor cared to ask—about his status with Lexi.

"Hope they have good squash courts down in DC," said Gregory. "Because I'll be coming for your spot next year."

Clint laughed. "I will keep that in mind if I'm ever having trouble staying motivated."

"Well," said Tyler, "we'd better go find a place to sit before this food gets cold and the band comes on. See you all next year?"

"Yep," everyone chorused. "Have a good summer!"

"Callie," said Vanessa, rounding on her immediately. "How are you ever going to 'see Tyler next year' if you don't stay in the Pudding!"

"Oh no!" Callie pretended to look horrified. "I hadn't thought of that!"

Vanessa sighed. "Lexi's gone. As in 'Ding dong, the *witch* is dead—'"

"Watch your language!" Dana snapped.

"Meaning," Vanessa continued, "that we have the opportunity to finally change the club! Make it a better place! Run for the board and get rid of the Punch Book and everything else like it forever!"

Callie raised her eyebrows.

"She's right, you know," said a voice from over Callie's shoulder.

"Grace!" Callie cried, leaping to her feet and giving the older girl a hug.

"You should never quit an institution if there's a chance that you can change it," Grace continued, appearing somewhat uncomfortable to find herself agreeing with a girl in a Marc Jacobs romper and four-inch wedges.

"Sounds like good advice," Callie replied.

"Feel free to take it or leave it." Grace smiled. "And also, congratulations on landing that gig at *The New Yorker*."

"Thanks, and same to you," said Callie. "I heard Dean Benedict was able to reverse their decision over at the *Times*."

Grace nodded, breaking into a smile. "Maybe I'll see you around at some point before next year. . . . Speaking of which, are you quite sure you won't reconsider accepting a spot on the *Crimson*?"

"Yes," said Callie. "I think I finally figured out what I'm supposed to be doing, and the paper isn't it."

"Football!" OK cheered, eavesdropping from where he sat. "Please say it's football! Your gifts are too precious to be wasted!"

Callie laughed. "Actually, the woman's varsity coach did e-mail me. . . ."

"What?" said OK sharply. "She didn't e-mail me—"

"*Parce que tu es un garçon*," said Mimi, "duh!"

"Still." OK sniffed, folding his arms. "I'm just as good as most girls, I should think."

"You are," Callie agreed, laughing.

"So it's back to sports for you, huh?" asked Grace.

"We'll see," said Callie. "Think I can play Division One soccer *and* keep trying to write fiction *and* maintain my GPA *and* . . . ?" She nodded at Gregory.

"Actually," said Grace, "I do."

"Thanks," said Callie, unable to resist hugging Grace again.

"No," said Grace. "Thank *you*. For . . . you know."

"I know," said Callie. "I'll e-mail you about getting together this summer."

"Sounds good," said Grace, walking away to join Marcus and some of the senior *Crimson* staff members who were camped out on the far side of the tire swing.

"A toast," said Mimi, holding up her can of soda. "First to Dana, who cares for our well-being so much so that she has superglued her 'Rules to Use the Common Room' to the wall such that we will all owe a fine since it remains permanently attached."

"Hear, hear," said the boys, raising their sodas, too.

"It was a good list," Dana muttered. Adam rubbed her back. "I never meant to deface public property. I can only hope that it will prove useful for the incoming freshmen."

Wow, thought Callie. How trippy to think that next year a whole new set of girls would be living in their suite. Would they read "The Rules" and wonder who came before them? Would they be just as different from one another or their year half as crazy? She looked at Gregory. Would the boys across the hall be even close to this cute? He kissed her on the cheek. Yes, Probably, Maybe, and *No way!* she decided.

"Next, to Vanessa," said Mimi. "I am not laughing *with* you; I am laughing *at* you."

Vanessa's jaw dropped and she pretended to look angry. "The best university in the entire world and yet they still couldn't teach you English," she said. "How tragic."

Mimi smiled. "And finally to Callie: you are a much better human being than would seem to otherwise be indicated by all the trouble you have gotten mixed into. I am glad that once I return from my summer traveling through Europe I will have *le plus grand plaisir* of living with you all *encore*."

Callie, Vanessa, Mimi, and Dana all clinked soda cans, smiling at one another under the hot afternoon sun.

"And to *mes nouveaux* roommates," Mimi continued, looking at the boys who, having joined their blocking group, would also be living in Kirkland House next year. "Adam: if you are ever needing to borrow a dress . . ."

"Don't," Dana warned. "I mean, no thank you."

"Yes, thank you, but Dana has plenty," said Adam, earning himself a *look*.

"Matthew," said Mimi, "someday, if you just keep on believing, your prince will come."

Matt laughed.

"Actually," said Callie, "I think his 'prince' might be in California, where he is planning—purely by *coincidence*—to spend his summer doing research for some Stanford professor's hot new book about the history of the newspaper industry."

"Oh my god," said Vanessa. "Is *Jessica* going to be there?"

Callie giggled. "Yes," she said, putting a hand on Matt's shoulder in an effort to calm his blushing. "So you guys are guaranteed at least one visit—probably more. My parents are still in denial that I'm 'suddenly running off' to New York."

"Thank god for that," said Vanessa. "I need somebody to hang out with while I attempt to avoid *my* parents."

Callie grabbed her hand and squeezed. "It's going to be a fun summer," she said, resting her head on Gregory's shoulder.

"Ah yes, to Gregory." Mimi resumed her speech. "We," she said, gesturing to herself and OK, "have always been on the Team Gregory, *pas le* Team Sweater Vest. So to your ultimate *triomphe* and becoming *moins d'un trou du cul*—"

"That's French for you're an asshole," OK explained.

"No!" Mimi cried. "I said becoming *less* like the hole *du cul*." She expelled a frustrated gust of air through her lips. "What I am trying to say *est la suivante: Grégoire, tu as enfin surmonté ton orgueil. Callie, tu as enfin surmonté ton préjudice. Comme le livre*." Mimi narrowed her eyes in response to their blank faces. "Oh, *quelle que vous tous, les Américains*," she gave up. "Cheers!"

"Cheers!" the others echoed, raising their sodas again.

"Hey!" said OK after taking a sip. "What about me?"

Mimi smiled at him, that familiar mischievous glint in her eye. "*Pour toi, mon amour secrèt Ne sois pas une un idiotte*!" she toasted him. "*Retrouve moi sur scène dans cinq minutes.*"

"Huh?" asked Callie. "What did she say? Where is she going?" she cried as Mimi stood and ran away.

"No clue!" OK shouted over his shoulder, getting up and dashing after her.

"Don't look at me!" Dana said a moment later, even though the only reason everyone was staring was because she had just harrumphed with a very knowing look in her eyes.

"What time do you think the band is supposed to start?" asked Matt.

"Probably any minute," said Gregory, shaking a cigarette out of his pack. "Last one," he promised Callie, showing her that it was empty.

"I didn't say anything," she said.

"Yes, but I can read your mind," he said, pressing his forehead against hers and then kissing her.

"Oh yeah?" she murmured, tilting her head back the tiniest bit. "Then what am I thinking right now?"

"Guys! Ew! Seriously! Get a room!" shrieked Vanessa. "And preferably not the one separated from mine by a very, very thin wall. God! Is this what it's going to be like all summer?"

Callie and Gregory looked at each other, cracking up simultaneously. "We apologize . . . in advance," he said.

"Yeah," echoed Callie, "we're sorry we're not sorry."

"Matthew," said Dana pointedly, "do you know which band is playing?"

"No idea," he said, glancing at the huge red curtain that was currently obscuring the stage. "Didn't the Yardfest flyer say it was a surprise?"

"I believe so," Adam agreed. "Something like special or surprise guest appearance from a 'certain international musical sensation'?"

Callie nodded. "I heard a rumor that—"

"Wait!" Vanessa cut her off. "I think I saw movement behind the curtain!"

Callie looked at the stage. The curtain might have rippled—but then again, it could have been the wind. Suddenly a student mounted the stage wearing a black headset and dragging a microphone with him.

"Er—attention, fellow Harvard students," he called, tapping the microphone. "As you know, the concert should have started a few minutes ago, but we just got word that our guests have been delayed on the second leg of their flight from Germany. We have a car waiting for them at Logan Airport now, but we're not really sure what time Sexy Hansel—oh, crap."

Cheers and shouts had broken out among the crowd.

The student onstage smiled. "Oops," he said. "Well, I guess now the secret's out. Yes, for this year's Yardfest we did somehow manage to book the techno pop sensation Sexy—what the hell?" he cried, turning.

The curtain, suspended from only a thin makeshift rod probably built that morning, seemed to be collapsing as if a weight had been hurled against it from behind. The rod curved as the curtain continued to drag it downward until finally it snapped. Red velvet splashed down like water tumbling from a glass, still writhing after it hit the stage as if someone—or someone*s*—struggled to escape.

There was a collective gasp from the blanket where Callie, Gregory, Vanessa, Matt, Dana, and Adam sat. OK's head had just popped out from under the curtain. Another face soon surfaced after him.

"Mimi?" screamed Vanessa, causing a few people to turn in their direction even though most eyes were riveted on the stage.

OK crawled out from under the curtain and then pulled Mimi up after him, taking both of her hands. He continued to hold one of them as he grabbed the microphone from the confused-looking student and said:

"Er—ah—pardon the interruption. I just dropped by to say that Sexy Hansel are a bunch of wankers—and also this."

The microphone made a loud plunking sound as it hit the stage, and nearly everyone from Wigglesworth entryway C gasped again.

OK and Mimi were kissing.

After a few seconds the crowd burst into applause, even though most of them couldn't truly have known what they were clapping for. No one, however, cheered louder than the inhabitants of C 24 and C 23, who looked at one another with wide-eyed expressions that all seemed to agree: *Finally*.

Grinning, Mimi picked up the microphone. "*Merci beaucoup*

et bonne soirée!" She curtsied, handing the mike back to the still dumbfounded MC.

"How long has this been going on?" Vanessa demanded as she and the others surrounded OK and Mimi upon their return.

"Er . . ." Mimi and OK exchanged glances.

"Oh, come on!" said Dana to Mimi. "The secret's out just like that boy said onstage and in more ways than one."

Mimi smiled at her. "You are right. It is time."

"Wait—Dana knew?" Vanessa was indignant.

"We both did," said Adam. "OK and I share a double. Why do you think Dana started letting me stay over so often?"

"I thought," Vanessa sputtered, "that maybe you'd decided that Third Base was no longer a sin?"

"So those noises we heard coming from OK's bedroom—that was you?" Callie asked.

"I should hope so," answered Mimi, narrowing her eyes at OK.

"Of course it was, my *petite baguette*," he said, mussing up her hair and lavishing her with looks of utter adoration.

"*Non*," she responded, her grayish blue eyes huge. "*C'est exactement* why I wanted to *garder le secret*!" Backing away, she started slapping his hands.

"Fine," he grumbled, sticking them in his pockets. "Have it your way. You always do."

"*Oui*," said Mimi, smirking.

"So you've been seeing Mimi secretly this entire time," Matt said to OK slowly.

"*Oui-oui-ouuiii,*" said OK, *avec une "fraaanch" accént*. "Ever since that day at the date auction when she realized she could no longer live without the fresh prince of—" He grimaced as Mimi held up a warning finger. "Uh. Yes. No big deal. Whatever. I, like, like her, and stuff," he amended, trying for an American accent.

Mimi smiled in spite of herself.

"But I don't get it," said Callie. "Why did you want to keep it a secret?"

"Really?" said Mimi. "You do not get it?" She nodded at OK, who seemed so brag-happy he was on the verge of doing a jig—or mounting the stage again to "Pull a Matt" by grabbing the microphone and telling the world that he loved Mimi Clément.

"*I* detested it," OK interjected, "but *she* seemed to enjoy all of the sneaking around. It really turned her o—into a . . . sneakier . . . person."

Mimi rolled her eyes.

"Well, hey, man," said Gregory gruffly, pulling OK into a half hug, "congratulations. Now, Vanessa," he said turning to her. "Have you met my friend Matt?"

"Wha—" Vanessa looked from Gregory to Matt.

"No," said Matt, slowly shaking his head.

"Nuh-uh," Vanessa cried, shaking hers, too. *"No way."*

"Not a chance," Matt countered.

"Don't even *think* about it, Robinson—"

"I wasn't!"

"Good, because if—"

"Okay," said Callie. "We get it."

"Great," said OK. "Time to go, then!"

"Huh?"

"We have to leave. Immediately," he said, starting to fold up the blanket.

"What!" shrieked Vanessa. "Why? Sexy Hansel could show up any minute!"

"Exactly." OK nodded gravely. "And we cannot be here when it does."

"Why not?" asked Adam.

"Because when I am on my deathbed," said OK, "I need to be able to tell all of *our* little princes and princesses"—he looked at Mimi—"that Daddy died never having suffered through a Sexy Hansel show."

Vanessa gaped.

"They are probably just going to lip-synch and Auto-Tune everything," Callie said to her, eager to avoid splitting up the group. Everyone else seemed game to leave except Vanessa, who stood her ground, chewing her lip.

"*Wellll*," Vanessa said eventually, "I guess there is one more thing left on the Birkin List that we still need to do.

"Uh," said Callie. "How are we going to pee on the John Harvard statue with all these people around?"

"Oh." Mimi raised her eyebrows. "Some of us already took care of that one after the Pudding party last night."

"Ugh," Dana groaned, plugging her ears.

Callie frowned. "Well then . . . you can't mean . . . But Widener isn't even open today!"

Obviously her hands weren't enough to stop the references to statue urination and library fornication, because Dana started singing loudly.

Vanessa shook her head. "We decided to take *that* one off the list since there's still plenty of time to try before we graduate."

"Well, then, *what*?" asked Callie.

Dana pulled her hands off of her ears. "You want to jump off that bridge, don't you?"

The banks of the Charles River were lined with people sunning themselves, tossing Frisbees, or jogging the dirt paths along the edge of the grass. The John W. Weeks Bridge jutted out over the calm gray-blue water, connecting Cambridge to Boston. This brick and white stone structure rose less than thirty feet above the river's surface, making it ideal for jumping.

Laughing and chattering nonstop, the inhabitants of Wigglesworth entryway C mounted the pedestrian footbridge, the grass turning to concrete beneath their feet. Callie paused halfway through their journey to the middle, turning back to stare at the Harvard campus fanning out behind them across the streets of Cambridge.

She'd survived the year. They all had, in spite of their various individual struggles, and she couldn't ask for better friends—or a better maybe-just-might-be-the-love-of-her-life boyfriend—

than the ones who currently stood examining the bridge's wide, white stone railing and yelling at her to hurry.

They had all climbed onto the railing by the time Callie caught up, even Dana, who didn't look nearly as afraid as Vanessa did when she turned, motioning at Callie to join her.

Smiling, Callie hopped up onto the railing in between Gregory and Vanessa and peered down at the tiny ripples in the water below. It felt a little higher from up here than it had looked from the shore, but it definitely seemed manageable—especially in present company.

Gregory took Callie's hand.

"Ready?" he asked, his blue eyes twinkling in the summer sun.

Callie beamed. "I am."

And so they jumped.